BLOOD ON VINES

THE MATAKANA SERIES

MADELEINE ESKEDAHL

SSP

This edition published by Squabbling Sparrows Press 2021

ISBN 978-0-9951369-3-9

Cover design: Jeroen ten Berge

Squabbling Sparrows Press

To Adrian, Holly and Olivia, your love and support kept me going and encouraged me to finish this book.

PROLOGUE

M *artinborough*

THE CHARMING DEMEANOUR, the talk about life insurance and the smart suit had convinced Peter to let him in. They never made it as far as the kitchen. The initial punch at the top of the stairs caught him by surprise. Before he could get his hands up, the second blow connected with his nose and mouth. He fell backward like a rag doll, hitting each step of the narrow stairs with a heavy thud, until it all came to a stop in the basement. The man from the bank said nothing.

As Peter came to, gone was the man's smile and dark suit. Instead, he was wearing disposable overalls and blindingly white gumboots. A blue sports bag sat on the floor. From the corner of his eye he could see a discarded syringe, but had no memory of it being used. Peter's legs were spread at an uncomfortable angle; it was as if they no longer belonged to him. A multitude of jagged tears covered his jeans, each leg blood-soaked from rage inflicted stab wounds.

Waves of pain rolled over him and he had lost control of his bladder.

The cold damp seeped into him from the grey schist floor.

His right arm was heavy and numb, hanging down by his waist like a dead tree branch. He just wanted to close his eyes and drift into the serene peace he knew was inevitable.

Lurching forward, the man pushed a pneumatic nail gun in Peter's face before grabbing his left arm, slamming the hand to the wall and squeezing the trigger.

Peter's screams echoed in the basement as a six-inch nail was pushed through the middle of his palm, penetrating just below the third finger, splintering ligaments on the way. As his left hand was fixed to the wall, the world went black.

Peter had no idea how long he had been sitting there. Was it still Friday? The small windows in the basement didn't let in much light. He had meant to trim the hedge in the flower bed, but like a lot of things in life he hadn't got to it. His failed relationships and lack of motivation for most things were going through his head. Not that it mattered now.

He'd had a funny feeling that someone had been in the house a few days ago, his things subtly rearranged, but had shaken it off as nonsense.

Slipping in and out of consciousness, Peter could just make out his attacker, his cold eyes full of hate. He could see the man's lips moving but all he could hear was the swooshing in his ears. Shaking his head, trying to focus, he could just make out, "I've got what I came for."

Peter's nose throbbed, broken and swollen shut. Breathing through his mouth was difficult, globules of blood making him gag. Thick saliva dribbled down his shirt in long pink strands.

The man pulled a carving knife from the sports bag and launched himself at Peter again. Blood splattered against the wall and pooled on the already sticky floor. Peter's femoral artery was severed; a cascade of blood squirted rhythmically.

"You should have kept your nose out."

Peter rested his head on his arm. Crushing tiredness overtook him. He didn't care anymore, his body beyond repair, and a deep cold spread through his body.

If I just close my eyes for a moment, he thought, as his heart pumped the last drop of life from his battered body. His head fell forward, and he was gone.

1

M atakana

LEXI WAS ENJOYING the early morning peace in the garden, clasping her cup of Earl Grey with its scent of bergamot and citrus. The warmth of the sun caressed her bare legs. A light breeze rolled over the gently undulating hills of Matakana wine country. A rogue gust caught her nut-brown tresses, and Lexi remembered she ought to book an appointment to have a cut, and the odd grey hair eliminated. Sweeping it off her face, she reached for the elastic band around her wrist and tied it up. The haircut would have to wait until after the harvest anyhow.

It was early; the family was still sleeping. She loved the quiet contemplation and appreciated the surrounding beauty, highlighted by the morning sun shining through the treetops, making the dewdrops in the garden sparkle like diamonds. The sweet, pungent smell of late summer fruit in the warming air was comforting, the gentle buzzing of honeybees flitting from flower to flower. Her mind was wandering. She glanced over her shoulder at her childhood home, the grand old homestead that held so many fond memories, and took another sip of tea. It had been a tough year for the entire family. Their vineyard was doing well, the operation had expanded a lot in the last few years, but with that came the stress, not the least on her and Avery's marriage. Gabriel, their eldest, had mixed with the wrong crowd at school and got into some trouble which hadn't helped either.

The soft yellow two-storey villa's crisp white trim had been looked after over the years. The large front porch, framed by beautiful fretwork, was used only for special occasions. It was easier to use the side entrance straight through to the kitchen. Gabriel had just been a baby when they'd moved to Matakana and taken over the family property sixteen years ago. Since then, the two girls had come along, Samantha was now fourteen and Evie nine.

With the development of the motorway and the tunnel from Auckland, the range of cafés, restaurants, art galleries and the famous Farmers Market on Saturdays, the Matakana Valley was flourishing. Being on the main road to Matakana Village helped, and the influx of visitors during weekends and holidays benefitted their cellar door and farm shop.

In the early days, Lexi's father had grown vegetables and kept a herd of dairy cows, like his father and grandfather before him. Thankfully, in the 1980s, Bob had the foresight to join a few of the progressive farmers planting the first grapes to produce wine. The valley's cool maritime climate during the winter months, combined with a pleasant prevailing north-easterly during the warm summer, made it ideal for growing cabernet-based reds, chardonnay, pinot gris and riesling.

Avery planted more vines when they bought the property, putting his heart and soul into the business, expanding production from a relatively modest operation to a label respected locally and overseas. The first few years had been tough, with a lot of work and not much money coming in. The area produced some award-winning reds, and even their Matakana Valley Wines had won accolades. They had dreamt big, been full of ideas and enthusiasm. Lexi still had the odd night of insomnia, lying in bed and staring at the ceiling. Avery was always calm, not at all like her — prone to stress out about the minor things around her. The kids, the homestead — there was always something.

Now it seemed they had drifted apart, especially after what happened last year. Not that it had gone as far as Avery sleeping with that woman, but it had been close. Avery had been full of remorse and had tried to make it up to her. Even though it was a year ago, it broke her trust, not helped by having a couple of moody, hormonal teenagers around and a prepubescent tween in the house. It had been much easier when the children were small, she thought and sighed.

Beau, their black Labrador, stirred at her feet and stood up, looking her deep in the eyes, tilting his head while his right paw gently tapped her leg. It was time for breakfast, he intimated. Lexi smiled and gave him a scratch behind the ear. In the distance, she could hear the faint alarm of the bread maker she had set the night before.

Pulling her cardigan across her chest and taking the last sip of the now lukewarm tea, she closed her eyes for a moment. It was seven-thirty, and the family would soon be awake. Lexi grabbed her empty cup and walked towards the house, the dew making her feet slip around in her jandals. She paused by the row of white iceberg roses at the front of the house, reaching forward, smelling the pleasant scent of her childhood summers and smiled. Planted by her mother, the brilliant white blooms set off perfectly against the warm yellow weatherboards and had a special place in her heart. She climbed the stairs and kicked her jandals off in the small but welcoming entrance. The delicious smell of freshly baked rye filled the kitchen, and she wondered what the day would bring.

2

"Mum!" roared Samantha from the top of the stairs, her agitated voice an octave or two higher than normal. If the rest of the family had not been awake before this outburst, they were now. Lexi made her way from the kitchen to the bottom of the stairs where she met her older daughter wrapped in a faded blue towel. Her face was red with anger and eyes black like thunderclouds, water streaming from her long hair onto the golden rimu floor.

"What on earth is the matter?" Lexi asked.

"There's no more water! There was only a little burst, just enough to wet my hair and lather up the shampoo. When I turned the tap on again, there was nothing. Look," Sam snapped, her hair full of suds and twirled into a loose topknot, water trailing down her back from a few loose strands. Her face said it all; the world as she knew it was ending.

"That's strange. Just calm down and I'll have a look." Lexi checked the tap in the kitchen. It too had run dry. Going upstairs, she bumped into Avery on the landing. He had heard the commotion and got out of bed. Wearing a pair of faded shorts, he yawned and stretched his broad neck and shoulders to wake up. He ran his fingers through his wavy brown hair which was sticking up, desperately trying to tame the wild mop. She couldn't help but look at his sun-kissed and freckled back, his muscles rippling as he went down the stairs. He was still in good shape, didn't look bad for a man in his early fifties.

It seemed like a long time since she had noticed him; they were always like ships passing in the night. She wondered what had happened, where they had gone wrong. She was a year younger than Avery, but that feeling of middle-age spread was definitely threatening, she thought as she glimpsed herself in the hall mirror. She pulled at the skin on her neck and scrutinised the tiny crow's feet at the corners of her eyes. She could definitely do with some jazzing up.

AVERY TOOK one look at his exasperated daughter, who at fourteen was definitely going on twenty-one, complete with a severe attitude to match. She was a carbon copy of her mother, athletic-looking, with long dark hair and a smattering of freckles across her button nose. They would have to monitor her as the boys would be along soon. She had her mother's stubborn streak too, so hopefully she would Sarge the boys, not the other way around.

He grabbed a clean T-shirt from the folded laundry at the bottom of the stairs and threw it on. They collected all the water from the vast roof spaces and water conservation was always at the front of their minds, especially over the warmer summer months. The rainwater in this part of the world was clean enough to drink unfiltered. As for the rest of the farm and vineyard, they were fortunate to have a stream running through the southern side of the property, which irrigated the land and the livestock. Avery stuck his bare feet in the tatty old Red Band gumboots by the door before walking around the back to the three large water tanks, camouflaged behind the glossy leaves of the olearia hedge. Even though he'd checked the water level only last week, it had been hot and dry since. Avery climbed the ladder with ease and twisted the large round plastic lid open and peeked in, the beam from his flashlight bouncing off the surface. To his relief there was still a third left, enough for a little while yet. Hopefully the rains would come after the harvest; if not, they would have to order a tanker. Putting the ladder back, he decided to have a look at the pump under the house.

The small trellis door was barely a metre square and protested loudly on its hinges as he pulled it open and peered into the darkness. A pungent smell of soil and warm air hit his face. A strong and unpleasant aroma of rat urine and something dead assaulted his nostrils, and he flinched. He swung his above-average height and broad-shouldered body through the small opening, feet first, and held on to the door frame for support. Trying to block the worst of the foul smell he put his hand under his nose while getting the torch out of his pocket. He hunched his body in the cramped space, losing concentration for a moment and not ducking low enough, hitting his forehead on one of the supporting beams. His head rang and he saw stars. He swore under his breath and wondered why on earth they hadn't moved the hot-water cylinder and pump closer to the door. He felt the top of his head with his fingers and knew there was a cut as soon as he touched the warm blood. Wiping his face and ignoring the discomfort, he moved closer to the pump in the corner. The air seemed denser and more stagnant the further in he went. The unidentified waft of the putrid matter was intensifying. It was probably the dead carcass of an unlucky rat or possum. Avery screwed up his nose and made a mental note to put some bait traps out. The last thing he wanted was to have a large nest of rodents congregating under the house as the weather turned cooler.

The pump itself was old, something Lexi's dad had installed a long time ago. Perhaps it had finally given up the ghost. Avery shone the torch over it. A slight smell of plastic and electric burn hung in the air. Without hesitation Avery reached forward and yanked the short power cord out of the outlet. Sparks flew. The unit was hot to the touch, and on closer inspection he could see evidence of flames having licked the plastic cover around the front. He breathed a sigh of relief, thankful that the damage had not spread. Cold shivers went down his back — the old homestead could have gone up in flames as they slept. He turned around to head back outside, away from the terrible odour, when a movement in the corner caught his eye. He shone the torch, letting the beam slowly illuminate the dirt on the ground. Apart from a few old planks and some other building materials, there wasn't much there. Out of nowhere, a massive rat ran right in front of him. The sudden movement startled him. *Damn rats.* He couldn't believe how brash they were. Avery shone his torch in the direction where the rat had disappeared, glad that he was wearing gumboots. He stood still and listened for a moment. There was a definite scurrying behind a nearby pile of Leca blocks left over from when Bob built the internal wine cellar many years ago. The scuttling intensified and so did the awful stench. By the sound of it, there were several. The smell of a dead animal was rife, and he took care where he put his feet, not wanting to step on whatever it was. He leaned in for a closer look.

"What the hell!" He recoiled back. It looked like a Halloween decoration that the kids had used at last year's party — if it hadn't been for the flesh of two of the fingers completely gnawed down, and the skeletal bones of the hand protruding like spokes in a wheel. Skin and flesh hung like torn bits of rags. Its centre had a large circular wound, the blackened edges looking ominous. The cut at the wrist was clean. As the realisation set in, something squeezed his insides. It was a human hand lying there in the dirt in front of him.

He grabbed hold of the pile of blocks to steady himself, in the process kicking a piece of corrugated iron that was leaning against them. The almighty bang made three or four rats scatter in all directions. The rat closest to Avery made its way up his right boot, until his reflexes kicked in. Swiftly shaking it off, he catapulted the creature on to a pillar with force. The rodent hit hard, making a sickening thud as it connected, falling to the ground, motionless.

Avery made a hurried escape towards the door at the far side. He flung the door open, scraping his arms as he pressed himself through the narrow entrance before collapsing on the dewy grass.

Lexi came around the corner. "What happened to you?" she said, her nursing training kicking in at the sight of him on the ground.

"It's just a scratch," Avery said, trying to keep his voice from wavering. A South Island man, he was used to feeling in control. "I knocked my head on a beam in there," he said, looking towards the trellis door. "You are not going to believe me, but there's a fucking human hand under the house. We'll have to call the cops." Lexi looked at him with disbelief.

"I'm serious," he said.

"It's probably a joke, a prop the kids have hidden under there," she said, picking up the torch. She peeked through the small opening. "What's that awful smell?" she burst out, pinching her nostrils with one hand.

Avery stood in the doorway directing her to the pile of Leca blocks. "Hopefully, the rats are still taking a break," he said.

LEXI SHIVERED, she couldn't bear rodents. Her face serious as the apprehension was building, and she braced herself for what she would find. There was no mistaking it for being anything else than a human hand. The foul odour made her gag and she swung on her heels, desperate for fresh air in her lungs.

Avery grabbed her before she fell over, pulling her close, his stubbly chin resting on top of her head. She couldn't remember when this had happened last and she took his scent in, savouring it. She felt safe and melted into his firm embrace. Touching her back, he cradled her.

"We have to call Bill," he said loosening his grip, breaking the spell. Lexi nodded, unable to get any words out. She desperately wanted to recapture the early-morning calm, sipping tea in the garden, when the day still had promise in the air.

Avery still looked pale, but was slowly regaining his normal self. He went to get his mobile and called Bill, the local policeman, and family friend.

3

Tiny dust particles gently swirled in the beams of early morning sun shining through the gaps of the Venetian blinds and landing on the bed like treasure at the end of the rainbow. Bill wished that the shrill ringtone of his mobile phone hadn't woken him. He sighed and rolled over, putting his phone back on the nightstand. It was Sunday; the police station was closed and he had enjoyed a rare sleep in, not something he normally did during the busy holiday season when the village and surrounding areas brought hordes of visitors from near and far.

Annika's side of the bed was empty, her pillows put neatly at the head of the bed. She was an early riser and probably already out in the studio painting. A slightly annoying headache radiated across his forehead. Thankfully, it wasn't too bad, but a few hours more sleep would have helped. By the time he had got into bed, Annika had been snoring gently and it was past two a.m. It had been a lovely barbecue last night; the neighbours had come over.

Stretching his back and shoulders he swung his legs over the edge of the bed and stifled a yawn before standing up. Scratching his back he felt the round scar on his shoulder, and automatically his eyes went to the puckered crater on his lower abdomen. Sometimes he went days without thinking about it.

Bill reached for yesterday's uniform trousers, draped over the back of the chair in the bedroom, and threw them on. He splashed some water on his face and brushed his teeth. On his side of the built-in wardrobe, there were no light-blue uniform shirts hanging. Even though Annika did most of the laundry, he helped as much as he could. He wasn't as quick as her, but it was a weird relaxation. Over the busy summer months, however, they had fallen into a routine where it was easier that she did them, as he was often home late. He knew he was lucky to have such an amazing wife and mother of his children. Sometimes he didn't know what he had done to deserve this stunning woman he had met in London on his working holiday. He had been flatting with Lexi and Avery. When Lexi had brought her new friend Annika to the pub after work one day, Bill thought he had died and gone to heaven. She was a stunner, almost as tall as him with an athletic build, long blonde hair falling in soft curls down her back. Her blue eyes were full of life with an infectious laugh to match. Annika was like an open book, when she was happy she shone and if something upset her, you knew it. He fell head over heels. A whirlwind romance followed, and they married within the year, with the festivities celebrated over a few days on the Swedish island of Gotland, with Bill's immediate family flying over. The medieval setting of cobblestone streets and heritage buildings added to the magical atmosphere. He had felt so far away from his ancestors and local marae, but so close to his adopted culture that dated back to the Vikings and beyond.

"Annika, have you seen any of my work shirts?" he called as he made his way down the stairs.

"Have you looked in the laundry?" Annika responded.

Bill, woken from his daydream, went into the cramped room tucked in next to the stairs. Sure enough, there they were, an entire week's worth of clean shirts, hanging on the rack.

"Thanks, darling," he said walking into the kitchen while doing the buttons up, leaning forward and giving his wife a kiss. Annika smiled and ruffled his short inky hair, her glance lingering on his bright emerald-green eyes. Bill pulled her close, swallowing her slim frame in his broad embrace savouring the mixture of old-fashioned soap and floral shampoo.

"I take it you are going to work?" She smoothed out the front of his shirt, feeling his firm chest.

"I just had a call from Avery. It's probably nothing, but he sounded upset." Bill dialled his colleague Niko.

With the increase in population over the summer months, Headquarters had thought it appropriate to transfer a second officer to the Matakana police station. A young Samoan constable, Falaniko Sopoanga, had applied and now lived in a small flat above the bakery in the village. Bill really enjoyed the company, and having the backup should he need it. Not that there was much trouble around, apart from the odd theft or an overly refreshed holidaymaker having had too much to drink at one of the many eateries in the village. Bill had been back in the area for ten years now and hadn't minded the automatic demotion to Sergeant in the slightest to take the Sole Charge position in the village.

"I'll pick you up in ten minutes," Bill said after having explained what was going on.

On his way out, Annika handed him a smoothie. "It's green superfood, full of antioxidants, and will give you a great start to the day." Annika was a bit of a health nut, and unfortunately for Bill vegetable smoothies were the latest craze that she was trying to get the family to embrace.

"What's wrong with a piece of toast and a smear of Marmite?"

"This will give you the energy to think, rather than a piece of toast sitting like a lump in your stomach. Not to mention that horrible black yeasty spread on top." She rolled her eyes. "I don't know how you can eat it."

Bill put the empty glass on the table, grabbed her waist and gave her a kiss. "Darling, I was only teasing."

"Ugh yuk, do you have to carry on like that?" It was their older daughter, Katie, tall and blond like her mother, cringing at her parents' affection.

Bill winked at Katie. "That's my cue to leave. I'll see you girls later."

He said it cheerfully, but in the pit of his stomach he could feel an element of worry. Avery was the quintessential hard-working, tough-as-old-boots kind of man, and he had sounded shaken. Bill started the ute, reversed, and drove along the long gravel driveway. It hadn't rained properly for weeks and a dust cloud enveloped the police car. He turned right on the sealed Leigh road and headed towards Matakana. There was no one else on the road so it didn't take him long to get into the village, turning right into the main street, passing the cinema and pharmacy with the bakery in between on the right. The large old pub on the left, the surf shop, Four Square supermarket and Black Dog Café were all quiet. He continued down another hundred metres until he got to the police station.

Niko was sitting on the front step of the old house, the slightly overgrown, bright pink bougainvillea shading the entrance. Bill quickly turned the car around and Niko jumped in the front, dressed immaculately as always. His hair was slicked back, still wet from the gym. His burly frame looked massive compared to Bill, even though he was close to 190 centimetres and broad-chested himself. His light brown skin was flawless, and he had more than once been mistaken for the movie star, The Rock. A Samoan tattoo showed below his short shirt sleeves. Niko came from Manurewa, one of the toughest Police districts in the country. He had been transferred up north over the summer months, and was about to go back home again as the season was coming to a close. As this was his second year in a row, Bill thought he must like it.

"Okay, Sarge, what's your take on the call this morning?" Niko said.

"Avery is an old friend. He sounded really shaken when I spoke to him. I'm hoping the kids have pulled a silly prank on him. It's the kind of stuff we did as teenagers."

"Jeez, Sarge, you had a sheltered upbringing. Me and my mates were hot-wiring cars for fun," Niko laughed.

Bill knew about Niko's misspent youth and how close he had been to getting sucked into the seedy world of gangs and crime. Sport was his saviour.

Turning right at the roundabout and on to Matakana Road towards Warkworth, Bill didn't have far to drive. Within a few kilometres they were at the entrance to Matakana Valley Wines.

Mature pohutukawa towered above a sea of wildflowers along the driveway. Bill remembered counting the trees as a boy; thirty to be exact, fifteen on each side. Lexi's great-great-grandparents had planted them when they came out from Scotland in 1857 on the famous brigantine *Spray*. Back then they had run cattle, cows and sheep on the land, and a trip to Auckland was only possible when it was dry enough for the horse-drawn cart to get through.

Now the trees were massive, their full canopies stretching across the dusty gravel drive, meeting in the middle, shading them as they drove up to the house. Niko's mouth dropped as they arrived at the beautiful old dame of a homestead. The yellow weatherboards and crisp white trim framing doors and windows made it look like something out of a storybook for children, a long stretch away from the cramped state houses where he had grown up. The inviting veranda with the cracked stone steps, edged by flowering white roses, made him forget for a moment why they were there.

Bill's mind was equally wandering. Having been friends with Lexi's older brother, he had spent many an afternoon after school here, exploring the outbuildings and surrounds.

The white picket fence surrounding the garden looked freshly painted and well maintained. At first glance, it looked idyllic, but as Lexi and Avery hurried down the path towards them, their pale faces told another story.

"Bill, I'm glad to see you mate." Avery shook his hand firmly.

"I picked up Niko on the way."

Avery shook Niko's hand. "Really appreciate it."

Bill opened the boot to get the equipment out. "Now, show me where it is."

"The entrance is at the back," Avery said, his discomfort clear.

As they walked across the parched lawn, Beau came bounding across to say hello, his tail wagging. Bill knelt down and gave him a good old pat.

"I'm sorry," Lexi said, mustering a weak smile. "He's in the habit of ambushing people and getting them to give him lots of attention." As quickly as Beau arrived, a rabbit appeared by one of the old apple trees, and the black dog shot off like a flash.

Still on his haunches, Bill was scanning the surrounding area. It felt like a long time since he had been there. He and Niko put booties and gloves on to go under the house.

The warmth of the late summer sun caressed their backs, and an ominous feeling hung in the air. Even before Niko opened the small trellis door, the unpleasant odour permeated through. He screwed up his nose involuntarily.

"Why don't you go back and keep Lexi company? It looks like she could do with some support," Niko said to Avery, who seemed relieved he didn't have to cast eyes on the limb again. Instead he just pointed out where it was. Bill pulled the door open, recoiling at the odour. He squeezed through with not too much of a problem, but Niko had to contort his body to get through. Bill switched his torch on. Even though he had to walk bent in half, he was glad the space was relatively airy, the mere thought of a cramped space was making him sweat. The smell was putrid, and the heat made it so much worse.

His brain quickly found the scent memory and brought him back to his first couple of months as a newly graduated constable. They had recovered the remains of an elderly man who had died in his small flat in the middle of a heatwave. It wasn't until the neighbours complained of the odour that the body was discovered. The overpowering sweet cheesy stench of human waste and fluids seeping from it had made him run outside to be horribly sick. For days afterward he struggled to eat and felt unable to get rid of the terrible smell, despite how many times he showered and changed. He hadn't smelled it for a long time, but it was etched in his memory forever.

Niko covered his nose. "Sarge, it smells like death in here."

Bill was sure that Niko had seen his fair share of unfortunate deaths in his brief time in the police.

There was a faint buzzing from the corner. Bill saw it first. It was a human hand. The flesh of two fingers were missing, a few torn bits hanging as if he and Niko had interrupted some creature having a meal. A circular wound in the centre of the palm didn't look like a gunshot wound — it had been made by force. The cut at the wrist was clean, probably made by a power tool as the edges were immaculate and even.

"That's a man's hand," Niko said, leaning in to get a better look. "It's swelled and not looking too great, but that definitely belonged to a bloke." He pointed at the coarse black hair on the bloated limb.

Bill nodded. The rats had definitely had a go, he thought, but now the flies were having a field day. The stifling air combined with the intense buzzing in the cramped corner made the familiar sensory overload raise its ugly head. The space was slowly closing in, blurred vision taking hold, he needed to get some air. "Come on, Niko. We've seen enough."

It was a relief to be in the open and take deep breaths, but questions whirled around; Who did the hand belong to? Where was the rest of the body? Or was the person still alive? And why was the hand under Lexi and Avery's house?

"You all right, Sarge?" Niko asked. Bill was standing with one arm against the exterior of the house, head bent down, large sweat stains spreading under his arms.

"Yes, all good mate. Just got a bit overheated." Bill was a proud man and had hidden his claustrophobia for most of his career. At seven he'd gone exploring behind the old marae, close to his childhood home.

His mother, Whina, had been helping the other women with a communal cook-up in the large kitchen at the marae. It was the start of the summer holidays, and his brother Hemi and sister Ata were supposed to be looking after him. Being older than him, they were more interested in doing their own things and had left him to his own devices. Bill had got bored and wandered over to the old meeting house to see if any of his friends were there. Getting side-tracked, he deviated and went to explore around an old cottage on the way. The doors were all locked, and he went looking around the overgrown garden. The thigh-high grass tickled his bare legs, and he was happy. He saw the door to the old shed was slightly ajar and walked towards it, not looking where he put his feet. It wasn't until he stepped through the rotten old planks that had covered the unused well that his brain registered what was happening. Scraping arms and legs on the way down, it felt like an eternity until he hit the cold murky water, completely submerging him, sinking into the silty bottom. Scrambling to get on his feet he clawed his way up, grabbing on to the uneven walls, coughing and spluttering until his head was above water. The muddy bottom was disgusting and full of rocks, and things like old bottles and God knows what. Once he found his balance he could stand up, the water reaching his belly button. Shivering, he moved around as best as he could, trying to warm himself. Gazing up, he realised it was too high to climb out on his own. As the cold and darkness set in and his voice grew hoarse from desperation and fright, he never thought he'd see his family again. It wasn't until late on the second day that they found him.

At that stage, he was too weak to call out, just wide-eyed and shaking uncontrollably from shock and hypothermia. His father lowered a ladder down the five-metre shaft and squeezed himself down the narrow well.

Bill didn't speak until several days later.

"Niko, let's cordon the area off and I'll call it in to Orewa," Bill said. "We need to inform the big boys." He wondered who they would send.

4

B ill pulled out his notebook and looked at a pale Avery as they sat down on the outdoor furniture at the front of the house. Avery went over the events leading up to finding the hand while Bill took notes.

"Did you hear a vehicle driving up in the night or early hours of the morning, or was Beau alerted to someone on the property?" Bill asked.

"No, I can't say that we heard anything. The bedroom is on the second storey. Beau sleeps on his rug in the kitchen. I would have heard if he'd got unsettled and barked."

"Any other vehicles that have driven up in the last few days that seemed out of the ordinary?"

"Not that we've noticed. With the farm shop and cellar door, there are quite a few cars coming up from time to time," Avery said, absent-mindedly stroking Beau's head. "I guess the old boy's hearing isn't what it used to be."

The lush greenery of the mature hedges cocooned them, providing a comforting embrace and some escape from the harsh reality of the scene under the house. A soft rustling of leaves and a tinkling of delicate notes from the wind chime on the veranda in the

distance was a welcome distraction. An earthy tang of the first wind-
fall apples lingered in the air, the sour cider smell reminding Avery of
his carefree childhood running around in the family apple orchard in
Central Otago. He had inherited his love of the land from his hard-
working parents, with most of the family's income coming from the
sale of apple cider in the autumn. The process had mesmerised
Avery, and that's what had got him interested in viticulture.

LEXI BROUGHT a tray with morning tea out and put an enormous pot
of coffee and the new white porcelain mugs on the table. The smell of
fresh bread and strong coffee permeated the air and Beau was
happily snoozing in the sun, twitching ever so gently, chasing rabbits
in his dreams as he slept by Lexi's feet.

A pair of fantails fluttered in and out of the old oak tree within
metres of the table, no doubt feeding their last lot of young for the
season. The birds' dark grey plumage and orange chests glimmered
in the morning sun. Beau stirred momentarily before losing interest
and going back to sleep. It was like any other lazy Sunday morning —
if there wasn't a human hand under the house. Lexi shivered, despite
the warmth of the sun.

BEAU RAISED his head sleepily as the second police car pulled in, then
set off to say hello to the two men stepping out of the vehicle.

Bill's heart sank when from the driver's side an older man stepped
out, his weathered features and stern mouth framed by tufts of coarse
grey hair, slightly thinning on top. A gust of wind caught the combed-
over tresses, whirling them around. His hand immediately smoothed
them down.

The younger cop, in his mid-thirties and lanky, had a friendly
smile and bent down to scratch Beau behind the ears, making them
best friends immediately. The older man completely ignored him on

his way past. A disappointed Beau's ears went down and he slunk away.

"Granger, what do we have here?" The voice was as gruff as his grey demeanour.

Before answering, Bill gestured to his right. "This is Constable Niko Sopoanga."

Niko grinned and put his hand out to say hello. Rudd ignored the introduction and had already turned away, addressing Avery first. "I'm Detective Senior Sergeant Brian Rudd from the CIB in Orewa. I understand you found the limb. This is my colleague Andrew Copeson," Rudd said, turning back to Bill before Avery answered.

Andrew Copeson was the complete opposite of his colleague and smiled warmly when introduced. "Copeson, get the kit. Granger will show us the way." Rudd turned his back on them while scanning the surrounding area.

"Okay, tell me what you know," Rudd said brusquely. If Bill had been a rookie it would have intimidated him; instead he felt annoyance rising. He disliked bullies.

"We arrived on the scene at eight twenty-one," Bill said, looking Rudd in the eye.

"What time was the call logged?"

"The call came in just before eight this morning."

"How did they discover the severed hand under the house? It's not like it was visible."

Bill had to bite his tongue in order to not snap and tersely relayed the morning's events from start to finish.

Rudd grunted, making notes without looking up or making eye contact. "Have you got the equipment set up, Copeson? And where is that photographer?"

Another car came up the driveway covered in a dust cloud, and a youthful man hopped out. The boy barely looked older than Gabriel, not helped by his uniform being slightly ill-fitting.

"I'm Jono," he said, his curly hair flopping as he walked over. "Sorry, I got a bit lost and had to turn around."

"About time," Rudd huffed and turned away, his footfall

crunching on the dusty white path as he walked to the back of the house, Jono pulling a face behind his back. Niko followed, giving Jono a hand with the lighting stands.

Copeson and Rudd got suited up in the protective gear. As they opened the trellis door, the putrid smell was worse than ever as the air had warmed up. Bill's green smoothie from this morning was threatening to reappear. He was pleased it wasn't him going back into the cramped space.

"Granger, show us where you found it, but take care where you put your feet," Rudd said.

Bill gritted his teeth. He remembered why he couldn't stand the grumpy old git. They had crossed paths before, each time as difficult as the last. You'd have thought the Orewa station would have got rid of him by now, either on a disciplinary matter or transferred him somewhere else, but obviously not. Thankfully he wouldn't have too many years left before retirement. Bill was sure he wasn't the only one counting down.

Bill stood at the entrance, trying not breathe in. He pointed. "It's just over there by the blocks."

"Okay Granger, wait for us outside." Rudd didn't even glance at him. He was in work mode, concentrating to the max as his flashlight swept the scene.

As Copeson's eyes got used to the dim light he could see the pieces of building material that had clearly been there for a while. He had put stepping plates down on the dirt floor and squatted down. He liked to change the viewpoint and looking at things from a fresh perspective. He and Rudd had their own investigating styles, but somehow it worked well; they complemented each other. They had worked together for a long time and he was used to Rudd's abrasiveness. Even though he didn't always like his manners, Copeson had a lot of respect for the man who never took shortcuts or compromised a situation. Even though Copeson had been in the force for the last fifteen years, the last five at Orewa CIB, Rudd still treated him as a rookie, although things had improved since he started standing up for himself on occasion. It seemed Rudd respected him more, but he sometimes forgot and fell back into his old ways of being gruff and plain rude.

"Let's go from here, Copeson. We'll move the lights as we need to," Rudd said.

"Sure." Copeson bent himself in half, trying not to hit his head on the low rafters. The stepping plates didn't help as they elevated him a couple of centimetres. At first glance, apart from a few shoe prints left in the fine dirt, which they marked, there didn't seem to be much of interest.

The strong rotting smell was getting worse. The severed hand was quickly deteriorating in the warm weather and decomposition was in full force. Copeson, an active member of the local Entomology Society, never tired of studying insects in the field and was glad he got to pursue his hobby in his line of work occasionally. The interesting thing with flies is that they rarely travel further than one or two miles when looking for food, but can fly a lot further when attracted by the unmistakable odour of rotting flesh.

With the buzzing in his ears, Copeson leaned forward. "This needs to be bagged up." He wiped the sweat off his brow while moving backward out of the cramped space.

Rudd grunted in reply and moved to have a closer look. "It doesn't look like it's been here that long, I would guess less than twenty-four hours. Any longer and there would be nothing left by the looks of what the rats have gnawed off already."

They went through the rest of the area methodically and marked anything else that might be of interest and finished as they were back at the door.

Rudd and Copeson emerged from under the house covered in cobwebs and dirt, faces striped from the sweat running down them. Being back in the fresh air was a relief.

Rudd stretched his aching back. "All yours, Jono. Take plenty of photos, and don't forget that burned-out water pump unit."

Jono pulled on the protective suit and got going.

"Is there anywhere we could rinse the dirt off?" Copeson asked Avery.

"Come with me. There's a tap by the water tanks. Rounding the corner, the men walked straight into Samantha washing her hair with the garden hose.

"What the hell? Take a photo, it'll last longer," she snapped, embarrassed at being seen rinsing her hair out and looking less than impressed with an audience watching.

"Sorry, sweetheart, we didn't mean to startle you," Avery said, but Samantha stomped away in a huff.

"Teenagers," he said. "I completely forgot, I need to call Ben Wilson, the electrician, to come and have a look at the water pump. That's if he isn't surfing and will come out on a Sunday." He turned to Rudd "When do you think we could get the pump seen to? There's no running water in the house without the pump working."

"ESR might want to take it with them. By the looks of it, you'll need a new one." Rudd washed his face under the tap.

As the car from Environmental Science and Research pulled up next to the police cars, Beau got up on stiff legs and stretched before bounding to meet the visitors. Emma Stansfield had legs that seemed to go on forever, Bill thought, accentuated just enough by her slim-line navy trousers. A crisp sleeveless white blouse neatly tucked in cinched her slim waist. Her blonde ponytail swished as she walked. With her brilliant white smile, bronzed face, and well-sculpted arm muscles, she looked as though she belonged on a surfing billboard. Avery looked mesmerised. Lexi had noticed her husband overtly staring, and did not look pleased.

Emma's partner Graham Rossi, an experienced Crime Scene Analyst in his early forties, was a good fifteen years older than her and was carrying most of the kit. His figure-hugging grey trousers and loud short-sleeved shirt exposing his dark hairy chest made his

Italian heritage clear. Bill smiled; he didn't think women fell for the stereotypical look. Still, Graham was in exceptional shape, his muscular body bulging in the right places through his clothes. Bill was sure he was well aware of the fact. Emma said hello to Rudd and Copeson and made the introductions to the rest. "Right, I guess that we'll leave it to you two," Rudd huffed, eager to get away. The two ESR Crime Scene Analysts headed around the back.

AS RUDD WALKED towards the car, he scowled and turned to Bill. "Orewa's dealing with multiple inquiries and I'm short staffed. You will have to handle some of this case from here, if that's not too much to ask," Rudd said, looking down his nose.

"We'll do our best," Bill said, slightly bemused at the decision.

"Good, that's settled then," Rudd said and turned on his heels and walked towards the car. Turning to Niko, Bill wondered what he'd agreed to. Returning his attention to this morning's event, he walked over to let Lexi & Avery know that they were leaving.

Bill could see that Lexi was exhausted so suggested that if they thought of anything else to pop in to see him at the station later today. Lexi gave him a look of relief. He could see she needed a reprieve and to catch her breath.

"That sounds good," she said, managing a weak smile. "I need to check on the children anyway." She walked towards the house, with her faithful companion Beau in tow.

"It's been quite a shock for her," Avery said. "If we're all done here I'd better go inside as well."

"ESR will stay on for a while. Once they leave you can have the electrician come around," Bill said.

"Thanks, mate," Avery said, gratitude in his eyes.

AVERY MADE his way up the stairs and into the kitchen where Lexi was staring out the window "Are you okay, darling?" he said.

"No, I'm not okay. Someone's bloody hand is under our house! Are we even safe here?" Tears welled up in her eyes. "And it doesn't help you making eyes at every pretty girl you meet, either." She bit her lip, looking down at the floor.

"We'll be fine," Avery said and took a step closer, opening his arms. Grudgingly at first, she melted into his chest, and for a few seconds, she let go.

5

Lexi phoned her best friend Annika who promptly invited them all to come over and freshen up. Once in the car, the pent-up nervousness and the uncertainty of the morning finally erupted. Samantha and Gabriel, even though they were too old for this, argued about whose turn it was to sit in the front seat. Evie was losing her temper because she could not find her favourite unicorn T-shirt and was whining like a three-year-old. The noise level reached a ridiculous level. Halfway down the driveway, Lexi's reasoning flew out the window and she stood hard on the brake, lurching everyone forward, cloaking the car in a cloud of dust, the shock silencing them all. It wasn't often that Lexi lost her patience.

"I know this is stressful for us all but will you behave yourselves. You're not pre-schoolers," she snapped.

"I'm not sure I want to come back home again. What if the person comes back to hurt us?" Evie said, her voice trembling. She sounded close to tears.

"Me neither. It's so creepy," Samantha said. "I think we should stay with Aunty Annika."

"What about Dad, I should have stayed with him, in case this nut job comes back." Gabriel was trying to sound older and more grown-up than his sixteen years.

"Listen, everyone, Dad will be perfectly fine," Lexi said, sounding more confident than she felt. "The people from ESR are still there, then the electrician will come over. It's not like he'll be on his own. Besides, he's got Beau there."

Lexi rarely lost her temper, but it seemed to have the desired effect as the children sat quietly for the rest of the drive. Unfortunately, her own mind was working overtime and the thought of some unhinged individual walking among them frightened her to the core. When she was younger, true crime, and the people behind it, had always fascinated her. That was what got her into nursing, specialising in psychiatric care. But it had been a relief to give it up when she had children, as emotionally it took a toll on her.

Driving through Matakana Village and on to Leigh Road, they went past Rusty's on the corner and then The Stables Restaurant, both family favourites, before arriving at Annika and Bill's house. The sight of the hundred-year-old white villa framed by dense hibiscus and a sea of bright pink flowers swaying gently in the breeze felt like a warm embrace. Lexi parked the car and everyone piled out.

Annika appeared on the front porch, her blonde hair swept up into a soft topknot, loose strands framing her face. Even though she was in her late forties, her skin still glowed from within, something Lexi put down to her good Scandinavian genes. She was dressed in workout gear, her figure almost as athletic as it was when they first met all those years ago in London. The twins, ten-year-old Anna and Veronica, pushed past their mother and ran down the narrow brick path, closely followed by their older sister Katie, who recently had turned fifteen. The girls looked like their mother, tall with golden flowing locks, although Katie's had been cut into a bob which made her hair look slightly curly, something she seemed quite pleased about.

Annika gave Lexi a hug. "How are you guys doing?" The twins and Katie all talked over the top of each other, asking lots of questions with Sam and Evie trying to answer as best as they could.

"Did you see it? What if there are body parts hidden all over the farm?" Veronica said with great animation.

"Girls, that's enough." Annika gave her daughters a stern look. "Have they not been through enough this morning?"

"Sorry Mamma, I didn't mean to be insensitive," Veronica said, downcast.

"No problems, V." Lexi put her arm around the young girl. "We've all got so many questions too."

"Hey, guess what, Mamma has made her yummy Swedish Socker Bullar," Anna said with a hint of the melodic Gotland dialect.

Samantha and Evie looked unsure for a moment.

"You know, those cinnamon rolls with pearl sugar on top," Anna continued excitedly.

The girl's face lit up and Lexi smiled.

"Who wants the first shower?" Annika asked, and the stampede up the stairs started.

Lexi gratefully sat down on the long wooden seat in the kitchen where the two families had enjoyed many a noisy dinner. Lexi had held her emotions together until now, but she could feel tears burning behind her eyelids.

Tears flowed down Lexi's cheeks. "What is happening to us?" She reached over the table for a tissue. "It feels personal somehow, don't you think?"

"I'm sure the police will get to the bottom of what this is all about," Annika said, trying to put her friend's mind at ease. She put her hand on Lexi's arm. "You're very welcome to stay here with us. The guest cottage is vacant at the moment."

Lexi gave a weak smile. "Thank you, that's very kind. I'm sure we'll be fine to return home once the water is working."

6

_____

It was eerily quiet. There was no sight of Beau who was still having his afternoon snooze in the kitchen, and had missed the entire thing. Avery went into the garage and got on the quad bike. All his jobs this morning had gone out the window. He needed to check on the livestock and make sure there was enough drinking water. He went up to the northern paddock, next to their neighbour, grumpy old Trevor. The cows were happy as ever, the water trough was full and he made a mental note to replace the salt stone, breathing a sigh of relief there was no sign of Trevor, who always seemed to stick his nose into everyone else's business. Avery was in no mood to listen to the old man's gripes with the world, not today.

On his way down, he parked the bike on the terrace hill and paused for a moment, looking out over the land they loved. The phone startled him with its loud ring signal. It was Bill Granger, wanting him to come down to the police station for another chat.

"I'm not sure what else I could tell you apart from what I told you this morning," Avery said.

"Have a think. Has anything happened prior to this morning, something strange or out of the ordinary? Sometimes even the smallest details can help."

"Well, we received some mail with cut-out letters, just like you see in those old B-grade movies." Avery was aware how silly he sounded.

"Have you still got them?"

"No. I'm sorry, I thought they were juvenile empty threats made by bored kids, to be honest. I didn't want to worry Lexi either, so I threw them away."

"That's a real shame, but try to remember what they said and come down later."

"I just have to feed the chooks, then I'll pop down."

When he arrived at the enclosure for the hens, the flock greeted him with a noisy display of displeasure. The leader of the flock and her sisters in the pecking order asserted themselves by squawking loudly and flapping their wings, letting him know that he'd better hurry.

Riding past the vines on his way back to the homestead, he stopped for a moment to check them out. Wine was his passion, and he tended to the vines as if they were his own babies. The abundance of plump purple grapes was pleasing to see. It looked like a bumper harvest.

After having a wash at the outside tap, he found a clean shirt and some faded shorts. He had a tendency to only wear old and comfortable clothes, but the washed-out and worn look didn't always appeal to his wife, at least not when they were in public. He fed Beau who ate with gusto as his mealtime was long overdue, and then invited him to come along in the car. Tail wagging, Beau jumped in on the passenger side of the beat-up blue Holden ute. It started making its usual rattling noises. Avery knew he really ought to upgrade to something newer. Gabriel could drive this one in a few months — it would be a great first car for him, sturdy and steady, with barely enough horsepower to pull the skin off a rice pudding. Gabriel had been driving for years on the farm, but it was very different on the road.

Avery's train of thought was disrupted when he saw Trevor at the end of the driveway. He sighed. Now he would have to stop to chat. Trevor was leaning against his metallic blue Hilux, waving vigorously to make sure Avery stopped. He had never seen Trevor in anything other than his faded jeans and a plaid shirt, sleeves rolled up exposing his wiry forearms. There wasn't a scrap of fat on the man, the deep furrows in his face telling a story of a less than a peaceful life. His grey stubble matching his short hair, reminded Avery of a pad of Steelo.

"Gidday, I was just on my way up to see you," Trevor said, tilting his head slightly, his cloudy blue eyes straining to focus. " You've had a lot of traffic to and from your place this morning. My eyesight's not what it used to be, but I could see you had a visit from the boys in blue. It's not that wayward boy of yours again, is it?"

Avery could feel the irritation rise from the pit of his stomach. He squeezed the steering wheel until his knuckles turned white, to control himself. "No, it had nothing to do with my son," he said. "Now, if you'll excuse me, I have to go into the village."

"Oh, I just wanted to give this to you." Trevor handed Avery a shrink-wrapped copy of *New Zealand Wine*, the winegrowers magazine he subscribed to.

"Thanks. How on earth did you get hold of this?"

"Well, the damned new NZ Post rep, must be blind, keeps putting your mail in my mail box, and doesn't read the address or the names properly." Trevor's face screwed up, showing his displeasure.

AVERY'S RELIEF was immense as he drove away, escaping his prying neighbour who seemed hell-bent on causing an upset with everyone in his path. The nit-picking and complaining had been going on since Lexi's parents owned the farm.

Beau, sitting on the front passenger seat, leaned over and put his sizeable paw on Avery's shoulder, cocking his head as if to say, "I'm here for you." Avery gave him a pat and said, "Thanks, mate. How about we stop for a coffee before we see Bill?"

They continued through the roundabout and onto Leigh Road to Bramble Café. The girls working there loved Beau, who was a regular visitor. The pair sat down under one of the enormous shade umbrellas. The café was busy, but as they were regulars one girl brought Beau an enormous bowl of water with ice cubes floating at the top. Avery took a sip of his flat white, made with full-fat milk, not that low-fat, watery rubbish. It was strong and just what he needed.

He cast his eye on today's paper. The *Sunday Star-Times* had no startling news, just the usual bleating about the current housing crisis and the need for new builds to accommodate the influx of people moving to Auckland. *As long as they don't all move up here*, he thought.

7

I n the comfort of Annika's kitchen, two coffees and a hot shower later, Lexi had changed into clean clothes and twisted her damp hair into a knot, securing it with a hair clip. Bill had called her earlier, asking her to pop by the station for a formal statement when she could. She knew she couldn't put it off any longer and drove into the main street and met Bill at the police station. Opening the heavy black painted kauri door, an original to the house, she felt as if she was in the middle of some crime drama on television. Bill got up from his desk and guided her through the small unmanned reception area, and into an open-plan room. He gestured for her to have a seat opposite him. Lexi squirmed on her seat, nervously chewing on her thumbnail. She just wanted to get this over and done with.

"Have you noticed anything that could be connected to this in the last few weeks?" Bill asked.

"No, we've been busy getting the winery ready for harvest and I've had some large orders for our cheddar and brie to fill. Apart from that, nothing I can think of."

"What do you make of it?"

"I don't really know. I could be wrong, but my gut feeling is chilling me to the core. I think it's personal. I'm not sure what the connection would be but the fact remains, there was a severed limb under our home, placed there or otherwise. The question is, why? The weird thing is that if Avery hadn't gone to check the water pump, we might never have made the discovery. The rats would have finished the remains and there would have been nothing left."

There was nothing more to add, but the question remained.

Avery pulled up as Bill walked Lexi to her car. Beau jumped out of the passenger side and ran up to greet Lexi. "Hi boy," she said, giving him scratches behind the ear.

"How are you doing?" Avery asked.

"Okay, I guess. Everything feels surreal."

"Ben Wilson's coming later this afternoon. I'm not sure if he got hold of a new pump. If not I guess we have to wait till tomorrow for the running water." Avery smiled. "It's not the end of the world."

"I'm sure we'll be fine," Lexi said, trying to sound cheerful.

BILL NOTICED a slight emotional distance between them and thought it unusual that they didn't display more affection towards each other. Lexi and Avery had always been a tight unit, so he put the lack of warmth down to the stress of the day and shook it off.

"Why don't you head back to catch up with Annika?" He could sense she was rattled.

"Thanks, I will do," she said and bent down to say goodbye to Beau.

"Is it okay to bring him inside, Bill?" Avery asked. "It's too hot to leave him in the car."

"Sure, no problem. I'll get him a bowl of water and we can get started."

Bill pressed Record. "You mentioned on the phone earlier that you'd received some letters in the weeks leading up to this. Can you tell me more about those?"

"Well, I'm not entirely sure it has got anything to do with this," Avery said, fidgeting on the uncomfortable plastic moulded chair. "I guess the first one arrived about six weeks ago. I didn't think too much about it. The simple text was something like, 'I know what you did'. It rattled me at first, then I thought it must be kids. Crudely cut-out letters pasted on a plain A4 piece of paper, put in a standard envelope, no postmark and addressed to me. It seemed silly. The second one was a few weeks later, with a similar message. The juvenile presentation convinced me that kids were having some fun. The third one came a week ago or so, and this time the message was different."

Bill leaned forward. "What was different this time?"

"It was written in black marker pen and said, 'You will pay'. The handwriting was urgent and angry, if you know what I mean." "I've got no idea what it could be about," Avery said sounding worried.

8

Lexi got into her car, the warm sun shining through the windscreen. She couldn't shake the spine-chilling cold from this morning, despite the hot shower at Annika's. As a nurse, she knew it was the effects of shock. Shivering, she pulled her cardigan tight and removed the hair clip that dug into the back of her head, letting her almost dry hair fall over her tense shoulders. Leaning back onto the headrest, she closed her eyes for a moment, wishing she could just stay there in the warm comfort of her car.

On the drive back to Annika's, she cracked the window just enough to feel the pleasant warmth of the late summer breeze. The blow out felt good, and she could taste the salt in the air. Oh, how she wished it was an ordinary Sunday. She took a deep breath, the fresh air filling her lungs, making her feel a little better. The last thing she felt like was having Avery's friend Isaac arriving tonight. He had called yesterday and wanted to come up from Auckland for a few days. He usually brought his wife Petra along, but this time he was coming alone. Perhaps she couldn't get time off work, Lexi thought. She would have to stop at the Four Square Supermarket on her way home to pick up some things for a barbecue. Thankfully she'd already made a large tiramisu that was sitting in the fridge; it was Isaac's favourite.

Lexi stepped through the open front door. In the kitchen, Annika was busy preparing tonight's dinner. Lexi could hear the familiar music from the Harry Potter movies.

"The girls wanted to watch *The Philosopher's Stone*. They assured me Evie would be all right," Annika said, hoping she had made the right call.

"Sure it is. We've read the first few books over the summer holidays. She's been busting to see it."

Annika smiled at her friend. "You're very welcome to stay for dinner. It's a large pork roast, plenty of food to go around."

"That's so kind of you, but we've got Isaac arriving tonight. He's staying for a few days. We haven't seen him in ages. It'll be nice, but I must say it's not the best timing."

"Is Petra not coming?"

"Apparently not, and of course Avery didn't think to ask why." Lexi rolled her eyes.

"At least have another coffee. The kids are just finishing their movie." Annika set some fresh cups on the table.

"Sure, why not," Lexi said and sank into the soft seat.

"Zac took Gabriel to Warkworth to catch up with a few mates. I hope that was okay." Annika leaned forward to take a sip of her coffee. Zac was a few years older than Gabriel, but they were still good friends. He had graduated with top results from Mahurangi College, was now in his second year of veterinary science at Massey University, and was a significant influence on Gabriel. "He'll drop him off at home on the way back later tonight. Now, I saved these for you. The rest the kids hoovered." Annika pulled a plate of cinnamon buns out of the pantry.

The white sugar crystals on top of the fluffy coiled bun crunched as Lexi bit into it, the butter and sugar layers coating her mouth with sheer delight as she closed her eyes. "God, I'd forgotten how amazing these are."

"I'm glad you like them," Annika said, pushing the plate closer, insisting she have another one.

"Thanks, but I'd better grab the girls and head home." Lexi called Sam and Evie, who came running into the kitchen.

"Thank you for having us, Annika," they said in unison.

As the girls ran to the car, Lexi lingered. "Are you sure you don't want to stay here? Isaac can come too," Annika said.

"Thanks for the kind offer but I'm sure we'll be fine," Lexi said, her smile strained. She was barely convincing herself.

The calm she had felt during the afternoon slowly disappeared as she headed back into the village to pick up a few things for dinner. Turning right into the main street by the cinema, she found it was busy with not a single park available on the road. She pulled in behind the shops and walked up the steep steps between the cinema and the surf shop, crossing the road to the Four Square. Close by, patrons at the pub were enjoying delectable food with glasses of wine in the late afternoon sun. The smell of soft cheese and charcuterie tickled her nose, enticing her to buy a selection of antipasti to serve before dinner. She would add some of their own cheese, perhaps the award-winning syrah cheddar. To complement she would serve the double-cream brie, its velvety and luxurious feel on the palate would match perfectly. Perusing the chiller, she decided on some aged grass-fed beef that she would pair with a home-grown salad. She made her way back to the car and with a slight feeling of dread, headed home.

9

The white Wilson Electrical van, the name in bold blue letters, pulled up to Matakana Valley Wines. In his old denim shorts with frayed edges and faded light-blue singlet with a Bintang beer logo, Ben Wilson looked every bit the stereotypical unkempt surfer. In the late afternoon sun, his bleached blond boyish tousled curls shone as they reached his tanned shoulders. Avery guessed he was in his early forties, although at a glance, he could have passed for ten years younger. Avery didn't know him well, as he was a relative newcomer to the area. His handsome appearance and reclusiveness made him a topic of curiosity among the young women in the village. That he always had surfboards strapped to the roof of his van added to his image.

"Hi, mate, glad you could fit us in today," Avery said.

"No worries. I didn't have much planned. " Ben pointed to the cordoned-off area around the house.

"What's with all the police tape?"

"Oh, it's just routine. It was a suspicious fire, so we had to call them. Not that I think it was anything deliberate, but you know how the insurance companies want the official process done before they pay out a cent." Avery was scrambling to find the words. "They had to remove the pump."

"How did they draw that conclusion?" Ben's piercing blue eyes went straight through Avery.

"It looked like the fan blade had got jammed, causing a short circuit which then overheated the unit. Thankfully, the house didn't go up in flames." Avery felt uncomfortable lying to the man's face, especially since he had given up his Sunday afternoon to help.

Ben nodded. "I see. I popped into Warkworth after you rang. My mate opened up his shop, so I have a new pump in the van for you." He peered into the darkness. "Well, I suppose I'd better get it hooked up."

The last thing Avery wanted to do was to go into any more details. The rumour mill in the village would go in to overdrive, anyway. While Ben was under the house, Avery's thoughts were swirling. It was a beautiful late summer's day and the harvest was around the corner. Everything seemed peaceful, just like before, but something had changed. His senses were heightened, and he felt jangled. He had to get a hold of himself. What if this had to do with the letters he'd received in the mail over the last few weeks? He had dismissed them; perhaps he shouldn't have.

"Ben, how are you going?" Avery called, peering into the dark void.

"I'm just about done here. Give me a minute and I'll be out," Ben said out of the shadows.

"Fancy a cold beer?"

"That'd be lovely, mate. Won't be long."

Avery went inside, Beau following him like a shadow, nearly tripping him up as he walked into the kitchen. "Come on, boy," Avery scolded. Beau's ears went down.

"It's okay, boy," Avery said, scratching the back of the dog's neck. "What's the matter with you today?" Beau was whimpering and pressing his ample forty-kilo frame against Avery's legs. "Come on, boy, how about a wee drink?" Avery picked up the metal water bowl and refilled it with cold water from the pitcher in the fridge. Beau stuck his entire face in the water bowl and guzzled.

Avery reached into the fridge for two beers, the bottles clinking as he went down the stairs to the table and chairs on the front lawn, Beau following closely behind. Avery sighed as he sat down and opened the beer, savouring his first refreshing sip. Ben walked around the corner, covered in dirt, wiping his forehead, streaks appearing on his face.

"The new pump works well," Ben said as he sat down, wiping his dirty hands on his shorts. Avery passed the beer over, reaching across with his own, banging the two necks together.

"Thanks, mate. I appreciate that you could come over on a Sunday afternoon," Avery said.

Ben nodded as he took a sip of the beer. Beau was snoozing under the table, enjoying the little shade the table was providing. Ben reached to give Beau a pat, giving him a fright resulting in a sharp bark of displeasure, his lips curled back and baring a row of brilliant white teeth.

"Sorry, boy, I didn't mean to startle you," Ben said as Beau moved away to lie under a tree at a safe distance a few meters away, observing from afar.

"Beau, you behave yourself," Avery said, feeling embarrassed. "Sorry about that."

"No worries. It was my fault. I gave the old boy a fright." Ben downed the rest of his beer.

"Would you like another?" Avery asked.

"No thanks, I'm fine, I might try to catch some waves at Tāwharanui before it gets too late."

Avery walked him back to the van, both men skirting around the uncomfortable subject of arson. "At least things are working and back to normal," Ben said as he loaded up his tools.

"Thanks. It's great you could sort everything out so quickly." Avery smiled. "Being without running water in a household full of women isn't easy. Will you email the invoice?"

"Sure, I'll get it out this week." Ben said and jumped in the van.

The uneasy feeling from this morning almost gone, Avery felt better as he sat back into the chair. The beer had done the trick, and it felt almost like any other Sunday afternoon. Beau had returned to his usual spot under the table and rested his head on Avery's foot, his intelligent brown eyes looking up, gently nudging Avery's leg with his paw.

"I know, boy. It's dinnertime."

10

A white van was parked in front of the farm shop when Lexi and the girls arrived back home. A smartly dressed man in his late fifties stood in thigh-hugging navy trousers, matched with a light pink polo shirt, the short sleeves squeezing his bulging biceps.

"Hello, I was just wondering if the shop was open," he said.

"Sorry, we're closed today," Lexi managed in her friendliest voice. "You're welcome back another day if that suits." Out of nowhere, Beau approached stiffly, his head and tail rigid, the hairs on the back of his neck bristling, his ears pricked forward, bailing the tourist up against his vehicle.

"Beau, behave yourself," Lexi said, her voice stern.

Beau's eyes were fixed on the man, a vibrating growl deep in his chest.

"Sorry, I don't know what got into him. He's normally such an easy-going dog." After the man got into his van and drove away Beau turned around as though nothing had happened, wagging his tail.

〜

FROM THE KITCHEN WINDOW, Avery could see the Audi pulling up and the girls getting out. He met the girls halfway across the lawn, scooping Evie and Sam into his arms. Evie melted into his embrace; Sam played it cool. "Who was that?" he asked.

"Some tourist wanting to have a look in the farm shop," Lexi said. "Beau didn't like him, and I'm in no hurry to lay eyes on him again. He gave me the creeps."

"Where's Gabe?"

"With Zac in Warkworth, catching up with some friends. Zac will drop him home later tonight." Lexi opened the boot to get the shopping.

"Ben just left," Avery said. "He got hold of a new pump and everything's back to normal and working. I suppose it was well overdue — the old pump was ancient, something your dad put in thirty or forty years ago."

"Did you say the fan blade was bent in the old one, causing the engine to short circuit?"

"Yes, that's why ESR took it, but in all honesty, we're lucky that there wasn't a fire." Avery's feeling of unease was returning.

Lexi glanced at her watch. "Goodness, is that the time! We'd better hurry to get dinner organised. Isaac will be here soon."

"Crikey, I'd totally forgotten he was coming up this evening," Avery said, a slight annoyance rearing its head. Isaac had been his best friend since university in Wellington. They might not see each other very often, but when they did, they just picked up where they left off. Isaac had sounded strange on the phone last night and had not alluded to why. It was a pity that James, their good mate from university, would not be joining them, although he lived only a stone's throw away in the valley where he ran his own vineyard. The falling out between him and Avery had been two years ago. They were both at an industry event, someone blew things out of all proportion and it had got out of hand. They had attempted to mend the bridges, but as time passed the more difficult it became. Perhaps he ought to reach out, see if James wanted to catch up over a beer at the pub, meeting on neutral ground. He missed his friend and was sure Isaac felt the same.

Lexi had it all in hand in the kitchen, the glistening steaks evenly placed on the wooden cutting board. A green salad topped with flecks of ruby pomegranate and plump figs sat on the bench next to thick slices of crusty sourdough bread. She was plating up the antipasti on the lid of an aged French wine barrel, the subtle aromas of cinnamon, fruit and allspice mixing with the deeper layers of coffee and tobacco. Avery's stomach growled and he realised he had eaten little today. He grabbed some bread with a hunk of cheese and a slice of salami. "I'll pop down to the cellar and get a couple of bottles of wine," he said between mouthfuls. Lexi nodded and moved on to the potatoes.

Avery switched the light on in the stairwell and descended the narrow stairs to the dugout part of the cellar. When Lexi's father Bob had first grown grapes, he had added a wine cellar. It was a generous size, floor-to-ceiling shelves and air conditioning keeping the temperature and humidity to an optimum level. The old unit rattled. Avery thought that if he knew Bob right, it would have been second-hand and something he'd picked up as a bargain. Bob had an eye for a good deal, but being penny wise and pound foolish did not always work out, as Avery found out when they took over the house and had to change most of the old appliances.

The bulk of their own wine was stored in large commercial wine cellars in the winery building. They also had a large library stock of Matakana Valley Wine, with vintages spanning over the history of the winery. And they always had some of their own label within reach in the cellar under the house, for drinking and sharing with friends.

Avery's other passion was collecting wines from all over the world. He was quietly fond of pinot noir. In his mind there was just nothing like the exuberance of a Central Otago pinot, cherry with a touch of spice, or on occasion the elegant balance of a French burgundy.

After perusing the racks along the wall, he decided on two

different pinots, brushing the dust off the bottles and making his way up the stairs.

"Shall I pour us a glass?" he asked, holding up the bottle. "Yes, please."

After all the drama and unpleasantness, Avery's heart swelled with love for her and he realised how much he had missed their closeness. He reached over for a kiss, taking her by surprise. He was well aware that the last few years had put a tremendous strain on their relationship. The stress of the ever-expanding business, plus having hormonal teenage kids at home, had put them on the back burner as a couple.

Lexi's cheeks glowed, and she regained her composure after the kiss. "It's still nice outside. I'll take the plates and the antipasti, you bring the wine. Let's sit outside and relax for a moment." She lit a citronella candle, sending the few buzzing mosquitos packing.

Avery put the Zalto wine glasses on the wooden table; hand-blown Austrian crystal, they were his favourites. He poured the wine and passed the fine-stemmed glass to Lexi, who pulled her cardigan close over her chest. Even though it was still a pleasant temperature, she could feel the evening damp slowly rising from the grass. In the far distance the cows were mooing, apart from that it was silent. Avery put his arm around her shoulders, enjoying the warmth and closeness.

"What a weird day, don't you think?" Avery said slowly.

"I'm not sure what to think. It's strange and disturbing," she said and took a sip of wine. "You'd think if someone was under our house last night that we'd have heard something, or at least Beau would have barked."

Avery swirled the wine in his glass. "I suppose so, but don't forget Beau is getting on. His hearing isn't the best. He was probably sleeping soundly, possibly on his good ear, deaf as a post."

The crackling howl of a V12 engine could be heard long before it got to the homestead, interrupting the peace. Moments later a silver Aston Martin pulled up.

"God damn," Isaac boomed as he stepped out of his car. "I'd

forgotten how dusty your driveway gets in summer." As a corporate accountant, he normally wore something dark and conservative. Being the weekend, today he was casual in a pair of unfashionable jeans that must have sat in the back of his wardrobe for the last decade, and a short-sleeved blue-and-green gingham shirt. It amazed Lexi that Petra had allowed him to leave the house looking like that.

"Love your wheels, man," Avery said. " Very James Bond."

"I picked it up last week," Isaac said brimming with pride. "It's got custom leather interior and is all built by hand."

Avery sat in the driver's seat and ran his hand over the leather finish. "There's nothing like the smell of a new car!"

"Come on 007, you boys can drool some more over the car tomorrow. Let's get the barbecue fired up. I'm starving." Lexi pushed the two men towards the house. "The spare room is all made up for you." Isaac was a partner at PWC in the city and Petra was a corporate lawyer, both were busy professionals and loved getting away to the stillness and calm of the country, and had stayed with Lexi and Avery many times.

Dinner cooked quickly, the smell of the grilled meat enticing the girls outside. "I can't believe how much you girls have grown," Isaac said. "I can remember when you were tiny babies — I could hold you in one hand. I can't keep up."

Avery was pouring another glass of wine for Isaac when Zac pulled up to drop Gabe off. Despite already having had dinner he was starving.

"There's plenty of leftovers. Help yourself," Lexi said. Gabe piled his plate high with steak and potatoes, completely ignoring the leafy green salad.

The candle had gone out and the temperature was dropping, and the night sky was putting on an impressive show while they enjoyed the last drops of wine.

"I can't believe how beautiful the stars look up here. In the city you barely see anything for the light pollution. You are so lucky to have all this." Isaac said, his voice cracking up.

"We sure are, mate," Avery said, seemingly clueless about his friend's emotional state. Lexi put her arm around him, giving him a squeeze. There was no need to speak.

"Shall we go inside for coffee? I don't know about you guys, but I'm getting eaten alive by the bloody mozzies," Avery said.

Once the dishwasher was chugging along and the coffee was ready, they went into the lounge on the other side of the hallway. Sinking into the weathered sofas, the soft leather sighing softly as they sat down. Updating the decor hadn't been a priority, although they were thinking perhaps over the quieter winter months it would be good to address.

"How about some dessert?" Lexi put the overladen crystal dish on the coffee table.

The cold, luscious mascarpone layers smothering the coffee-soaked sponge fingers and sprinkled with dark chocolate Vahlrona balls looked heavenly.

"I can't believe you remembered tiramisu is my favourite," Isaac said, his eyes shining. "This is nice. I'm so glad to be here." "We're glad to have you here too," she said.

Avery shook his head. "I'm glad you weren't here this morning."

"What happened?" Isaac's jaw dropped as they told him about the macabre find under the house. "You are shitting me!"

"I wish we were. It feels surreal," Lexi said.

"Well, that makes my news pale in comparison," Isaac said, his normally confident voice wavering.

"Petra has left me."

"I'm so sorry to hear that," Lexi said and leant over, giving him a hug.

"The worse thing is, I don't really know why, and she refuses to talk to me." Isaac said, his voice tinged with sadness. "We've had our issues over the years, but doesn't everybody? Last year was difficult for us. We gave IVF one last go. It was a hormonal rollercoaster and tougher than I realised on Petra. The truth is, I'm not sure if I was there for her enough." He twisted his wedding band nervously round and round. It wasn't easy for him to open up like this, Lexi knew.

"Then against all odds, we became pregnant. Unfortunately it wasn't to be and we lost the baby."

"I had no idea mate," Avery said.

"Were you able to talk about your grief?" Lexi asked.

"No. Petra distanced herself from me, and point-blank refused to see a professional. In fact, we gave our marriage one last push with a trip to Fiji over Christmas. Things seemed to improve a little. I really thought we'd been through the worst of it. Then last week, out of the blue, she packed her bags and left a note for me when I came home from work. She said she couldn't take any more and needed space."

"Where is she now?" Lexi asked.

"With her sister. At least I know she's safe and not on her own." Isaac wiped his nose with the back of his hand.

"Oh Isaac, perhaps she just needs some time to heal. You've both been through a lot."

"Well, getting you out of the big smoke and into the fresh air up here will do you a world of good." Avery gave Isaac a friendly punch on the arm. "I hope you've brought some old clothes, because I'll get you up nice and early tomorrow to give me a hand with the chores. Get you doing some real work for a change," Avery said. Isaac smiled, it was apparent he couldn't wait.

11

———

Bill was enjoying the early morning in the quiet house, and got up to let Maggie and Finn, the four-year-old standard poodles out for their morning toilet stop. Maggie, the alpha dog and more sensible one, meandered through the open door, sniffing the morning air, her curly chocolate coat making her look like a teddy bear. The jet-black Finn, who was much bigger than his sister, scampered past Bill, nearly knocking the cup of tea out of his hand. He was a handsome boy, but not the most intelligent.

It was still dark outside; summer was ending for sure, the damp from the ground rose with an early autumn freshness in the air. Bill liked it as it was the beginning of peace up here. His hand automatically went to check the teapot which was still hot and he poured himself another cup before he sat down and opened his iPad to browse the *Herald* online. They had stopped receiving the paper edition well over a year ago. He had to admit, he still missed not holding a paper in his hands when reading the news. It had been Annika's idea; she was going through a serious recycling phase, saving the trees and all that comes with it. As a family they were environmentally friendly, recycling household waste, they had a worm farm and he had even installed solar panels on the roof. Although it was a pain putting in the extra work, he remembered with a smile, that's why he fell in love with Annika. She was a passionate and caring woman who embraced many things in life, and he loved her quirky traits and whims.

Nothing particularly interesting had happened over the weekend, but soon enough journalists would get wind of the hand found in Matakana, and the phone would ring off the hook. The thought made him sigh out loud.

He cast an eye on the clock, it was nearly time for the children to wake up and the morning madness to begin. The Nespresso machine on the bench was Annika's favourite appliance and took pride of place. He reached up into the cupboard for the caffeine-free capsules, inserted one and waited for it to do its magic. The toaster popped, and he smeared a generous amount of butter with jam on top before walking upstairs and waking his wife with a gentle kiss.

"You are a darling," she said as the aroma of coffee spread through the bedroom.

"I know," he said.

"What's the plan for today? I suppose there's a bit to do with the recent investigation."

"Yes, no doubt Orewa will issue directives, so I'd better get going."

Annika savoured her coffee, momentarily thinking of the George Clooney ad. She was looking forward to a productive day. As soon as the children went off to school she would go out to the studio to start a fresh canvas. She often had two or more on the go, as she loved the freedom of going between pieces as they developed organically.

"Mamma, where are my school shoes?" Veronica shouted from downstairs, shattering the morning's peace.

"Mamma, where is my PE bag? I can't find it," Anna yelled, competing in volume with her twin sister.

"I'll be there in a minute," Annika called. She took a last sip of coffee, got up, threw her old floral dressing gown on, and stuck her feet in the sheepskin slippers by the end of the bed. She headed downstairs towards the noise, carrying her half-eaten toast with her. The kitchen table was chaotic with cereal packets, yoghurt pots, fruit and Katie's Spanish textbooks.

"I thought you said you'd finished all the homework over the weekend," Annika said with a slight annoyance. "It's too late doing it now, don't you think?"

"I did most of it on Saturday, I just forgot about this one page of verbs," Katie groaned. "I meant to get it finished yesterday, but then Sam and Evie came over and I forgot."

"As long as you're up to date with your work and don't get into trouble with the teacher."

Annika scanned the pantry for lunch box food. "Veronica, did you have a look in the entrance for your shoes?"

"Yes, found them."

"That's great. What about you, Anna? Did you find the PE bag where it normally goes when it's laundered and clean?" Annika said, barely able to contain her laugh.

"Yes, sorry."

"I'm glad everyone's found the things they need for school. How about checking that you've got everything you need the night before?" Annika suggested.

"Mamma has a point, you guys," Bill said, his voice as terse as he could muster. "Preparation is key."

"Yes, we know. We'll have to try harder, won't we," said Katie, ever the diplomat.

"Dad will take Katie to the bus and drop you two at school," Annika said while making ham and cheese sandwiches for the twins and a quinoa salad topped with leftover roast pork from last night's dinner for Katie, and finally a piece of home-made ginger cake and some fruit in each lunch box.

Bill normally came home for lunch, it was a full-time job cooking and looking after her busy family of six, but she loved her crazy big lot and wouldn't have it any other way.

"Time to get going, girls, or we'll miss the bus," Bill said, herding the twins towards the door.

"Do we have time for hot chocolate after we drop Katie at the bus?" Veronica asked.

Bill said, "Sure, why not," but Annika shook her head. He was such a pushover, and he knew it.

"Awesome," the twins shouted in unison and ran to the car.

Goodbye kisses all around, then the peace set in. Annika looked at her half-eaten toast and made a fresh cup of coffee. As if on cue, as soon as she sat down there was a short sharp bark from the front door. She let Molly and Finn in from their morning scamper around the garden, giving them a little fuss, then putting their breakfast in the usual spot on the porch. As she was stacking the myriad of plates and implements in the dishwasher, Zac sauntered into the kitchen, bleary-eyed and yawning, his hair sticking straight up.

"Morning, I'm just going to grab a piece of toast and get going, I have to be at Uni early today," he said, scratching his unshaven chin. He looked so much like Bill when he was younger, Annika thought; bright green eyes, olive skin and, by the amount of young women he socialised with, a real charmer.

"Okay darling, just let me know if you're home for dinner so I know." Annika playfully tousled his dark glossy hair.

Annika went upstairs and had a quick shower, getting dressed and ready before seven-thirty, not a scrap of makeup on and her long blonde hair tied in a loose bun. By the time she got back downstairs, Zac had already left. She struggled with the concept of their first-born being all grown up.

She loaded the food-scrap bucket and went outside to feed the chickens, going past the front paddock to check on her beloved Gotland sheep on her way. She was happy to have been able to get hold of the breed here on the other side of the world, making her feel connected with her birthplace. The ewes were of medium build, fine-boned, the small horn curling to the back graciously. The dense pelt with its lustrous tight curl ranging in colour from light greys to charcoal, highlighted by their jet black faces with a lighter-coloured muzzle. Their large brown eyes looked at her inquisitively. The single ram was a big boy and was strutting around, puffing his chest out as if he owned the place. His thick and grooved horns twisted around to the front majestically, showing the annual rings like a tree trunk. The ewes felt safe with him around and the small flock gathered along the fence line as she gave each of them some fuss, their sweet and greasy lanolin coating her hands. A happy chorus of bleating immediately reciprocated the affection received. Not raised for meat — Annika used their wool in her artistic endeavours — they were more pets than anything, and were shaved at the beginning of summer to make them more comfortable.

She made sure there was enough water in the trough before she carried on past the hen house to her studio in the old barn, with the airy gallery to the side. She felt very fortunate to be able to pursue her passion. Maggie and Finn followed behind as usual, lying down on the large rug inside the door in the gallery while Annika continued to the studio at the back. She liked to work on large canvases on the floor. Taking out a range of paint pails from the cupboard in the corner, she turned the music up loud and got to work.

12

Lexi dropped Gabriel and Samantha at the bus stop and continued into the village to drop Evie off at school. A tight band was setting in around her head, the exhaustion after last night's terrible sleep catching up. Not a brilliant start to the week. She sighed while massaging her throbbing temples. Avery and Isaac had set off early, well before she'd got up. The harvest was upon them, and Avery spent most of his time tending to the vines, testing the sugar content and working out optimum picking. It would probably be another week, she thought, looking around the old kitchen, breakfast dishes piled up high. It annoyed her that it always was up to her to tidy up. Venting her frustration, she slammed the plates and cutlery as she stacked the dishwasher. The stomping around woke Beau from his slumber, and he raised his head with a startled expression.

"Sorry. I didn't mean to wake you, boy," she said. Beau stretched and walked over to the bench where she was standing. Much of the irritation drained away, and she bent down to pat him.. "Come on, boy, let's collect the veges for the shop." Beau followed her like a shadow as she entered the large greenhouse behind the winery building. A few lazy flies greeted her, the buzzing somehow comforting as the warm earthy air hugged her like a blanket. She filled the cane basket with courgettes, cucumbers, leeks and a couple of bunches of celery. Wiping the dirt off her hands before stepping further in, she picked a few handfuls of perfectly ripe tomatoes. The heavily laden specimens were staked and tied with string to the ceiling, securing the long spreading stems. The moist air mixed with the herbaceous green scent of the fruit brought her back to her childhood in an instant. As a child she used to sit in here for hours, it was her special place of serenity. Taking a bite out of a warm tomato, she walked next door to the farm shop, Beau still close behind.

In the last few years they had expanded the business to making the award-winning syrah cheddar and double cream brie, as well as an aged cheddar, parmesan and a popular super-stretchy mozzarella, all made from milk produced from their own cows, and matured here on the farm. It had long been Lexi's dream to break into boutique cheese production, and they had installed the commercial kitchen last year. Roger up on the ridge tended the Jerseys, it wasn't a large herd, but it was more than enough for what they needed. The arrangement was that Roger milked and looked after them, and in return got to keep the milk Lexi didn't need. It was a mutually beneficial arrangement.

Lexi switched the lights on in the shop, a feeling of happiness washing over her. She'd worked hard for this and was immensely proud. The fridges along the back wall were full of fresh cheeses, all produced by herself and two local women who came in once a week. The day-to-day running of the cheese-making she managed on her own. Lexi went behind the counter, putting today's float in the till. She caressed the thick slab of solid kauri, left over from the shipbuilding days in nearby Matheson Bay, and acquired by her grandfather many years ago in a trade. It must have been sitting in the barn for the last fifty years until Avery had put his heart and soul into handcrafting a beautiful shop counter for her.

In the quiet winter months, Lexi would make various textile products such as aprons, pot holders and tote bags she displayed on the tall shelves behind the counter. The latte-sipping crowds from Auckland seemed to like anything rustic, and she assumed it made their expensive kitchens with thick granite benches look homelier.

After setting up for the day, Lexi put the "Back in 5 minutes" sign on the door, got on the quad bike and headed towards the orchard. She didn't lock the door; no one ever did around here. Most road stalls were unattended and had honesty boxes. It was all part of country life and she loved it.

In the orchard she gathered handfuls of ripe stone fruit and figs, slightly sticky to the touch with a sweet smell of dry earth and scorched sun. The passionfruit vine was out of control on the sun-kissed side of the trellis, a sea of large white-and-purple flowers swaying gently in the breeze, delicate curly tendrils holding the vigorous plant in place. Lexi filled the tray on the bike with as much as she could. She cut a passionfruit in half with her pocketknife, enjoying the sweet fragrance as she squeezed the fruit into her mouth.

Next, the chicken coop. The hens were free-range and could come and go as they pleased, but thankfully mostly laid their eggs in the hen house. The old wicker basket had seen better days, but hadn't collapsed yet. Lexi gently put the fragile eggs in one by one, laying them on the bunched-up rags to stop them moving around. The two old hens strutting completely ignored her, scratching and pecking around her feet.

Back at the shop she cleaned the eggs, putting them into cartons of six with a best-before date of four weeks from today. After finishing her chores, she went back to the house. Waiting for the jug to boil, her mind wandered to yesterday's drama. The room suddenly went gloomy, as if mirroring her state of mind, the ragged edges of the ominous thick, dark-grey cumulus blocking the sun completely, its outer edges glowing softly against the darkened sky. Beau sensed her discomfort and buried his wet nose in her palm. She poured the tea, grabbed the biscuit tin and sat down at the kitchen table. Beau gazed up at her, forever hopeful of a piece of biscuit to share.

"You've just had breakfast, boy," Lexi said firmly, but quickly gave in, breaking the shortbread in half.

It was only ten o'clock; she had a ton of paperwork to get through for the accountant, but was in no mood to tackle it. The concentration was just not there. Perhaps she should call one of her old colleagues who now worked in the School of Psychology at the University of Auckland. He sometimes did profiling for the police. Perhaps he could shed some light on what kind of nutcase they were dealing with. One thing was for certain, none of this was anywhere near normal.

13

At Matakana Police Station, Bill was going over the information from yesterday's crime scene. They didn't have much and there were still so many question marks. Niko had called all the hospitals north as far as Kaitaia and south as far as Taupo to see if anyone missing a left hand had presented. Having no luck with the hospitals he had tried the morgues, but no luck there either.

"It's a bit of a mystery for sure," Niko said looking through his notes. "The Special Search Group went through the farm and the area surrounding it yesterday and found nothing of interest."

"I spoke to Rudd just before," Bill said. "They should have a preliminary answer, perhaps by the end of the day, on how long since the hand was severed." He was grateful that Orewa felt so inclined, as to keep them in the loop. "It's lunchtime. Let's head over to Matakana Valley Wines for another look. We can grab a sandwich on the way."

AVERY AND ISAAC had finished their chores and the inspection of the vines and continued to the paddock up the hill to check on the cows.

Even though Roger milked them, Avery still had the primary responsibility for their welfare. They refilled the drinking water in the trough and got a couple of salt stones out of storage in the milking shed, as the old ones were just about gone. A few of the fence posts needed straightening so Avery decided to return after lunch to fix them.

The gentle ride downhill and back to the homestead took only a few minutes. Isaac parked the quad bike next to Avery's before going inside. "You should have become a farmer. It suits you," Avery said, knowing how much Isaac enjoyed riding the farm bikes.

Isaac smiled. "Perhaps I should have. It would have saved a lot of crap in my life, and would be a pleasant change from wearing a suit every day. I much prefer shorts, singlets and gumboots."

"You're just in time. There's frittata and salad on the table for you," Lexi said. The smell made Avery realise how hungry he was. They chatted like old times, Isaac telling them about some of his more demanding clients. He was finally relaxing.

Then he became serious. "We've had a terrible couple of years, rounds of IVF, the hormone treatment for Petra with its horrible side effects. I was merely a passenger. It was her body and mind that copped the full brunt of the ordeal. I could have been more sensitive to what she was going through."

Lexi touched his hand. "These things take time to heal. Just let her know you are there for her, no matter what."

"It was tough to lose the baby for me as well, but I chose to bury myself in work, leaving Petra to cope with the grief on her own. That wasn't fair on her." The look in Isaac's eyes said it all.

"You should call Petra," Lexi said. "Let her know you are there for her."

"We are here for you both, you know that," Avery said.

"When is the Matakana Film Festival on again?" Avery said, changing the subject.

"Opening night is tomorrow. The first movie is *The Dark Horse*." Lexi turned to Isaac. "Would you like to come along?"

"Sure, but isn't it a few years old?"

"Yes, but they're showcasing the best of New Zealand film over the next week. Annika is in charge so it will be a fabulous event."

"Talking about doing well, how is James?" Isaac asked.

Avery rubbed his stubbly chin before answering. "I saw him down at the pub last week. He said a quick hello before he took off in a hurry."

"I can't believe it's still dragging on. I thought you said you'd talk to him before Christmas."

"I tried. I drove up to his house with a basket of goodies from the farm shop. No wine — I didn't want to inflame the situation further. Instead, I put in a single malt, one I know he likes. I just wanted to apologise for my part of the upset, offer him my hand and sort it out."

"What did he have to say?"

"James was in a terrible space, completely crushed. Tina had just left him and taken the two boys with her."

"I knew they were having a few issues, but it would have been tough on him that she just up and left like that. Did you manage a truce?"

"I guess we did, of some sort. We agreed that there had been a misunderstanding at the International Wine Show, and that our tempers had got the worst of both of us. Even though he admitted he didn't think I cheated when I submitted my wine, it seemed like he wasn't thinking we deserved winning the syrah gold."

Isaac frowned. "Serious accusations."

"Absolutely, and completely without merit, James admitted he was going through a crappy time when it happened. I reacted like anyone would when accused of cheating."

"I guess you have to feel sorry for the poor bloke, he must have gone through hell these last couple of months," Isaac said. "We should call him, see if he wants to catch up over a cold beer."

"Yes, why not? I'll call him later, but first let's get the fence fixed up before we have some escapees."

～

BILL AND NIKO pulled up in front of the homestead just as Avery and Isaac came down the steps.

Bill stretched out his hand. "Isaac, it wasn't yesterday that I saw you, mate."

"Great to see you too."

"I suppose Avery has filled you in on recent events?"

Isaac nodded.

"Would you mind if we have another look around the place, Avery?"

"Yes, no worries. I haven't noticed anything else out of the ordinary, but you never know."

"Great. We'll start with the outbuildings and work our way around the property if you don't mind."

"All good. If you want to use the quad bikes, I park mine over there and Gabriel's is parked in the barn, the green one," Lexi said. "Key's in the ignition."

Bill pointed to the sleek Aston Martin. "You wouldn't be able to leave the keys in this beauty."

"No, mate. I'm sure it would go quickly, especially in Auckland," Isaac said, making them all laugh.

Avery got on the motorbike. "Isaac and I have to head up to the corner paddock and tend to the fence. We'll catch up with you later."

Lexi took the men into the outbuildings where everything looked fine until they got into the back of the winery where Avery had his office. "Bloody hell!" Lexi cried out. The small windowless office looked as though a tornado had gone through it. The desk drawers had been pulled out and left overturned on the floor; books from the wall unit were all in a jumbled mess, thrown everywhere in a rage. The metal filing cabinet was the same, although the heavy drawers were still in place, the files dumped and scattered all over the desk. "Avery can be a messy bugger, but not like this!"

"Touch nothing," Niko said as she reached for the files on the desk.

"Can you please call Avery and get him to come back," Bill said as he stepped cautiously between the piles of debris on the floor.

Lexi tried his mobile, but it went straight to voice mail. "Typical when we need to get hold of him. He's hopeless with his phone. Half the time it's turned off. I'll try Isaac."

The signal rang twice before she heard Isaac's voice. "Hi Lexi, are you all right?"

"Yes, but can you send Avery back to the winery? We just need to check something."

"Sure. He'll be there in a few minutes."

Bill and Niko carefully worked their way around the room. Lexi felt uneasy and leant against the wall for support.

Bill picked up on her worried demeanour. "Don't worry," he said and put his arms around her shoulders. "We'll sort this out." Bill was like a big brother to her, and had always looked out for her since they were kids. She knew she could trust him.

Avery walked through the door with Isaac in tow and stopped in his tracks when he saw the mess in the office. "What the fuck is this?" He was visibly shaken. "It was fine when I left the office on Saturday afternoon. Well, perhaps a little untidy, but nothing like this." His normally straight back and shoulders sagged; the air had completely gone out of him.

Bill took a well-thumbed notebook from his pocket. "Who else has had access to the office since then?"

"We rarely lock the door," Avery said. "The harvest is just around the corner and my workers are coming in next week for the final clean of the vats and the equipment."

"We'll get a few photographs," Bill said, "but could you stay here? It would be good to see what's missing."

AVERY FELT as if someone had punched him in the stomach. *This is far from over.* "Sorry to have to bail on you, Isaac."

"No problem. This is important. Perhaps I could go back up the hill and finish the repair job in the meantime?".

"Thanks, mate." He shot his friend a smile. "I just wish you'd have come up last week instead, and not in the middle of this bloody mess."

~

"I'M GLAD TO BE HERE," Isaac said and walked back to the quad bike. Adrenalin coursed through his body as he sped up on the uneven ground, his hair flopping in the wind as he went through the vines and up the top paddock. For the first time in a long while he felt useful and needed and a little of his self-worth was returning.

It didn't take long to finish the job. Isaac leant back and admired his handiwork. The electric fence was still turned off. Turning the switch, Isaac felt a tremendous jolt cursing through his body. The last things he saw before landing head first in the tall grass were the blue flames licking his fingers and up his hand where the electric current entered his body.

~

LEXI WENT BACK INSIDE. There wasn't much she could do until they'd finished in the office. Standing at the large double sash window, she pushed the ceramic pot with the red flowering geranium aside, making enough space for her to perch. She could see the farm shop and the winery from there. This late in the season, there weren't many customers anyway.

Finding it impossible to just sit there and wait, she dashed across to the winery. They'd made little progress by the looks of the state of the office. "I can't see anything that's missing," Avery was saying as Lexi walked in.

"What about the framed photo that used to hang on the wall behind your desk?" she said. "Have you found that?"

"What's it of?" Niko asked.

"It's an old photo," Avery said. "Crikey, we're going back to my university days. It was the summer we all graduated. Peter Evans, my friend from Martinborough got us all jobs at one of the local vineyards over the holidays. Peter, James and I had just got our viticulture degrees, but had very little experience, so this job was perfect. We would assist the resident winemaker, a grumpy old sod. But it wasn't all that we thought it would be."

"What do you mean?" Bill asked.

Avery laughed. "Well, we didn't get to do as much as we thought we'd be doing, and the pay was piss poor. We still had an outstanding summer, though. The world was our oyster."

"Who was in the photo?" Bill said, scribbling some notes.

"There was Peter who got us the jobs, James Smith, who lives here in Matakana now, Isaac Miller and myself."

Bill looked up from his notebook. "Isaac was there too, but he isn't in the wine industry, is he?" "No, he's an accountant. He got a job as a caretaker, so he could hang out with us guys."

"Who took the photo?"

"I think I did," Lexi said, piping up from behind.

"Do you still have the negative?", Bill asked.

Niko tried and failed to stifle a laugh.

Bill glared at his younger colleague. "It's not like now with everything being digital, and accessible immediately."

"Sorry Sarge," Niko said, still grinning.

"We may still have a copy in one of the photo albums in the attic," Lexi said. "Is it important?"

"It might be of significance. If you can locate it, that would be good."

14

Isaac lay flat on his back in the grass, his jaw clenched shut as he tried to open his eyes. A burnt-flesh smell mixed with the scent of fresh dung wafted over him. He could not decide which was worse, the searing pain piercing his brain every time he looked up or the bashed-up feeling from top to toe. Where was he? What had happened?

He willed his body to move, the nerve endings screaming with every attempt. He had no idea how long he'd been unconscious. His scrambled thoughts whirled around his head until he remembered where he was. Matakana, on the farm. The cows came in closer, gathering around his battered body, large inquisitive eyes staring at him from above. Thick warm breath laced with notes of fresh-cut grass washed over him. A strong sandpapery tongue licked the length of his face and snapped him out of his daze, making him shout out, and the herd dispersed. He could see the blue sky again.

Bit by bit he could move his fingers and then slowly his arms, all while angry pain impulses radiated through his body. He sat up, and his head felt as if it would explode. The weird sensation in his body remained, a tenderness from the inside out; surely wild horses or mad cows had kicked the crap out of him. A heavy smell of flesh and rancid fat hung in the air. He realised it came from the raw burn etched on the inside of his hand just below his right thumb.

He stood up and hobbled over to the quad bike to have something to lean on. His backside was on fire and his chest ached with every breath. Heart racing, he tried to catch his breath. He fumbled his mobile out of his back pocket to call for help and realised why his rear end was sore — a $2 coin in his pocket had melted onto the back of the phone, causing the screen to crack. It was completely fried. He started the bike and carefully rode down the hill.

"WHAT THE FUCK HAPPENED TO YOU?" Avery said.

Isaac attempted a smile. "That pissing electric fence gave me a real kick. Jolted me good."

"That's impossible. There's no way it would kick like that."

"Unless someone's tampered with it?" Bill said.

"The current went through my hand." Isaac held it up to show the wound. "And exited through my bloody arse." He turned around, lost his balance and toppled over.

Avery and Bill went over to help him up and propped him against the bike. "We can take you down to the doctor to have a look at those wounds," Bill said.

"Why the hell didn't you call us?" Avery said, irritated and embarrassed Isaac had got hurt while helping him.

Isaac held up the damaged phone. "This copped the brunt force of the current. It's good for fuck all now."

"I'm sorry mate, I didn't mean for you to get mixed up in this mess," Avery said shaking his head.

"I'm fine," Isaac said, trying for a smile. "Just feel a little bashed up."

"Let's call it a day. Lexi will plaster you up while I hop on the quad to check the fence. Can't leave it like this while we've got livestock in the paddock."

"If you're sure you're okay, we'll get going," Bill said, still concerned.

Isaac shook his head. "Really, I'm fine." He grinned. "It'd take a lot more than that to kill me."

Lexi had returned with the first-aid box. "Let me have a look at those burns and bandage them up for you," she said, taking him by the arm and pushing him towards the house. "Let's take care of the hand first."

Isaac held his right hand out, the wound looking angry and red. "I think I must have leaned against the metal post with one hand and accidentally come into contact with my right hand with the fence. Not sure how else I can explain it."

"You were lucky. It looks like it's gone through two layers of skin, with a slightly deeper burn in the padded part of your hand. We may have to take you to the doctor tomorrow, depending on how it looks," Lexi said, cleaning it gently.

Isaac flinched, but said, "I'm sure it will be fine." Lexi added a soft gauze dressing and wrapped it up with an outer layer to keep it sterile.

"Let's have a look at your bum," she said. Isaac turned around and pulled his shorts down enough for the top of the buttock to be exposed. An angry outline of the iPhone was seared onto his skin. Thankfully this wasn't as severe, but it was still a large, red and partially blistered area. As the skin wasn't broken she applied burn ointment to soothe it before bandaging him up.

"At least I can still sit on it," Isaac joked.

WHEN AVERY ARRIVED at the top paddock the cows seemed content and everything looked like it usually did. Walking along the fence line, he inspected the solar-energy box which seemed fine too, the power was on and at the correct level. How on earth could Isaac have got such a jolt? Then he spotted a power cable along the top end of the paddock leading into the milking shed. There he found it was plugged into the mains.

"What the hell?" he burst out. How could this be? It sure wasn't here when they were up before lunch. Someone had been here and beefed up the voltage.

ANGER HAD TURNED to fear by the time Avery arrived back home. "Did you see the extension lead hooked into the mains when you straightened up the fence posts?" he asked Isaac.

"No, but I saw you turn the fence off before you left, so assumed it was off when I did the repairs. Are you telling me the electric fence was going through the mains?"

Avery nodded. "I've let Bill know. There's not much we can do now. How about a remedial beer for the patient?"

Isaac accepted without hesitation and leaned back in his chair, savouring the first mouthful. "Shit, that hits the spot," he said.

Both men quietly contemplated the day's events. "Strange though, don't you think?" Avery said, fiddling with the beer label.

Isaac nodded. "Was anything missing from the office?"

"The funny thing is, all I could see that was missing is that framed photo of us, Peter and James from that vineyard in Martinborough," Avery said, still picking at the label on the bottle.

"That was the best summer. We had the time of our lives," Isaac said. "I can't believe I got the caretaker's role — I'm the least handy person I know. Are you sure it's not just lost in the mess? Why would someone steal a framed photo, for christ sake."

"Yeah, strange, but who knows?" Avery finished the last mouthful of his beer. "Another?"

Isaac smiled. "Go on, then you silver-tongued bastard."

Just then Lexi said as she walked into the kitchen, "I have to go into Warkworth to pick up groceries. Can you ask Sam to mind the shop when she gets off the bus? I shouldn't be long."

After she'd gone Isaac asked Avery what had been on his mind since he arrived. "Are you guys okay?"

15

Back at the station, Bill typed up the report on the burglary at Matakana Valley Wines. They were still none the wiser, he thought. Who had planted the hand under the house, and what was the connection with the ransacked office? Niko had uploaded the photos from today and printed them out, adding them to the wall of information from the day before. Staring at the photos, Bill pondered for a moment and decided he needed some fresh air to get his brain engaged. He stepped through the front door and the heavy humid air instantly made his long polyester-blend trousers stick to his legs like glue. He wished he was wearing shorts instead. Wearing a stab-proof vest on top of the regulation shirt in the height of summer was like being in your own portable sauna.

On the way down to the Black Dog Café he saw Ben Wilson crossing the road heading the same way. Ben had already ordered his coffee when Bill walked in. Apart from the two of them, the café was nearing closing time and empty. The comforting sound of the sputtering old La San Marco coffee machine overrode the buzzing noise from the row of fridges, a rich aroma tickled his nostrils and a calm set in.

Ben nodded, leaning against a table. "I hear there's been some trouble at Matakana Valley Wines. I was there yesterday helping Avery out. Terrible story."

"Yep, strange goings on. How's work going otherwise?" Bill said, unsure how much Ben knew and keen to change the subject.

"I'm doing a job at the cinema. The film festival starts tomorrow and they're in a bit of a panic."

Bill felt his insides squeezing, the festival was Annika's project this year. "Will you have it all sorted in time?"

"Course." Ben grinned, picked up his coffee from the counter and left.

Poor Annika, Bill thought. Issues like this were the last thing she needed before the festival started. He tried to call her mobile, but it went straight to voicemail. He grabbed his takeaway flat white. It was hot and strong, just the way he liked it. He ambled back to the station, stopping in the shade and leaning against the brick wall, the cool rugged surface scratching through his clothing. The hot coffee had an immediate effect — he could feel the caffeine coursing through his veins, invigorating his brain. His thoughts went to the events over the last days. What did it all mean? He had a terrible feeling that this was only the beginning, and there was lots more to come before they could make sense of it all.

When he arrived back at the station, Niko said without looking up, "They called from Orewa while you were out. The initial findings were that someone had cut the hand off post mortem, but get this — indications are that it's been frozen, or at least kept on ice for a period."

Bill shook his head in disbelief. "Well, that doesn't make things easier if there's no way of saying when it happened. But where's the rest of the body?"

"I've done an extensive search in the database. Nothing comes up for any corpse with a missing hand in the last five years."

Bill rubbed his jaw. "We could be dealing with a murder predating that."

16

Lexi drove into the underground carpark of the Warkworth Countdown off Neville Street. She cast a wary eye around before stepping out of the car. People were walking past and she almost collided with an old man struggling with his shopping trolley. She apologised and his warm smile in return made her feel a little better. The supermarket wasn't very busy and she hurried around as quickly as she could, picking up ingredients for lunch-box fillers and the next couple of meals. Almost at the checkout, Trevor the nosy neighbour appeared in stealth mode from behind. Lexi let out a squeal when he tapped her on the arm.

"Sorry, Lexi, I didn't mean to scare you. Though with all the goings-on at your house it's no wonder you're jumpy." Judging by his smirk, she thought, that was precisely what he intended. "I suppose it's been upsetting with the chopped-off hand found under the house and all."

Lexi held onto the shopping trolley, her knuckles turning white. "How do you know about that?"

"Heard it at the pub last night. People are talking about it." He watched for her reaction.

"Are they now?" she said. She could feel the anger rising in her face. She blurted out she'd forgotten something in the frozen section and took off at a light jog. It really didn't matter how much she had tried to excuse the old bugger, he seemed to take great delight in upsetting everyone and sticking his beak where it didn't belong.

Lexi hid out at the other end of the shop until she was sure Trevor had paid for his groceries. Her body was still shaking with anger and annoyance. Her first instincts had been to leave the laden trolley and run. She was relieved that she hadn't, as it would have further fuelled the fire. The older woman at the checkout chatted away, making her relax a little. Focusing on slowing her breathing down seemed to help. In a small community, if the word was out already, the rumour mill would start and the story would spread like wild fire.

While she drove home, her thoughts swirled. Her family was at risk and she was at a loss at what to do. As she pulled into the dusty driveway, a blue Nissan Skyline turned off the main road. She didn't recognise the car, it wasn't one of their regular customers. She parked close to the gravel path to the house as she had a lot to carry, but before she'd even swung her legs out, the passenger in the Skyline threw himself out of the car and hurried over to where she was. The driver turned the ignition off with a thud and joined his friend. Lexi thought they were customers and gave them a warm smile, but then a recording device was thrust in her face. The passenger, a gangly middle-aged man with slicked-back hair, fired questions at her with machine-gun speed. "I hear there was a severed limb found on the property," he said. "Who made the find? Where was the rest of the body found? Do the police have any suspects?"

Lexi's head was spinning. Only when the driver pointed a camera in her face did she snap out of her stunned state, slamming the boot and pushing the man aside as she hastily carried the grocery bags up the garden path.

"Hey, careful, lady," the passenger said. "We're only doing our job."

"I think you should do your job somewhere else," Lexi said, running the last few metres up the cracked stone steps to the house and safety. She dropped the grocery bags in a heap on the kitchen floor and sat with her back against the wall, trying to catch her breath. Waves of anger rolled over her as the pair kept shouting through the closed door to get her to come back out.

They gave up after a few minutes. Lexi got up and peered out of the window. Her blood boiled when she saw the photographer taking dozens of photos of the house. How dare they come and accost her in this way? She marched to the front door, swung it open and strode across the lawn towards the pair, who were now skulking around the outbuildings and the winery. The last few days of pent-up emotions erupted and she let them have it. "You two, piss off!" she yelled.

"We just want to ask a few questions," the reporter tried.

"Then you should have thought of your manners before ambushing me as I arrived home. Shame on you!" She was seething with anger.

"Sorry, we didn't mean to startle you," the reporter said.

Lexi folded her arms. "On your way. If you have any questions I suggest you direct them to the police." She turned on her heel and walked into the farm shop, closing the door with a firm thud.

Samantha was standing at the large wooden counter, earphones in and hadn't noticed a thing. Lexi had to walk right up to the counter before Sam noticed. She pulled her earphones out and said, "Hi, Mum."

"Hi, darling. Thanks for helping, I really appreciate it, but perhaps turn the music down so you notice customers walking in the shop."

"Sorry, Mum, I didn't think," Samantha said sheepishly.

"Let's close up. I don't think we'll have any more customers today." Lexi started tidying up while Samantha chatted away about school.

"Listen, Sam, somehow the media has found out about the hand under the house. We knew they would eventually."

Samantha nodded, embarrassment spreading across her face. "I might have Snap-chatted some people yesterday. Perhaps that's how they found out," she said, looking down at her feet.

"It doesn't matter how it happened," Lexi said and put her arms around her daughter.

"Mum, do you think this crazy person will come back?"

"I don't think so, sweetheart." Lexi did her best to sound convincing. "It'll be all right, darling. I don't want you to worry. Come on, let's go inside." Lexi locked the door, pulling the handle a second time to be sure.

As they walked up the path to the house, she wondered where Avery and Isaac were. She had last seen them sitting outside enjoying a cold beer. She poked her head into the winery, Avery's office was still a tip. She thought, *Well, that's another day's problem*, and shut the door. She would have to remind Avery to lock up. They wanted no more unwelcome visitors.

Inside the house, there was still no sign of the men but the door to the cellar was ajar and she could hear them.

"Mum, when's dinner?" Evie yelled from upstairs. "I'm starving."

"Let me check on Dad, then I'll get dinner organised."

Lexi went down the creaky old stairs, smooth to the touch from years of polishing by feet. Avery's loud laughter greeted her before she got to the bottom. Judging by the empty bottles on the table, that wasn't strange at all. For all her dad's skimping on the building materials, the antique table he had bought and lovingly restored was the centrepiece of the room. The honey-coloured waxed timber top gleamed like Baltic amber in the dim light. It was over a hundred and fifty years old, and Lexi's mother had been aghast when he sawed off the legs to get it down to the cellar. The two chairs were rumoured to be from the *Spray*. Two bench seats flanking the table were originally floorboards from an old shearing shed, hence the smooth surface from years of exposure to lanolin and wool.

"It looks like you boys have had a grand afternoon," Lexi said with a hint of sarcasm.

"We got a bit carried away," Avery said, trying not to laugh.

There were three complete floor-to-ceiling shelf units with bottles of all varieties, all arranged in verticals. To the untrained eye it looked as though there was no system, but Avery had them all catalogued in an app on his smartphone, which synced with his laptop.

"How are you feeling, Isaac?" Lexi asked.

"Not too bad, thank you. The wine has been medicinal," Isaac said slurring a little and trying not to giggle.

"Dinner's in thirty minutes." Lexi stomped upstairs, making her feelings known. She wasn't mad at them for drinking all that wine, it was the fact that she'd had to deal with the nosy journalist with no help from her husband.

17

It was late. James was driving home from Warkworth where he'd spent a fun evening with his boys. They had gone for a pizza at Domino's where his mate Jake worked, and the boys'd had way too much soft drink, but he didn't care. He wanted to spoil them, and the night had been great, lots of chatting and laughter. He missed having them around.

The drive home didn't take long, he knew the road like the back of his hand. The long sweeper before Ascension Vineyard, the right turn after the second-hand store — he had driven it a million times before. As always, you had to watch out for the critters crossing the road at night; possums, rabbits and the odd stoat. Some days they littered the road, poor mangled animals. He felt sorry for them, such an undignified death.

He turned right and pulled into the driveway. He couldn't wait to roll into bed. It had been an endless day full of emotions, so his heart ached having to go home to a quiet house. But he was pleased that he and Tina were sorting through some issues.

It was a typical 1970s red-brick house with mismatched aluminium joinery, the small windows scowling and making the house look tired. James was desperately trying to hold on to the happy memories of the evening, and it pained him to come home to his gloomy and depressing home. Tina and the two boys had left a gigantic hole in his heart when they moved out, and his surroundings mirrored his state of mind. They had been together for longer than he could remember, but she no longer wanted to be with him. It was sad they had waited so long to have children, he thought; the boys were six and eight and full of energy, the way it should be. It was no good for them to live in town; they needed to be here in the country where they had room to roam and discover and go on adventures. Thankfully Warkworth wasn't far away, but not close enough for them to remain in the village school. Greg was the oldest and missing the farm, Timothy was more settled with his friends in his new surroundings. A pang of bad conscience in the pit of James's stomach sent a reminder of the guilt he carried for not being able to give his children a happy and relaxed childhood.

He parked the beaten-up Ford Ranger in its usual place under the enormous oak tree next to the garden gate. The dim security light switched on as soon as he stepped onto the path, casting long shadows on the neglected and weed-strewn crazy paving under foot. Tufts of weeds stuck up in the cracked concrete and were long overdue for a spray. Tina had always enjoyed keeping the garden nice and tidy. It didn't look like that now. A feeling of despair and neglect surrounded him.

He needed to get a grip, he realised, and put some elbow grease and love into both the house and the surrounds. Perhaps if he got his act together, next time Tina dropped the boys off for a visit and saw that he was trying, she would reconsider and give him another chance. There had been a slight glimmer of hope tonight. Tina had seemed relaxed and friendly, they'd even chatted over a glass of wine when he'd dropped the boys back after pizza. Tomorrow, he decided, was the day he would stop moping around and start sorting his life out. The boys deserved more. The thought cheered him up and put a slight spring in his step.

Arriving at the entrance to the darkened house he halted. He was sure he had left the outside light on. The hackles on the back of his neck stood up. What was that on the doormat, and why was the door wide open? His heart was racing and he fumbled for his phone in the back jeans pocket, almost dropping it as he pulled it out. He had to press the flashlight option several times before the light bounced off the lifeless mass on the floral welcome mat. His once-proud rooster lay there, limp, lifeless. Its frame seemed so much smaller in death with its neck at an unnatural angle.

Fear set in, his throat closing up and his breathing becoming laboured. He needed his inhaler. He fumbled around his jacket and realised he didn't have it with him. *How could I be so stupid?* There was a spare inhaler in the bathroom cupboard. Casting the light into the entrance, he knew he had to get it quickly. Stepping over the dead rooster, he could feel the panic rising. The light in the hall didn't work either, but it wasn't far to the bathroom and he went for it. He flicked the switch. The bathroom was suddenly bathed in light, forcing him to cover his eyes for a second. He rummaged around in the top drawer and found the inhaler. Perched on the heavy porcelain bath he greedily sucked on the medicated puffs, opening his constricted airways.

Taking a few deep breaths and regaining his composure, James went to shut the front door. He tried the light switch again, but it still wasn't working. He shone the phone torch on the ceiling. The tight squeeze around his chest returned when he saw the empty light fitting. Someone had removed the bulb.

The fear came creeping back. Not sure if there was someone still inside, he proceeded cautiously down the dark hallway to the lounge, grabbing a broom handle from the cleaning cupboard. To his relief, the light switch there worked fine. The light bounced on the back wall, the scribbled message hitting him in the face like a clenched fist; *You will be next.*

The sinister blood-red lettering, dripped in the corners as if the intruder had used too much paint. Taking a second for the message to hit home, James stood frozen, struggling to comprehend what was happening. Then he bolted out of the house, almost tripping over the dead rooster, and sprinted towards the car. He threw the Ranger into reverse, gravel flying, the gear box protesting loudly at the rough treatment. Afterwards he had no memory of the quick drive into the village.

Perched at the back of the Matakana Pub, he swirled his third glass of whisky, the comforting sound of two ice cubes clinking making him think of his father. The amber liquid warmed his throat and belly and a slow calm unfurled the tension. He was glad to have people around. He wasn't easily frightened, but this had been a new level of fear, weighing heavily in the pit of his stomach like a pile of dark and slippery river stones. He waved Matt the publican over and ordered another one and explained that he needed a room for the night. To his relief there was a vacancy, saving him sleeping in the car. There was no way he was going home tonight — not that he could anyway after all the alcohol he had consumed. By the time his drink arrived, he had made his mind up; he would go to the cops tomorrow.

18

_____

Avery and Isaac, both looking worse for wear after their big night in the wine cellar, struggled with each mouthful of bacon and eggs. If they'd stopped at the couple of bottles they had polished off before dinner, things would probably have turned out all right, but Avery had insisted on opening a bottle of Pyrat rum, which inevitably had finished them off. Avery hadn't felt this unwell for a long time. There was a large percussion band in his head, and any movement sent off shock waves in all directions. Isaac was equally quiet, by the looks of it, doing his best to soak up the alcohol with the few mouthfuls of food he could manage and then fighting to keep it all down. Lexi thought, how silly two grown men could be.

"How are your burns today, Uncle Isaac?" Evie asked, gently patting his arm.

Isaac put his hand on hers. "Not that bad, darling."

"Could we have a look at the Aston Martin when we get home from school?" Gabriel asked, his eyes sparkling.

"Sure, but I think I can do one better. How about I pick you up from school instead?"

"Really? That would be cool." Gabriel's face lit up like a sun. "The guys will flip when they see it."

"You three, finish up your breakfast and get your bags." Lexi said. "We have to get going."

"I really envy you. That's three amazing kids you have," Isaac said, his voice tinged with sadness.

"It's not too late for you and Petra," Avery said. "You still have time."

"I suppose so," Isaac said, his eyes betraying his thoughts.

"Why don't you call her, see if she wants to come up for a few days? I know Lexi would love to see her too."

"I don't think she wants to see me at the moment."

"Hey, we should give James a call," Avery said to change the subject. "I know it was a lot of drunken talk last night, but I meant that."

"Sure," Isaac said perking up a little.

Avery scrolled his phone for James's mobile number and made the call. Just as he was about to hang up, a sleepy voice answered. "Hi James, it's Avery. How are you?"

"Not too bad," James croaked. "Sorry, I had a hell of a night and must have overslept."

"Listen, Isaac is up for a few days. We were talking about getting together for a beer. What do you think?" It felt like an eternity passed before James answered.

"Yes, sure. How about a quiet beer at the pub tonight?"

"Sounds great. We're going to the opening night for the film festival at eight. We could meet at six-thirty for a bite if you like." Avery wondered if he had pushed it too far.

"Okay. See you then," James said.

When Lexi arrived home from dropping the children off she was pleasantly surprised to find Avery clearing the breakfast dishes. She suspected he was keen to redeem himself after yesterday's carry-on in the wine cellar.

19

It had been a warm night; the only airflow came from the crack of a small window above his head. James's head was pounding from sleep deprivation. He remembered having had a few generous glasses of whisky, before falling into bed sometime around one in the morning, his mouth like the Sahara Desert. It hadn't helped that there had been a party in the room next door, a group of young backpackers having a singsong until at least three. When he finally got some sleep, one nightmare after the other had plagued him. The phone call from Avery had woken him with a jolt.

He cupped his hand under the antique tap above the original pedestal hand basin and drank greedily, droplets running down his chin and onto his bare chest. Splashing some water on his face, he felt better. His unruly hair was standing on end and he had to dampen it to tame it, not that it made a difference. When it grew beyond a certain point, it seemed to resemble a mushroom on the top of his head. Tina used to tease him about it. Looking in the mirror, he knew he desperately needed a haircut.

James paid for the room and wandered down to the Black Dog Café. It wasn't busy this Tuesday morning and he sat down in the courtyard outside, enjoying the sun on his bare legs. At the next table was an older man with a terrier sitting by his master's feet, gazing longingly. It was clear the dog knew the routine.

He'd had an Airedale when he was a boy. Perhaps he should get another one, he thought. The company would be good, and the boys would love it too.

He felt a little silly after last night's ordeal. He was a grown man, for Christ's sake. Had he over-reacted? It was probably just mischief by teenagers. The financial stress of the vineyard and the separation from Tina had taken a huge toll on him. It had been few tough years. After taking a gamble and ripping out some of the older vines, he had replanted a new variety, sangiovese, more suitable to the local climate and terroir, but it would take time for them to yield any profit.

The waitress delivered a plate laden with bacon and eggs, and a side plate with a large sausage, to the man with the dog. The terrier knew it was his sausage and was salivating yet didn't move a muscle. The man took his time to cut up the sausage in small, even bites, letting it cool, while continuing with his own breakfast.

The leggy waitress, barely out of her teens, her hair pulled up in a high ponytail, flashed him a friendly smile. He ordered a double-shot espresso and Eggs Benedict, sauce on the side. He glanced at the next table, not sure how long the dog could take it. He knew the drill, but it must have been torture to sit and wait.

"Okay, Tweed, it's your turn, my old mate," the man said. He put the plate down on the ground and the dog ate the sausage in seconds.

James had planned to go past the police station after breakfast but drove home instead. *Perhaps it won't look as bad in the light of day.* When he drove in, the house looked just like it always did, sad and desperately needing some TLC. The lush garden was definitely more than overgrown, but nothing he couldn't handle. He parked the car and walked up the pavers. The air was buzzing with honey bees, stocking up with nectar in the sun's warmth. The closer he got, the more trepidation he felt.

He shuddered when he saw the dead rooster. Poor Henry. Someone had broken his neck and after the signwriting, had tossed the paintbrush to the side, the tip of the bristles bright red. He hadn't seen it in the dark. There was something disturbing about the juxta-position of the two objects.

He stepped over them and went inside. His mouth felt dry and he swallowed hard, squeezing the inhaler in his pocket. The writing was harsh in the daylight. He had talked himself into thinking perhaps it had all been a dream, but there it was in bold letters. The whistling in his ears got louder and he felt faint. Steadying himself by grabbing hold of the back of the couch, he stepped into the lounge. He fumbled for the inhaler and took a puff, closing his eyes for a moment. He could still see the vicious message with his eyes closed.

The medication took effect quickly and his breathing slowed down. He looked around the sparsely furnished room; none of the obvious burglar targets like the TV or other electronic equipment was missing. The old stereo was sitting in the corner with the black faux-wood CD tower next to it. Someone had rummaged through the bookshelf, books and photo albums were tossed on the floor in a jumble.

James continued around the house. The kitchen looked like normal until his eye caught a large knife embedded in the tongue-and-groove wall, the tip of its blade piercing a yellowed newspaper clipping. It was from the *Martinborough Star*, a photo of him and his mates the summer after university when they worked at Stott's Land-ing. His focus shifted to where the knife had pierced the paper, the tip directly stabbed through the image of him. James swallowed hard and raced outside — he couldn't stand being in the house any more. His stomach was in knots when he called the cops.

WHEN THE OFFICERS ARRIVED, a pale James was leaning on the bonnet of his old Ford Ranger. Bill said, "So, someone broke into your house last night?"

"It must have been after five, as I was home until then", James said.

"You think you came home around nine thirty?"

"Yes, sometime around then I would say," James said, fidgeting.

Bill looked up from his notebook. "Did you see anything suspicious, any other vehicles or things out of the ordinary leading up to this?"

"Not that I noticed. Mind you, I wasn't looking, I had spent a marvellous night with my boys, I was happy."

Bill could sense James's pain. The despair and sorrow when families rip apart — he'd seen it all before. "If you wouldn't mind staying here, we'll look around," he said.

He stepped over the dead bird and walked into the house. They went through the house room by room, Niko taking photos as they went through. Concentrating on the kitchen they inspected the knife and newspaper clipping. Bill spotted what appeared to be a palm print on the lacquered wall panelling on the left side. If it hadn't been for the slight kitchen grime, he would never have seen it. The SOCO's would come through and process the area, but he would make sure to mention it.

James was sitting in the shade under the oak tree at the front of the house, his leg jiggling nonstop. "We've gone through the house, the prime areas being the living room and the kitchen," Bill said as he sat down, instantly regretting that he hadn't brushed the dirt off the seat before sitting down on the rickety old garden chair. "Start from the beginning. Can you go through what happened when you got home last night?"

James went through the whole scenario, including how he had thought it best to stay the night at the pub, omitting that he'd been frightened and had run out of the house screaming like a little girl.

"Any idea what the message on the wall is all about?"

James shook his head.

"What about the old newspaper clipping?"

James shrugged. "It's years ago, since my first job in the wine industry down country in the Wairarapa. They must have found it in one of the photo albums. Not sure what relevance it has," James said, still bouncing.

"Who are the other men in the photo?"

"It's the entire harvest crew of workers, including my mates from university, Avery McCall, Peter Evans, Isaac Miller and me."

"Can you think of who might have done this to you?"

"Not that I can think of," James said. "It has rattled me a bit. It feels strange to know someone has been rummaging around the house and done this."

"Have you got somewhere else to stay for a few days?" Niko asked.

James looked up. "I suppose I could stay at the pub. Harvest time is around the corner, so I really need to be here. Not that we have a massive production, but every dollar counts."

Niko nodded. He knew money trouble when he saw it — the sad looks, the hunched backs and beaten spirits. He'd been around it all his life.

"Bill, I hear they found a hand at Matakana Valley Wines. Any truth in the rumour?" James said out of the blue.

"Where did you hear that?" Bill said. He'd known it would get out eventually.

"Someone at the pub last night. News travels fast."

"For fucks sake, I might as well move my desk into the pub," Bill said.

"We're just about done here," Niko said changing the subject, sensing Bill's annoyance. "You don't look so good, mate. I suggest you go into the house, grab clothing and whatever you might need," he continued with a friendly smile. "Avoid the cordoned-off areas. You'll see the tape."

James stood up, his face ashen and eyes hollowed as if he hadn't slept for days. His grey stubble made him look like an old man. That he was in desperate need of a haircut didn't help.

He made his way along the path slowly, his pulse increasing with every step closer to the house. Keeping his head down he went straight into the master bedroom, pulled the sports bag from the top of the wardrobe and threw some clothes in, popping into the bathroom on the way out for his toiletries. Getting a whiff of his unwashed armpits, he felt desperate for a shower and a change of clothes. On his way out, he glanced into the kitchen catching sight of the ominous message when something nudged his memory.

Bill and Niko were leaning on the bonnet of the police car as James jogged towards them. "I just thought of something." He dropped the bag on the ground, putting his hand on his thighs, catching his breath. "The knife in the kitchen. It's not one of mine."

NIKO TOOK one last walk around the house to check that it was all secure and locked up before they left. James had given them a spare key, should they need to go back. On the way back to the station Bill pulled in to Ravish for coffee. The barista seemed happy to see them, directing her attention to the handsome young Samoan. Niko was completely unaware.

Both men chose a corned-beef and mustard doorstop of a sandwich, large enough to satisfy the most ravenous appetite. "My treat. You got it yesterday," Niko said.

"Thanks, mate," Bill said, seemingly happier again.

"I finish my secondment at the end of the month, Sarge. I'll miss this place. It's been another brilliant summer. I can't say that I'm looking forward to going back to the city," he said with a wry smile. "I much prefer the beach lifestyle to that of South Auckland."

"It's been great to have you here," Bill said. The winter months are quiet and I know you'd probably get bored with the pace of life."

"I guess you're right, Sarge," Niko said. They both laughed.

Bill's phone pierced the conversation. "Hi Bill, it's Lexi. I just wanted to let you know I had to deal with an intrusive journalist yesterday. Not at all what I would expect from a reputable newspaper. I told them to piss off. Hope that was the right thing to do."

"Yep, definitely. Thanks for letting me know. At least we know the news is out and can manage the situation."

Bill frowned at Niko. "Well, I'm not surprised the media circus has started." As he put his phone down, he could see there were several missed calls from the same number. He quickly checked his voice-mail. Sure enough, they all wanted a comment from him. Pressing delete, he went back to finish his sandwich. They would have to call back.

After finishing their coffees, Bill and Niko headed back to the station. The first thing they saw when pulling into the main street was a white One News station wagon parked outside the Four Square. A little further down trucks from TV3 and Newshub were parked, awaiting their arrival. Both crews must have been past the station, realised it was unmanned and waited. Bill pulled in and parked. It didn't take many moments before the TV crews pulled in behind them and reporters he recognised stepped out and thrust their cameras in his face. A hurried phone call to Orewa CIB had been made, they weren't happy, but there had been no choice.

Afterwards it all seemed like a blur, lots of questions that all seemed to ask the same thing repeatedly. He used the standard answers "We cannot disclose that information at the moment" or "As it's an ongoing investigation . . ." Bill went back inside feeling like a wrung-out dishcloth.

"You did great, Sarge," Niko said, slapping him on the back.

"I hope it was okay. They really put me on the spot. I hope I didn't put my foot in it," Bill said, the relief setting in. Pouring water from the dispenser, he went back to his desk and drank it all in one gulp. "Well, I guess we'd better get on with the break-in at James Smith's house. Have you uploaded the photos yet?"

"Already done," Niko said with a broad smile.

"Great work," Bill said, how far away are the SOCO's?" Bill had upgraded the investigation when they left James's house. It was no longer just a burglary.

"They should be here shortly," Niko said. "I'll drive over and open up as soon as I get the phone call they're near." Looking at the photos, Bill now knew the cases were connected.

20

M *artinborough*

PAT DROVE up the narrow driveway to the compact brick house on the hill, the dew still heavy on the grass and glistening in the morning light. It was a beautiful day. Peter would have already left for work. He commuted to Wellington three days a week, Monday to Wednesday. Today was Tuesday. From what she could gather, it was the modern thing to work from home, especially if there was a longer commute, saving on fuel and cutting down on emissions and being environmentally friendly and all that. It would have been unheard of in her time. Being retired, Pat supplemented her meagre pension with the part-time job of housekeeping for Peter, who was still a bachelor. She didn't understand why he was still single; he was a good-looking man with a great job and a kind heart. Working a few hours a week meant that she had a little over and above her pension, and she could afford a few treats now and then. Anything else would have been too hard on her body. She would turn seventy-three at the end of the year. Apart from arthritic knees and elbows, she was in good shape for her age, something she believed was because of keeping relatively active. Twice a week she spent a few hours doing a little cleaning, washed some clothes and did his ironing. It was enjoyable work and she felt needed. On a Friday when she came in and Peter worked from home, she normally brought along some home-cooked food she had prepared the night before, and they had a pleasant lunch together. It was a mutually beneficial arrangement as they were both on their own and had over the years developed a friendship.

As soon as the children were grown up and had left home, Pat left her domineering husband. She had met no one else to share her life with, but was content with her life as it was. She kept herself busy, particularly enjoying playing Canasta, the book club at the library, and her knitting group making tiny vests and hats for premature babies. Last year, an extra love had come in to her life, a little West Highland White terrier named McTavish. They made a good pair; he was a rescue dog and had not had an altogether uncomplicated life either. McTavish was a typical stubborn terrier, curious and full of beans. He adored Pat and came along everywhere. He'd even got special permission to accompany Pat to the library, and the community centre next door when she played cards. Naturally he came along on the quick drive to Peter's house on the days she worked, McTavish loved to snooze in the sun on the front porch.

The late-summer Tuesday appeared no different as they parked in the shade of the magnolia tree. McTavish hopped out of the car and went for a sniff around as usual, when suddenly the hackles on his neck stood up and he gave a low-pitched growl. His wiry tail at attention, all senses focused, his demeanour had changed. Something had upset him.

"Come on, McTavish, there are no rabbits around. You've chased them all away, boy." Pat gave him a reassuring scratch on the top the head. As she continued down the dusty gravel path, the crunching sound underfoot reminded her of her childhood home. McTavish did not let up, the growl grew deeper.

"That's enough McTavish," Pat said sternly. "If you don't stop this nonsense, you can wait in the car." The little dog wasn't used to being spoken to like this; his ears went back and his tail dropped, he followed behind Pat up the few wooden steps to the sun-drenched veranda, still sulking.

The front door was slightly ajar. Pat was just about to grab the handle when McTavish barked, making her jump.

"McTavish! What did you do that that for?" she scolded, but the little dog stubbornly got in front of the door, blocking the way. Grabbing his collar, Pat carefully opened the door, suddenly apprehensive. Peter was safety-conscious and would never forget to lock the door. Something didn't feel right. Her heart was in her mouth and she swallowed hard. Her vision blurring, she tried to calm her breath for the lightheadedness to go. It wasn't like her to frighten easily; there must be a perfectly logical explanation to this. Her hearing wasn't what it used to be — what if Peter had hurt himself and needed help? She had to go inside.

McTavish was still unhappy, but had calmed somewhat, giving a short low bark of displeasure. With her heart in her mouth Pat took a few steps into the hallway. It led into a compact kitchen that direly needed modernising — the faux-wood cupboard doors and Formica benchtops had been the height of fashion in the Seventies. In stark contrast was the top-of-the-line dishwasher and matching fridge-freezer with its own ice-maker and water-dispenser. On the other side was a generous lounge, and an entire wall dedicated to Peter's precious collection of World War II medals and police memorabilia. The two sparsely furnished bedrooms were a good size, one converted into an office. It was definitely the home of a bachelor, the only female touch being a few doilies that his mother had left behind when she died. Everything seemed in order and Pat breathed a sigh of relief. Perhaps Peter had just forgotten to lock up.

"See boy, it's all fine," she said to the little dog.

Pat put her cardigan and bag on the coat rack in the entrance, slipped her housecoat on and opened the cleaning cupboard, grabbing the vacuum and the small basket of cleaning products. The vacuuming and dusting didn't take long. She went back into the kitchen and measured two cups of tap water into the old stove top coffeepot, added three heaped tablespoons of coarse-ground coffee and wiped the cupboards down. The familiar smell of coffee permeated the room, making her feel a little better. She put the tray on the table and chose one of the delicate Queen Anne cups and saucers with the pink roses from the cupboard above the sink. She was the only one who used them, Peter preferring clunky ceramic mugs. Pat had brought along one of her ginger and banana cakes that Peter loved, to put in his baking tin. She would cut a slice off to savour with her coffee while sitting in the sun. She even had a little morsel that she had brought for McTavish. The little dog was sitting in the doorway, still huffing and letting out the odd growl, still unhappy.

"I don't know what's wrong with you today, boy. I'll be out with a treat as soon as I've put the washing on," Pat said.

Waiting for the coffee, Pat went to get the washing basket from the bathroom. The laundry was in the basement and the door at the top of the stairs was difficult to open. The trick was to put your shoulder into it and give it a little nudge, but only just enough, as there was only a small landing and the last thing she wanted was to fall headfirst down the narrow stairs. The door groaned and popped open without too much of a problem and she fumbled for the light switch.

Stale air mixed and a smell of something rotten hit her. Had Peter forgotten to close the chest freezer? In this warm weather meat went off so quickly. She covered her nose and took the first couple of steps down the wooden stairs, her knees protesting a little with every step, turning at a ninety-degree angle down the bottom. That's when she saw him.

Flies buzzed around the crumpled body. Pat let out a strangled cry, the basket tumbling the last few steps, bits of clothing scattering over the floor. Unable to move, her sensible lace-up shoes stuck to the step. Her scream alerted McTavish, who came careering down the floorboards of the hallway, coming to a stop at the top of the stairs.

The sudden short sharp bark roused her from the state of shock she was in.

"It's okay boy. Stay," she mustered, her voice weak. McTavish's low growl echoed down the narrow staircase, waiting for her next command. There was no way she wanted him down there with her. Her mouth was dry, making it difficult to talk. Steadying herself against the wall, she mustered all the courage she had and turned her head back towards the crumpled heap on the floor.

Peter was sitting in an awkward position, his head resting on his chest and his arms by his side. There was a lot of blood on the floor and up the wall. What kind of person could possess such rage and anger? Pat and her husband had owned a farm and she'd seen a lot of home kill of livestock, but this was something different. The musty smell of blood reminded her of the jar of coins she had kept as a little girl.

Peter had been like a son to her. Even though she knew in her heart that he was dead, she bent forward to check for a pulse on his neck. The strange sensation of waxy transparent skin and the cold of his body chilled her to the core. She pulled her hand away as if she had been burned. Then she realised that his left hand was missing. The nausea she had held at bay suddenly overcame her and she rushed up the stairs as fast as her arthritic body could manage and pushed the dog aside, barely making it outside and into the garden before emptying this morning's breakfast onto the lawn. As her blood pressure dropped and the world around her started spinning, she felt faint and keeled over on the dandelion-speckled lawn. When she came to, she had no idea how long she had been unconscious. McTavish was standing over her, frantically licking her face to wake her up.

"Okay, boy, thank you so much. I'm fine now," Pat said pushing herself to sit up. Bum-shuffling up the first couple of steps and turning around onto her knees, she ignored the shooting pains in her arms and shoulders, and grabbed hold of the handrail and pulled herself up. She stood on wobbly legs, her stockings laddered with large tears on the knees, blood slowly dripping from a scrape on one of them. She had to get to her handbag where her phone was to call the police — but that meant going back inside, something she wasn't keen on doing. Opening the front door, she could smell the burnt coffee grounds and smoke was filing the air. She quickly turned the element off and pulled the red-hot coffee pot aside. She dug deep inside her handbag, finding the mobile at the very bottom. Her hands shook as she dialled the police.

The operator assured her they would dispatch a patrol car straight away. Pat reached for her bag and a Werther's Original, the hard sweet's creamy texture of brown sugar caramel and butterscotch combating the shock. Tears rolling down her cheeks, she sighed. Her friend was dead; they would no longer have their Friday lunches. She would miss his quirky humour and the fact that he used to laugh at his own jokes. Her mind was in upheaval. Who could have done such a thing to him? And why so brutal? Precious Peter was dead, and he had been so full of life.

When the police arrived Pat was more than relieved to see them pull in from where she was sitting on the porch, McTavish by her feet.

"Are you Mrs Taylor?" the bearded police officer said.

"Yes, but please call me Pat."

"I'm Sergeant Archie Lawson." He gestured to the slightly younger officer with dark slicked-back hair.

"This is Senior Constable Dave Rogers," Archie said. "Pat, if you could please remain here while we have a look."

Putting on protective shoe covers and gloves, the two officers entered the house.

The smell of burnt coffee and death lingered in the air. From the call they knew the body was in the basement, but were not prepared for the mess that awaited them.

"Fuck me," Archie said covering his nose with the top of his hand. The many stab wounds and the missing hand looked like a lengthy and particularly vicious attack. Archie had recently been on a forensic course. By the looks of the bluish-purple complexion, the beginning of bloat combined with the blood-speckled foam coming out of the victim's mouth and nose, it was clear to him that the attack had happened several days ago. According to the four stages of decomposition, this was the second stage, around day 3 to 5 after death had occurred. Archie shivered. When he had sat at the lecture last week, he had no idea he would be looking at this now.

He wrote in his notebook, "Time of death: Friday?" then said to Dave, "I think we've seen enough. Let's leave it to the SOCO's and ESR to handle the rest."

21

M *atakana*

BILL STOOD BACK and gazed left to right. The wall had the latest photos from James's place added. They had added a photocopy of the newspaper clipping. The same four men as in the missing photo from Avery's office, who had all worked at Stott's Landing in Martinborough from November 1987 to April the following year.

"We need to talk to Avery and James again, and get hold of the other two," Bill said, absentmindedly tapping his fingers on the table. "What's the connection and what could have happened all those years ago?"

Niko, who was making a coffee, tried to ignore the irritating sound. Things like this could drive him crazy. "Well, three of the blokes are here in Matakana at the moment. That's kind of interesting, don't you think?" He handed Bill a cup of instant coffee to stop his incessant tapping.

Bill looked down at his notes as he sipped the steaming brown sludge. "What about the fourth man? This Peter Evans — where does he come in?"

"Avery mentioned that Evans still lives in Martinborough and was working as a winemaker at one of the premier labels. Apparently, he retrained and changed careers about ten years ago, and is now working in IT for a firm in Wellington."

"Surely we could get something more drinkable than this!" Bill exploded, and tipped his coffee down the sink. "Bloody undrinkable shit!"

Niko laughed. "Whatever you say, Sarge. I'll buy something more upmarket next time. Anyway, Evans shouldn't be difficult to find." He was already typing the name into the computer to do a search. "Looks like there is only one Peter Evans in the area. No landline, but a mobile number. I'll call him," he said, already halfway into dialling his number. No answer. Niko pressed redial again. Still no one picking up. He hated leaving messages — he always seemed to stumble on his words, and somehow there was never enough time to leave all the details. Pressing redial, he left a voice mail but was cut off mid-sentence, so had to call back one more time to leave his contact details. His frustration level was rising, putting him in a foul mood, the muscles at the top of his back twitching. He was in desperate need of a good workout and couldn't wait to finish for the day and head to the gym. At home in South Auckland the large police station housed a fully equipped gym where he started each day, working his muscles to the limit which, apart from keeping fit, was great for focus and general well-being. Since the Matakana police station was tiny and had no training facilities, one benefit he received while being up here was a complimentary membership to the local gym. Bill had one too but Niko had never seen him there. Judging by his girth, he didn't think Bill had set foot in the place for a long time.

22

The warm sun caressed James's back as he sat in the garden bar at the Matakana Village Pub. He felt slightly guilty as it was a regular Tuesday and a working day, and here he was. He wasn't used to sitting around doing nothing as there was always so much to do in the vineyard. In reality he could have done with more help, but the finances didn't allow it. He'd promised Bill he would visit the station later. The message on the wall was more disturbing than he had let on.

James finished his coffee, grabbed his phone from the table and crossed the main street. It was a sleepy afternoon. His eyes nervously darted around as he wracked his brain to work out who he might have made an enemy of. There was only one; Avery, even though he'd arrived before Christmas with a fully laden gift basket. No doubt Lexi had organised that. Avery had apologised, too, which had surprised James. Thinking about it now, he had been equally to blame. He should have reached out over the summer, but going through his and Tina's marital issues had been all-consuming, and nothing more had come of it. His failing marriage combined with the financial worries had just about broken him. He missed his friendship with Isaac and Peter and was sorry they'd lost contact over the years. In the earlier years they'd got together regularly. It was a shame they'd all got so busy and just focused on their own lives. They had been inseparable at university. What had happened to them?

The bougainvillea on the porch of the police station, tickled his nose, the sweet scent reminding him of his grandmother. The pleasant memories evaporated as soon as he stepped through the front door, and reminded him why he was here. He tried to swallow but the lump in his throat got stuck. He coughed, his nerves getting the better of him and ran his hands down his jeans. He needed to get a grip of himself.

BILL LOOKED UP, gestured for James to come in and buzzed him through the tiny reception into the main office. He was on the phone to the lab, confirming for the third time that he was in a priority queue. There were other high-profile cases and theirs was missing a body, which didn't help. Niko came over and James's hand just about disappeared in the large Samoan's warm handshake. He gestured for James to sit down on the chair next to his desk, which was meticulous. His friendly demeanour made James relax a little.

"Tell me about the vineyard you worked at in Martinborough," Niko said.

"I'm not sure there's much to tell. Avery and I had got work over the summer. We met the owner at a job expo on campus. He was looking for cheap labour over the summer and into the harvest season. We were keen for some work experience, but to be honest it was more like slave labour. Anyway, we got Peter in. He'd been doing the same viticulture degree as us." He paused "Not sure how we got Isaac in, but he was there as well."

A memory flashed through Niko's mind from yesterday; Isaac didn't look like he was used to doing much manual labour.

"The wine industry can be very up and down. I can say that I have first-hand experience of that." James paused again. "There's a saying in the industry, if you want to make a small fortune in wine, start with a large one."

Niko could see the pain in James's eyes and nodded.

"Anyhow, I digress. We were young and lucky to go into the industry straight out of University."

"What about your relationship with Avery? Did you get on well?"

"Avery was the natural leader. Just look at him — he's the whole package. People would congregate around him like a magnet. He was energetic and everyone loved him, especially the ladies, but he had only eyes for one — Lexi. We got on well most of the time. I found him annoying sometimes and we had the odd spat, but I would have thought that was normal among mates."

Niko caught Bill's eye and could see that he was listening in.

"At Stott's Landing, did anything happen?" Niko said, looking James straight in the eye.

James took a sip of water. "Not that I can think of, really. There was a fair share of action going on with the local girls, especially for Isaac and Peter who were notorious Casanovas."

Niko shifted his sizeable frame in the uncomfortable office chair. "What about yourself?"

"Well, I was a lanky kid with pimply skin and thick Coke-bottle glasses." James said, looking down, the lack of confidence and unhappiness flooding back. "I was a late bloomer. As soon as I could afford it, I had laser surgery on my eyes. It was hands-down the best thing that I could've done."

Niko felt a pang of sympathy. James's teenage years could not have been easy for him. "What happened after the harvest?"

"I went back home to Auckland, moved in with my parents while I worked for Kumeu River Wines. I stayed there for twelve years and learnt all I know from them, it was a great learning ground."

"How did you end up in Matakana?"

"My grandmother passed away and left me some money. I bought some land with existing vines on it, and the old farmhouse came with it." James smiled. "I felt like I'd won the lottery."

Niko leaned back in his chair. "Can you think of anything that might have happened over the years that might be important?"

"I don't think so, although I seem to recall some upset while we were in Martinborough. It happened on a weekend at the end of the harvest when I'd gone home to visit family. I'm not entirely sure what went on. All I know is, the mood of the place changed overnight. I asked the others what had happened, but they shrugged it off. Eventually I just dropped it."

Both Niko's and Bill's ears pricked up. "Any idea who could have broken into your house?" Niko asked.

"Not really. Probably the same bloody teenagers that have put the anonymous letters in my letter box, I imagine."

"Letters?" Niko sat bolt upright. "Why haven't you mentioned this before? What was in them?"

"Similar messages to what was scribbled on the wall, although it seemed a lot less sinister when you looked at cut out pieces of letters like a silly ransom note in a bad movie." James looked like a possum in the headlights, the connection finally dawning on him. "They seemed childlike and a load of bullshit."

Niko wanted to shake him. Why had James not divulged this before? "When did they arrive, and how many were there?"

"The first one arrived maybe four weeks ago, then every ten days another one. I thought they were a kid's prank, and just threw them in the bin." He looked sheepish. "Perhaps I should have kept them."

"Well, that would have been helpful," Niko said, doing his best to stay calm. "Never mind, not much we can do about it now."

"Can you remember what they said?" Bill asked

"Not verbatim, but it was all pointed towards some sort of thing that they knew that I had done. As far as I'm concerned, I haven't done anything wrong here. I have nothing to hide."

"What about your relationship with the other guys?" Niko asked. "Do you still see each other?"

"I guess we caught up sporadically over the years, getting gradually less when families and work commitments took over, especially with Peter living all the way down in Martinborough. It's a lengthy drive. But Avery and Isaac have always been thick as thieves." James sighed. "You might as well hear it from me. Avery and I had a falling out a while ago. It turned out to be a misunderstanding, but it's taken some time for the tempers to settle. Avery called me yesterday out of the blue suggesting that we catch up for a meal and a beer. Isaac is up also and I'm looking forward to seeing them. It's been a long time."

Niko didn't quite know what to think. James seemed to be on the verge of a mental breakdown, one minute he was chatting away, the other he was like a nervous teenager, not knowing what to do with his hands. It was obvious the man had issues.

23

The drive from Matakana Valley Wines to Warkworth was quick. Isaac enjoyed the lush open fields with undulating valleys in the distance. He loved it up here. It was like a parallel universe — every time he visited, he didn't want to leave. He was slogging his guts out in the corporate rat race in the city, and for what? The hellish long hours and difficult clients with impossible deadlines did nothing for his already strained marriage.

The howl of the six-litre V12 engine made heads turn as he pulled into Mahurangi College to pick up Samantha and Gabriel. He was ten minutes early and the carpark was almost full. Petra flashed through his mind, and he was glad he'd found his work phone in the glove compartment and pressed her name on speed dial.

"Hi, darling," he said, his heart racing while sounding as cheery as he could. He was missing her.

"Oh. Hi." Her voice had a cool tinge to it. An awkward few seconds of silence followed.

"I just wanted to hear your voice. I'm missing you lots," Isaac said, his voice close to breaking. Another long pause. "I miss you too," Petra said, barely audible.

Isaac's heart was beating faster, the sudden rush of blood to his head making him feel giddy. "I'm up in Matakana. Why don't you take a few days off and come up? Lexi and Avery would love to see you too," he pleaded.

"You know I can't," she said, sorrow heavy in her voice. "I have a lot of work on I can't get out of, and I don't know if I'm strong enough at the moment. I need some space to think about us."

"Can I see you when I get back?"

"Sure, I'd like that," she said sounding more upbeat. "Perhaps we could have dinner."

"I'd like that too," he said. Stepping out of the low-slung sports car, Isaac felt as though he was walking on clouds. If Petra was willing to talk, perhaps there was hope for their marriage. He was prepared to give her all the time she needed to get over losing the baby. He had to give himself time to grieve, he realised, it had been his child too. For the first time since the miscarriage, he could no longer bottle his feelings up. His chest contracted, squeezing every bit of air out of his body. The avalanche of emotions washing over him was overwhelming and all he wanted to do was crawl into a little ball on the ground and cry. Finally, he understood how Petra was feeling. One mother walking by stopped and put her hand on his shoulder to check if he was all right. Isaac was embarrassed and explained his pained face by saying he had pulled a muscle in his back. He forced himself to put a brave face on. The tight band across his torso was gradually letting up and air was filling his lungs again. He didn't want Samantha and Gabriel to see him like this.

The dull ringing of the school bell sounded out, and children poured through the large finger-smeared glass doors. The muted sea of students gradually morphed into a noisy, excited mob as they spilled out into the bus bay and carpark. He remembered what it was like when the school day was over, the excitement of being free.

"Whoa, look at that beast!" Gabriel said to the friends walking with him. Each one took a turn sitting in the leather driver's seat, feeling a million bucks. They took masses of photos, most likely to appear on Instagram before they'd even arrived home, Isaac thought. This generation seemed to live more in the virtual world than the physical one. He explained some features of the Aston and a growing crowd listened intently.

Samantha came along dragging her schoolbag. "Gabe, can you get your friends to stop drooling over the car, I'm sure Uncle Isaac would like to get home."

"It's okay, I don't mind if the lads have a look," Isaac said before Gabriel could say something nasty back to his younger sister.

The crowd eventually dispersed and they set off back to the farm with Gabriel talking nonstop about the special features and performance of the car, Samantha rolling her eyes in the back seat.

The smell of freshly baked scones greeted them as soon as they got home and Sam seemed to forget her annoyance. A bowl of freshly whipped cream sat on the table next to a large jar of home-made raspberry jam. The mood lifted and calm spread through the kitchen as everyone tucked in.

"Will you guys be all right here at home tonight?" Lexi said. "Dad, Isaac and I are going to the film festival, the one that Annika has organised."

"We'll be fine," Samantha said. "I've got lots of homework, and I'm sure Gabe and Evie are the same."

"Perhaps I should stay home?"

"We'll lock the door," Samantha promised, "and we've always got Beau."

Lexi was still worried. "I guess we're only a few minutes away," she said.

24

Standing back, Annika put the last touches to the decorations at the Matakana Cinema, she was very pleased how it had turned out. Opening night of their own Celebration of New Zealand Film was only a few hours away and she could feel the butterflies whooshing around her stomach. The opening movie was *The Dark Horse*, featuring an extraordinary home-grown cast, including Hollywood stars Cliff Curtis and James Rolleston. It was based on the New Zealand chess champion Genesis Potini, with the main character teaching disadvantaged children how to play the game. Even though it was a few years old, the committee had nominated it to open the event. It was one of Annika's favourites. Over the next week they would show a plethora of New Zealand films in the arthouse theatre, a far cry from the modern multiplexes that had, she thought, as much soul as a piece of toast. Tonight's movie was in the Tivoli, which had an old-fashioned and opulent feel to it, with its plush red velvet seats, chocolate-brown wallpaper and an enormous chandelier above.

She glanced at her watch. It was almost four o'clock and there was still so much to do. She popped her head into the projectionist booth to check if Ben had sorted out the electrical fault only discovered yesterday. She pushed the heavy door open, and warm stale air greeted her. She squinted and managed to just make out Ben kneeling in the corner with a myriad of exposed wires coming out of the wall.

"How's it going?" she asked anxiously. "Are you making any headway?"

"I've had to change this entire panel," Ben said without taking his eyes off what he was doing. "It's completely fried. But everything will be fine for tonight's screening. I shouldn't be long."

Annika sighed in relief. "Thank you so much, Ben. We really appreciate you dropping everything and coming in."

She could feel the weight coming off her shoulders. Everything would be all right. She was such a worry-wart! Rushing out of the Tivoli, she nearly collided with Lexi on her way in. "What are you doing here so early?" Annika said as she grabbed on to the swinging door to stop herself from toppling over.

"I thought I'd check if you needed any help, or perhaps a coffee. I love what you've done with the foyer." She glanced at the massive Ponga trees they had moved inside, framing a beaten-up old VW Beetle with a chess set strategically placed on the bonnet. "The committee sure are lucky to have your artistic flair."

"Thanks. It's been a lot of fun, although I must admit getting the Beetle in was a bit of a mission," Annika laughed. "We had to rely on brute force."

"Hope you evicted all the creepy-crawlies from the Ponga. I know how much you love Wetas."

Shivers went through Annika at the mention of them. "We only spotted two of them. Let's hope any others stay put deep in the fronds until they get put back outside in a few days." She grabbed Lexi by the arm. "I don't have anything else to do. Let's go downstairs to MMK and have a coffee."

They ordered at the massive timber slab counter by the entrance. Lexi gestured towards a row of tiered plates with glass domes covering a variety of baked treats. "Can I have one of the marshmallow chocolate Swiss Kisses, please."

"You mean the Swedish Mums-mums," Annika said, and ordered one too. "The Swiss just stole the recipe." They both laughed. It was a bit of a joke between them, Annika was fiercely patriotic and missed Sweden and its culture from time to time.

The staff at Matakana Market Kitchen were busy setting up for dinner and they found a table for two on the terrace overlooking the slow-flowing river running through the village. The warm afternoon sun and the sweet smell of the wildflowers on the bank enveloped them. The emerald water shimmered where the sun hit the mirrored top. Thick clumps of weed swayed below the calm surface of the water where a family of ducks were diving and frolicking.

The coffees and Swiss Kisses arrived. Lexi took a sip of coffee, the rich aroma of earth followed by cedar and clove with a well-rounded creamy finish. The barista was on form today.

"Hey, guess who Avery and Isaac are catching up with tonight," Lexi said.

That sparked Annika's curiosity. "Who?"

"They convinced James to join them for dinner before the movie tonight."

"I thought there were irreconcilable differences between them. Great if they can sort it all out. They used to be such good mates, didn't they?"

Lexi nodded. "James has always been a bit of a dork, but I've felt sorry for him since Tina left and took the boys with her." Lexi took another sip of her coffee. Her hands were trembling, and she narrowly avoided tipping the cup over as she sat it down on the saucer.

"How are *you* all doing?" Annika asked.

Lexi took a deep breath. "To tell you the truth, I'm scared," she said. Her voice was a bit wobbly. "I'm not sure leaving the children at home on their own is the best thing to do."

Annika put her hand on Lexi's arm. "I'm sure they will be fine. I can ask Niko to stay with them, if you like. That way you can relax and enjoy the event tonight."

Lexi's face lit up. "That would be great. Could you ask him?"

Annika dialled Niko, who said yes straight away.

"It'll be all right. You'll have one burly cop there keeping watch," Annika said. "Nothing will happen."

ANNIKA SLOWLY WALKED BACK UP to the cinema. It had been a busy few months getting everything organised; the movie selection, the decorations including the old VW in the foyer, the catering and the director of *The Dark Horse* himself, who would say a few words. The event had completely sold out. This was what she loved about this tight-knit community, that people supported their own. It didn't matter if it was an art exhibition or a market day, people turned out. Thoughts of her own upcoming exhibition crashed through her mind — opening night was less than a month away. She had completed most of the works, but still had a couple she wasn't entirely happy with.

On her way out, Annika poked her nose into the back of the theatre to look for Ben, but there was no sign of him, and the tangled mess of cables that had been on the floor were now tidy and back in place.

While scrounging around in her handbag to find her car keys, she bumped into the projectionist who reassured her that everything was in perfect working order. "Ben couldn't wait to get out of here. Perhaps he has a hot date for tonight," he chuckled.

Annika didn't find it funny but attempted a smile and went on her way. She was almost home when she got a call from Zac who was waiting by the bus stop. She had to force herself not to lose the plot and scream. It wouldn't help one bit, and would probably result in a whopper of a tension headache, something she could do without today. She took a few deep breaths, pulled herself together and turned the car around. She focused on the fact that she would be home soon and able to sit down for a moment before she had to cook the family dinner. They rarely bought takeaways, but perhaps she should have tonight.

Zac waved when she pulled up. "You forgot about me, didn't you," he said with a cheeky smile.

KATIE WAS CHOPPING vegetables as they arrived home and a delicious smell from the chicken already in the oven permeated the cosy kitchen. Annika's spirits soared.

"Thank you, darling, that's very thoughtful of you. I really appreciate it," she said, kissing her daughter on the cheek.

Katie smiled. "I knew you'd be busy and thought if I got dinner organised it'd be one thing less for you to do."

It had been a stressful day. "You are amazing," she said, and headed upstairs to have a quick shower and get changed.

25

Niko was already at the farm when Lexi arrived home. His racing-red Holden R8 was gleaming, not an easy feat considering the dusty country roads. You could tell it was his baby. Avery and Isaac were sitting in the garden having a chat with the off-duty cop who looked relaxed and very different in his board shorts and loud Hawaiian shirt hugging his bulging biceps. Lexi stopped to thank Niko for giving up his evening off, to hang out with the kids.

He smiled. "No trouble at all. I'm happy to help."

"We're very grateful anyway. Thank you again." Lexi liked Niko, he was only in his mid-twenties, but very comfortable with himself, she thought. She knew from Annika that there was a girlfriend on the horizon and she was pleased for him. Perhaps Gabriel would learn something from Niko's mature and positive outlook. Her son worried her sometimes. Last year had been rocky, with him putting in little effort at school. Thankfully, this year seemed to have started off better and he was doing well.

"Please help yourself to tea and coffee and whatever is in the pantry," Lexi told Niko.

"Thanks, but I'm trying to be good." He patted his taut stomach. "I have to be in some shape when I get home, or the guys will give me heaps. They think all I do is lie on the beach and eat ice cream. Sounds nice, but miles from the truth," he said with a laugh.

"Dinner," Lexi called out to the children, who were on their way out to see what was happening. "No need for cutlery, just grab the tomato ketchup." She opened a parcel of greaseproof paper wrapped in newsprint. This was the beauty of fish and chips, she thought.

Lexi had to make a quick turnaround as the boys were already meeting James at six-thirty. She had asked Annika to meet her for dinner at the same place. She had chosen the blue dress with the chiffon draping and wore a pair of silver sandals instead of heels. The days of trotting around in toe-pinching high heels were long gone, she didn't miss that one bit. She brought the curling iron out and made a few soft waves, framing her face nicely. Feeling more festive, she splashed perfume on her wrist and transferred it onto her neck. The floral notes of jasmine and rose, along with a touch of bergamot and Sicilian orange, enveloped her. It was her favourite and a standby birthday gift — Avery knew that she loved it. Before going downstairs, she ran her fingers through the curls and carefully slid her grandmother's antique Swarovski crystal hair clip through her tresses.

It was a long time since she had an occasion to dress up and look nice, although she was unsure whether Avery would even notice.

26

Avery parked the Audi at the back of the pub where there was plenty of space. The temperature had dropped a little from this afternoon and a slight musky autumn smell was in the air as the leaves were dropping. James was sitting at a table outside. He was freshly shaved and and looking good in his light-coloured polo shirt and navy trousers.

"Good to see you, James," Lexi said, hugging him, his soft after-shave enveloping her.

"Likewise. I'm sorry it's been so long." His chin dipped down and a flush spread across his cheeks.

"Don't worry about it," Lexi said and touched his arm. "I'll leave you guys to it." She went over to a table on the other side of the court-yard. Her phone bleeped. The message was from Annika, who was running late.

A handsome young waiter appeared and took her order, a glass of pinot gris from Matakana Estate. She scrolled through her emails while she waited for Annika.

The waiter arrived with her wine, an air of confidence radiating through his golden glow. He smiled and gave her a wink. Lexi was not used to getting such attention and blushed. Slightly flustered, she took a generous first mouthful. The wine was delicious and she relaxed a little.

"Hi, I'm sorry I'm late," Annika said as she rushed in, almost knocking over the chair as she sat down. "I had to wait for Bill to come home, then there was a homework emergency for the twins. Thank goodness Katie had cooked dinner for everyone." She was talking at a million miles an hour.

"Just breathe. Let's get you a glass of wine and have a look at the menu." Catching the waiter's attention, she pointed to her glass and put one finger in the air.

"I'm nervous about tonight," Annika said. "What if something goes wrong?"

"Nothing will go wrong. You've been planning this for months. I know it'll be great," Lexi said reassuringly.

The wine arrived at the table, the waiter exuding charm. Lexi blushed again, feeling like a schoolgirl. She had forgotten the feeling of butterflies fluttering in her stomach and the intoxication that comes with being appreciated.

Annika was oblivious and chattered away. They both decided on the snapper with seafood risotto and a green salad. After ordering Lexi excused herself and went to the Ladies' room. She didn't know what on earth had got into her. Why was she reacting in this way? She was a happily married woman. Or was she? The last year of work on the farm and vineyard had been exceedingly busy, and with the trouble that Gabriel had caused them on top of that, she and Avery had drifted apart.

When Lexi emerged a good five minutes later, there was a fresh glass of wine for each of them on the table. "I nearly sent out a search party for you, are you all right?" Annika said, looking worried.

"Sorry. I think the wine went straight to my head," Lexi said.

The meal arrived and they switched to sparkling water to keep their heads clear. Each time the waiter arrived he clearly found it amusing that he had such an effect on Lexi.

She glanced across at the three guys in deep conversation, having an enjoyable time. She was pleased for them; it would be good if they could put their troubles behind them. She and Annika paid the bill and, as they left, the waiter caught her eye again, flashing her a smile that left little to the imagination.

They made it across the road to the cinema. Annika was fretting and wanted to see that the wine and nibbles were being set up properly. She needn't have worried, the spread set up by The Vintry, the funky little bar inside the cinema complex, looked amazing. Soon people started arriving and Annika was busy greeting everyone, as were the rest of the committee. Lexi mingled and chatted to people she knew; it was shaping into a pleasant evening. Having finished a glass of champagne she switched to orange juice as she could feel the alcohol hit her. Avery and Isaac found her just before the screening of the film started.

Afterwards, the crowd cheered when the director of *The Dark Horse*, James Napier Robertson, spoke about the concept behind the film and the making of it. Annika made the closing remarks and got a standing ovation.

"You are a star! I'm immensely proud of all your effort," Bill said, and gave his wife a big kiss. A slight pang of jealousy hit Lexi in the chest. She wished Avery would sweep her up in his arms. As the evening was coming to a close Avery caught her eye and gestured for them to leave. Lexi didn't mind — she was tired and was looking forward to going to bed. It had been a tumultuous couple of days.

Avery and Isaac came over, complimenting Annika on a superb evening and took Lexi by the arm as the venue emptied. Crossing the almost-deserted main street they went behind the pub to get into the car. Lexi stopped dead in her tracks. In the dim light from the building she could see on the bonnet of the silver car someone had written *U ARE NEXT* in bright red paint. The run-off from the crudely drawn letters trailed down the side of the car like streaks of blood.

"What the fuck?" Avery took the few metres in two giant strides.

"It's still wet," he said, touching it with his finger. He circled the car to see if there was any other damage.

Lexi was scared and visibly upset by it all. Isaac grabbed hold of her and sat her down on one of the fencing posts. She just wanted comfort from her husband but he was oblivious, still pacing along the gravel parking lot.

Isaac darted across the road to get hold of Bill, who spoke to Niko on the phone. "The children are all fine. Everyone's asleep. Niko has peeked into their rooms to make sure," he told Lexi.

"Thank you," Lexi said, her eyes shiny and face drained of colour. Bill put his big brotherly arms around her, stroking her back gently as she disappeared into the haven of his chest.

Having calmed down a little, Avery came over and put his hand on her shoulder. Bill let go, but it was all too late. A moment of awkward silence followed.

"I'll drive the three of you home?" Bill said. "It's best if you leave the car here anyway. We'll have to take some photos and have another look at it."

No one spoke on the way home. The front lawn and the path leading up to the house were bathed in light and Niko was already waiting by the car.

Lexi hugged him. "Thanks so very much for being here tonight."

"My pleasure. They are awesome kids." He chuckled. "They remind me of my own big crazy family. We had a ball."

By the time the three of them got inside Avery had poured a generous night cap for each of them, and that's when the seriousness of the situation set in. Isaac filled Lexi in on what James had told them about the break-in at his house and the threats made.

Lexi's mind was working overtime. The priority was to make sure the children were safe so tomorrow she would take them to her parents' place in Orewa. It wouldn't hurt if Evie missed a few days of school, and the older two could catch the school bus to Warkworth. Avery and Isaac went around the house and checked that all the windows and doors were secure. Beau was snoozing on his large yellow rug in the kitchen as they all went to bed to get some rest.

The wind picked up, whining around the corners of the creaky old homestead, and a chill inched its way up from the base of her spine to the back of her neck. Lexi shuddered — not at the sudden drop in temperature, but at the thought of someone out there watching them.

27

A handful of people were still at the pub, most of them far too busy nursing a glass of wine or beer to notice Bill and Niko pulling in. Bill had got his tool kit from the ute and was lying on a piece of cardboard on the ground with a compact mirror and a torch, checking under the car.

"You don't think someone has planted a bomb, do you?" Niko said, barely able to hide his laughter.

"Of course not." Bill's voice was tight. "However, it is procedure and it would be foolish not to check. Don't just stand there, get on your knees and have a look."

Niko knew he had overstepped the mark. "All clear here, Sarge. "It's been a long day. Let's get this done so we can piss off home," Bill sighed.

"Is James staying at the pub?"

"He said he was. He also mentioned that he was going back to the vineyard tomorrow. Apparently Avery and Isaac will come over and help." Bill stood up and dusted off his clothes.

Niko drove the Audi back to the station where they rigged a pair of sturdy floodlights to give them enough light to examine it. The paint had dried — it looked like acrylic so it could be the same as in

James's house. They couldn't be sure until they had compared the two samples.

"The only thing I know is," Bill said, his brow furrowed, "if this escalates Orewa will take over the investigation completely and we'll be totally out of the loop."

"Let's hope it doesn't get to that."

Bill cast an eye at his yawning partner. "How about I drop you off on my way home?"

"Thanks, but I'm happy to walk. It's only up the road, it'll do me good."

"Suit yourself. See you tomorrow morning," Bill said and drove off.

Niko strolled to his flat. He loved the peace, so much nicer than the streets of Auckland. Not that he was worried — he had been in his fair share of scrapes as a teenager and had to thank the local community cop for setting him on a path to sorting his life out. Officer Loto Fa'amoana inspired him to work harder at school, building his self-worth and to take part in sport instead of roaming the mean streets of Manurewa. Loto was a coach at the local rugby club and got Niko playing. Having both aptitude and size, he was a promising rugby player, both at school and club rugby. He had even been selected for the development squad of the Auckland Blues, but his career came to an abrupt halt when he ruptured his knee ligament in his first season. This ended his professional dreams and sent him on a self-destructive downward spiral, connecting with his old associates, the petty criminals and gang prospects. That's when Loto was there again, convincing him to apply for the police and setting him back on a better path. His life could easily have gone the other way, with him joining a gang and becoming trapped. Niko knew he had a lot to be thankful for.

The street was quiet. Niko was looking forward to going to bed — it had been a long day. Reaching for the door handle to get upstairs to his flat, he heard raised voices and an argument unfolding across the street at the pub. Turning around and crossing the road, he recognised Piri and another of the old drunks well known to the police arguing about something, arms flapping.

"Hey, guys, what seems to be the problem?" Niko said, his towering frame casting shadows across the table.

"Fuck sake, mate, you know how to scare the shit out of an innocent bloke, don't you." Piri's unkempt white beard was almost luminescent in the moonlight. He had tucked his tatty old shirt into his low-slung jeans, revealing a bulbous spare tyre around his middle, hinting at a fondness for beer and fast food. The initial glance might give people an association with Santa, but Niko knew that was a long bow to draw. Once you got close and could see the furrowed face and lack of teeth, this bloke had not had an uncomplicated life.

Niko leaned on the outdoor table. "Well, if you hadn't caused such a racket, I would've left you alone. Now, tell me what you're arguing about."

The slightly younger one, whom Niko didn't know, piped up. "We're not arguing, officer, we're having an honest discussion about the city folk who come up here and throw their weight around." The greasy hair framing his pale face made him look a fright up close.

There was no doubt the comment was directed at him, but Niko took it in his stride. "Regardless, if you don't keep it down, I'll have you both locked up for disturbing the peace. Let's see how cheery you are tomorrow after a night in the cells."

"But there are no holding cells here in Matakana," the younger one said smugly.

"That's true, but there are in Warkworth. Those boys would gladly come and pick up a couple of mouthy old pricks. Up to you."

Piri, who had a few brain cells remaining, said, "We'll keep it down. Don't worry about us — it's nearly closing time and we'll get on our way," he said with a slight sarcastic undertone and a pious expression that betrayed his insincerity.

Niko ignored it. They weren't worth getting in trouble for. His temper had got the worst of him growing up and there were things he regretted from his troubled youth. The suffering he had caused still sometimes kept him up at night.

28

Lexi could barely lift her head when she woke up. It had been another restless night and when she finally dropped off she must have stayed in a peculiar position, hence the discomfort in her neck. The exhaustion was like a heavy veil and her eyes were gritty from not enough rest. Getting out of bed she felt as if she had jet lag. Taking the robe from the hook behind the bedroom door, she went downstairs while gently massaging the knot in her neck. Beau was ecstatic to see her, his fluffy plume of a tail wagging ferociously. She boiled the jug, dropped an Earl Grey tea bag in her favourite mug. The delicate aroma seemed to lift her tiredness a little. She dialled her parents' number. It was early, not seven yet, but she knew they would be awake. Her mother had either her walking group or a swim in the morning. It set her up for the day she said. Elsy had embraced the clean-living and exercise lifestyle since moving into retirement living, Lexi's father not so much. These days she made Bob lots of low-carbohydrate, healthy-fat meals, quite a contrast to the meat, three veg and potato that had been the staple during Lexi's childhood. Bob didn't make a fuss and knew his wife meant well, but Lexi knew that didn't stop him from indulging in the baking at local cafés.

"Hi Dad, it's me." Having held it together this far, she could feel her voice trembling.

"Hi, darling. You're calling early. Is everything all right?"

Lexi filled him in on the key points of what'd happened. "Oh dear. Do you want us to come up and help for a few days?" he said when she had finished.

"That's very kind, Dad, but Avery and I are okay. I was wondering if the children could come and stay with you for a few days instead."

"Of course they're welcome to stay with us. If the girls are happy to share the spare room, Gabriel could sleep on an air mattress in the lounge."

"Sounds great. Thanks very much. Could I drop them off this morning? They can all have a sneaky day off school."

Relieved that the children would be safe at her parents, Lexi took a sip of tea. She grimaced. It was lukewarm, but she wasn't too proud to put the mug in the microwave for thirty seconds. She smiled. Annika would have given her a lecture on how bad it was for you to use the micro.

Avery looked hollow-eyed as he joined her in the kitchen. Lexi made him a coffee and told him about the conversation with Bob.

"That's great of your parents to look after them," he said. "It's not like they have much room anymore."

"I had a terrible night's sleep."Lexi said. "It's playing on my mind that James and us have both received threatening messages, and the hand found here. Are you going to speak to Bill?"

"Yes, but first Isaac and I are going over to help James, give him a hand before the harvest."

That pleased Lexi. This was more of the Avery she had married. "I'm glad you've sorted things out. James seemed happy last night. He's had a tough year, poor man," she said as Isaac walked through the front door dressed in black Lycra leggings with stripes on the side and tight purple compression zip-up shirt.

"Look at you," Avery laughed. "You are such a trendy city boy."

"Morning. I had to clear my head. I couldn't run so I went for a good blast on your bike to blow some cobwebs out. That was nice, but

I might have overdone it. I can feel the top of my arse," Isaac said and grimaced. "And this didn't make it easier," he said and held up his bandaged hand.

A SHRILL signal cut through the noise and Avery reached for the phone. Both Lexi and Isaac could hear Trevor shouting, "Your blasted cattle are all over my garden, trampling and eating everything in sight! They've ruined my flower beds and demolished most of the vegetable garden. You need to come and sort them out!" It wasn't a request.

Avery was not looking forward to facing the old git. He would most definitely demand cash as compensation. He was just the type.

Trevor was standing in the middle of the lawn, swinging his arms like a windmill and shouting. The cows were grazing, paying no attention to the angry man. They had pushed the fence down and got out. Avery stepped off the quad bike and checked the power. It was turned off. How could that be? Yesterday, the mains had been hooked to it, making it potentially lethal. Avery and Isaac straightened the two posts that had been trampled, compacting the dirt around it. Once the electric fence was on again, the cattle wouldn't go near it. They had a sixth sense about things like this.

"Don't just stand there, get them off my property. They're a bloody menace," Trevor grumbled, throwing his arms in the air like a crazy person.

"I'll get behind them," Avery said, taking charge. "You two cover the flanks and we'll push them back into the paddock." Trevor muttered something under his breath, but complied. It didn't take long to get the cows corralled back into the top paddock, the animals seemingly happy and content with full bellies.

Trevor vented his dismay. "How the bloody hell could they have got out? I thought you had the electric fence on?"

Avery frowned. "It was on, but for some reason it's been turned off."

"Are you sure it was on in the first place?" Trevor asked, his bark settling down.

"I made a point of checking on it yesterday, as we had some trouble with it the other day," Avery said, looking at Isaac.

"Someone was up here on a two-wheeler this morning." Trevor's pointy chin jutted out, his arms crossed over his chest like a toddler throwing a tantrum. "Your delinquent son doesn't have one does he, creating more trouble for decent folk still in bed?"

"No, he hasn't," Avery huffed, "nor has he been up here this morning. Let us know what we owe you for the damage." He jumped on the quad bike and took off, dirt and gravel flying. His blood was boiling and he was so tired of the whingeing old bastard. Isaac followed, leaving Trevor standing there with a sly smile. He had the feeling that the old man was happy with the outcome.

By the time Avery had got back to the house he'd calmed down a little. "Let's get some breakfast, fix the posts then head over to James's before it gets much later," he said. "And get out of those clothes — this isn't the Tour de France!"

The early morning rush of adrenalin had made them both ravenous. Thankfully there was a mountain of bacon, eggs and piles of wholegrain toast with cooked tomatoes on the side, the smell greeting them as they stepped inside the house.

"Food of champions," Isaac exclaimed. Avery could only nod in agreement as he started stuffing his face.

"I'll have to take your car to drive down to Mum and Dad's when you come back from James's," Lexi said. "Mine is in police custody, remember."

"I'd forgotten. We shouldn't be long," Avery said. "You know, it wouldn't surprise me if Trevor is the one messing with the electric fence. I wouldn't put it past him to cause trouble."

29

J ames woke with a start. It had been the same recurring nightmare again. The crumpled bedsheets were wrapped around his body like a snake strangling its prey. He looked at his phone, and it was still early. The air was fresh and the dew covered the windowsill. The sweat-soaked sheets made him shiver. Fragments of his dream were still vivid in his mind, the obscure face and the stale, putrid breath of the person haunting him — or was it the smell of his own sweat-soaked body that made him feel a little queasy?

He forced himself to get up, turfing the bedclothes at the base of the narrow bed, grabbing the towel off the hook behind the door. It was still damp from his shower last night. The faded blue carpet had seen better days, but softened his step. Even though he was sure it was vacuumed regularly, it still wasn't great for his asthma. The shared facilities on the pub's second floor with its checkerboard tiles was a charming remnant from the eighties and the compact shower cubicle in the corner clean and sufficient. Someone had been in there before him as the warm steam had completely fogged the mirror. He put his towel on the wooden stool provided and got into the shower.

The hot water dispersed the terrible night's sleep, making him feel a little better.

With the towel wrapped around his waist, he walked back to his room and got dressed before going to the Black Dog Café a few doors down. The loud group of girls that had been in the rooms next to him and had partied until the early hours this morning again were exuberant and noisy. *Oh, the joys of youth*, he thought. From what he could hear, today's adventures included snorkelling at Goat Island. He ordered his coffee and some wholemeal toast, grabbed a newspaper, walked out into the courtyard and sat at the same table as yesterday. The sun was beating down and he was enjoying the warmth as he glanced over today's headlines. When the waitress brought his long black she gave him a friendly smile, clearly recognising him from the day before.

As James sipped his coffee, his mind wandered back to the conversation with Avery and Isaac. It had almost felt like old times. They had shown a genuine concern when he told them about the break-in at the house. Avery had also told him the full story of what had happened at the homestead which was disturbing.

The pile of toast arrived with an assortment of condiments. James smeared a generous layer of butter and Marmite on the first slice and tucked in. For a fleeting moment he was back in his mother's kitchen, ten years old and freckle-faced with no cares in the world. Finishing his breakfast he ordered another coffee to take with him. It was time to head home; he had neglected the vineyard for the last couple of days. As a passionate winemaker he wanted to be there, nurturing his vines and getting ready for the upcoming harvest. James gathered his things from the pub and paid his bill before getting into his car parked at the back.

The eight o'clock news came on as he turned the ignition. The presenter was talking about a man found dead in Martinborough, quickly moving on to a political faux pas made by an MP in Parliament yesterday. Switching off the endless drone of words he drove towards home, forcing himself to shake the foreboding feeling of doom.

Pulling into the driveway he glanced up at the house, and it looked just as he'd left it, devoid of the noisy family that belonged there. His heart was heavy, he missed them so much. He went straight into the winery. The massive old wooden doors creaked as he pulled them open. As far as he could see no one had been in there. He flicked the light on. This was his joyous place. He filled his lungs with the mix of French oak barrels and earth. There was a compact kitchen, very basic but perfectly functional, the slightly roomier office, both leading off the primary winery area. It wasn't large by industry standards, nor particularly well equipped, but nevertheless it was his and he was proud of it. Going back outside, the morning sun blinded him. He opened the garage and got on his quad bike. He glanced at Greg and Timothy's kid-size quad bikes that hadn't been used for a long time. A pang of torment hit him straight in the chest. Next time they came for a visit, he would make sure they went for a ride together. He knew how much the boys enjoyed it.

Reversing out, he parked out the front and popped back into the winery to get his testing kit. It was shaping up to be another gorgeous day; he was expecting a pleasant ride with the warm winds in his face. A movement at the corner of his eye made him turn around.

The large spanner hit him hard across the bridge of his nose and the last thing he heard before losing consciousness was the loud crunching of his nose and cheekbones.

JAMES WOKE to an excruciating pain radiating across his face and into his teeth and sinuses. His right eye was swollen shut, with only limited vision through the left. He felt as if he'd gone several rounds with Tyson Fury. He was sitting on the concrete floor with his back against an old wine barrel they used as a leaner for drinks, the damp seeping through his shorts. Both his arms were stretched around the barrel at an unnatural angle making his shoulders scream in agony — although that wasn't a fraction of the pain radiating across his smashed-up face. James's heart was thumping and fear oozed out of every pore. Running his tongue across his front teeth he swallowed hard to get rid of the clotted blood and the foul taste of metal in his mouth. The lack of saliva didn't help. His throat was dry and it made him cough, sending pain across his swollen face, globular gelatinous matter filling his mouth. He tried to spit but dribbled gunk down his chest instead.

The panic and lack of breathing through his nose was causing a tightness in his chest. James knew he had to calm down or there was an enormous risk of an asthma attack. He forced himself to breathe in deeply through his mouth, but the exposed roots of his damaged teeth sent shock waves of pain through his jaw.

The masked man just stood in the doorway looking at him, no expression at all. He was dressed in white protective clothing, the disposable kind that painters sometimes wear.

"Who are you?" James gasped. There was no answer. A tool box was set up in the middle of the floor. The man ran his gloved hand across a row of shiny objects, making a series of clinking sounds as they knocked together. James couldn't quite see what they were from where he was sitting.

"My friends are coming over. They'll be here any moment," James blurted to win some time.

"I thought as much," the man said. "I saw you all thick as thieves last night and overheard your plans."

James had a faint memory of hearing that voice before, but where and when? His brain hurt and he struggled to think.

"Don't worry, I've made sure your friends will be busy rounding up livestock before they can come over here. We have plenty of time."

James realised there was no way out. "Who the fuck are you?" he tried again through his swollen lips. "What do you want with me?"

Holding a small ampoule the man calmly filled a small syringe with the clear liquid.

"What are you going to do?" James could hear the desperation in his voice growing.

"Just relax. This won't hurt a bit." The man walked towards James and swiftly injected the liquid into his abdomen. He perched on a stool in the corner. He didn't say a word, just sat there and watched.

James felt the sweat running down his back pooling at the top of his butt cheeks. He was trapped and helpless, the air was stale with intent and fear. He clung onto the hope that Avery and Isaac were on their way — they had promised to come over early. He wondered what the time might be, remembering he had listened to the eight o'clock news on the way home but had no idea how long he had been unconscious.

The silence was deafening and seemed to consume all the air in the room. James's shoulders were screaming with the stress of the joints, his arms heavy and tingling from the cut-off blood supply while wrapped around the barrel. The man lifted the latex glove and looked at his watch, then suddenly stood up and lunged towards him, holding a long, narrow knife. All James could do was watch the knife being thrust into his lower body, hitting tendons and bone. The pain was indescribable. The blade stabbed into his flesh time and time again. His screams rebounded around the industrial equipment. He wasn't sure if he had bitten his tongue or if his nose was bleeding again. Either way the blood was choking him, making him cough to get air, while he slowly lost consciousness.

When he came to, the man was back sitting on the stool, just watching him. James looked down at his bloodied shorts. Pools of blood were on the floor, trickling out of the wounds like molten lava. Feeling like a spectator and getting weaker by the second, as minor rivers of blood trailed away from his broken body.

The man in the corner stood up and packed away his things, calmly wiping the knife blade and putting it back in the box.

James used all his strength to lift his head. "Why?"

"You and your friends should have let sleeping dogs lie."

"What?" James struggled to think. What was he talking about?

The man stepped closer. "Let me remind you."

That's when James recognised the voice.

His last thought was not what the man was saying — he had already stopped listening, it was how much he loved his sons.

30

They got into Avery's old hack and drove towards James's place. The driveway, sparsely planted on the sides, was full of potholes and neglect. The house looked the same as it had when Avery had been here last year, just more overgrown. You could see how things had got on top of James when the financial troubles started, he thought, with the last nail in the coffin being when Tina left and took the boys with her. But the outside was nothing a bit of elbow grease couldn't fix. Perhaps he should organise a little working bee, getting it all back in order for him. It would have to wait until after the harvest.

Avery parked next to James's Ford Ranger.

"Let's check the winery," Isaac said. James's quad bike was casually parked outside. The large wooden door creaked in protest as they pulled it open, light seeping into the cavernous space. There was no movement or lights on and Avery was about to close the door when they spotted what looked like someone sitting on the floor at the back.

There was a change in the air as they pulled the double doors wide open. Light flooded in, dust particles dancing in front of them. When they realised it was James slumped over at the back, they ran over, Avery desperately searching for a pulse, calling out his name. He was still warm to the touch but not responding. There was so much blood on the floor.

"Isaac call the ambulance," Avery yelled, hoping it wasn't too late. The dank smell of blood and human waste was overwhelming.

Checking for a pulse again, Avery felt nothing but clammy skin. He stood up slowly and walked away from the body on wobbly legs, leaving a trail of bloody footprints behind. He wiped his hands on his jeans, unsure if he would throw up. He sat on the ground outside, feeling faint, his stomach in turmoil. He put his head between his knees, trying to concentrate on one breath in, one breath out. He had never seen gore like this.

Isaac was equally quiet, and in shock. It seemed ages until he finally heard the approaching sirens from Warkworth.

AN AMBULANCE OFFICER jumped out of the passenger seat, dark-green shirt with a hint of white showing at the neck and navy cargo pants with a multitude of pockets down the leg. She looked at Avery's blood-stained jeans and asked, "Where are you hurt?"

"Not me, I'm okay but he isn't," he said, pointing towards the winery. The second officer, medical kit in hand, followed her into the building, pulling his latex gloves on, his face pale with shock at the sight. He checked for the victim's vital signs and confirmed he was dead. "Bloody hell," he said to his colleague as they both backed out from the crime scene.

WHEN BILL and Niko arrived Avery was sitting pale as a sheet with James' blood on his clothes and hands; Isaac was in shock and staring into the distance with a hospital blanket wrapped tightly around his shoulders. Leaving Niko with Avery and Isaac, Bill took a deep breath and walked into the building. He knew from experience that air could be difficult to get once you entered a violent crime scene. James's body was arranged like a rag doll. The ferocity of the attack was clear from the multitude of puncture wounds on his legs. There were no visible wounds on the torso; perhaps, Bill thought, the attacker hadn't wanted him to die straight away, but to suffer and bleed out slowly. The face was a mess, swollen and bloodied. Bill swallowed hard — it was one of the worst scenes he had been to.

"Fuckin' hell man," Niko said when he appeared in the doorway. "That's someone with a lot of hate."

"It looks like gang warfare. Only a really sick bastard could be this calculated."

"Seems unlikely James would have any dealings with a gang. He was too much of a soccer dad, if you know what I mean."

"Stranger things have happened, respectable guys getting involved in shit they shouldn't."

"I saw him at the pub last night. Poor bastard. No one deserves to go this way."

"I have to call this in to Orewa," Bill said. "Then we'll see if we can make sense out of Isaac and Avery." As he called the Senior Sergeant in Orewa, his heart was heavy. He knew that James had two young sons who would now grow up without a dad.

"Orewa is sending a team up right away," he reported to Niko. "ESR hopefully won't be too far behind. I'd hate for his body to lie out too long in this warm weather, the flies are already buzzing around."

"Well, there's nothing more we can do here," the female ambulance officer said. "The men are in shock, but they will be fine." Even though she was young, Bill guessed it wasn't her first crime scene.

"Sure, no problem. Thanks for keeping them separated. We'll monitor them." Bill thought of Tina. They had to inform her as soon as possible. He didn't know her personally, but had seen her with James before. He seemed to remember her working at the New World supermarket in Warkworth, but he'd try the home address first.

~

NIKO WAS SITTING with Isaac who gave his account of how they had found James. "I just keep seeing him sitting in there."

When Niko couldn't get anything more from Isaac he left him to sit with his back against the building, alone with his thoughts.

"I can't believe he's dead," Avery said subdued. "We agreed last night to come and give him a hand to get organised for the harvest in the next week. We must have only just missed the killer. The body was still warm, for fucks sake." He was angry now. If they hadn't been chasing cows they'd have been here earlier and maybe prevented the attack.

"Did you see anyone else leaving the property?" Bill asked.

"No. There was no one here when we arrived. We saw the quad bike parked outside and went straight to the winery, but there was no sign of him. I was thinking it was strange as we had agreed to meet today. We were on our way to shut the door when we glimpsed him sitting on the floor at the back, in the dark."

Suddenly Avery stood bolt upright. "Jesus, I have to ring Lexi. What if this deranged prick is on his way to our house?" He frantically searched for his phone, fumbling, missing it, the panic making him clumsy.

"It's in your back pocket, Avery." Bill said. "You need to calm down. It won't be helpful if you scare Lexi when you speak to her. I'll put a call into Warkworth. They can dispatch a patrol car and stay with Lexi and the kids until you get there."

He called it in and asked the Senior Sergeant there, "Can you let me know they're all fine when you've got personnel at Matakana Valley Wines?"

When Bill disconnected the call, Niko gestured at the two sad individuals slumped in opposite places. "Do you think those two have anything to do with this?"

31

Lexi put the phone down and slid down the wall of the farm shop, her heart beating almost out of her chest. James was dead. She swallowed hard, but saliva gushed from under her tongue like a fountain, resulting in her bolting to the toilet in the back room. Sticking her face under the cold tap she rinsed her mouth, her stomach cramping from the violent purging of her breakfast. She slammed the shop door and sprinted across the front lawn, throwing herself inside and locking the door. She perched on a kitchen chair, contemplating if she should go and brush her teeth and rinse the horrid taste out, but fear paralysing her to stay put and wait for the police to arrive.

Beau put his soft head in her lap and gave her hand a lick. She looked into his large brown eyes and stroked his soft head. "Thank you, boy. Everything will be fine," she said with her cheeriest voice, but she wasn't very convincing, least of all to herself. She glanced at the wall clock. *How long until the police will be here?* She knew that Avery and Isaac could not leave until the police and the forensics team had finished with them. How on earth could she defend herself and the children if the attacker came here? There was the storage locker next to the stairs with the gun safe, but where was the key? She had a vague memory that Avery kept it in the kitchen junk drawer. Rifling through, she found the key and put it in a wooden trinket box on the shelf in the hallway for easy access should she need it.

Suddenly Beau barked, which made Lexi jump. She peeked out of the kitchen window and saw two uniformed police officers walking up the path to the house. Lexi opened the door, while holding onto the dogs collar.

"Hello, I'm Senior Constable Gary Trenton and this is my colleague Constable Laura Rose. We're from the Warkworth station," the policeman said, his sidearm and smile making her feel a bit safer. Beau refused to move an inch from her legs, leaning in, wary of the strangers.

"We'll stay here with you until further notice." Laura said. "Would you mind if we came inside?" Her auburn hair was striking against her English-rose skin. She was at least ten years younger than her colleague, her warmth and kindness shining through. "I'll put the jug on," she said. Lexi immediately liked her.

Gabriel came thundering down the stairs and into the kitchen stopping dead in his tracks as he saw the two uniformed officers sitting at the table.

"Gabe, come and sit down," Lexi said. She put her hand on his arm as she told him that James was dead. Lexi watched her son struggle with the enormity of the situation. Even though he looked like a man, she realised, inside he was still only a boy.

32

Bill felt uncomfortable treating Avery and Isaac as suspects, but he had to follow protocol. The last thing he needed was his arse kicked by the team from Orewa.

He didn't believe that either man had anything to do with the death, but the fact remained that Avery and James had not been on the best terms. Stranger things had happened, and in this case there was both motive and opportunity. According to the grim statistics, eighty per cent of murder victims knew their killers.

Avery was sitting with his head in his hands. Isaac was now pacing around like a man possessed, muttering something under his breath. Niko had done it by the book; processed their witness statements, taken prints and photographed the pair. Detectives Copeson and Rudd arrived shortly after, with Mike Thorpe, a Detective Sergeant in his mid-thirties, looking hot and bothered in beige trousers and rolled-up shirtsleeves. Rudd was even more bedraggled than last time, if that was possible. The large dark circles under his eyes made him look perpetually grumpy. Copeson and Thorpe had youth on their side and looked fine, apart from large sweat stains under their arms and back of their wrinkled shirts.

"Thanks for coming up so quickly," Bill said, shaking Thorpe's hand.

"It's not like we have a choice in the matter," Rudd spluttered in his usual abrasive manner, continuing towards the winery with no pleasantries. "People seem to be frivolously killing each other, and my area is large enough to cover without this."

Andrew Copeson lingered for a moment, waiting until his superior was out of earshot. "Don't mind Rudd. He's pulled an all-nighter. It was a hellish car ride until he fell asleep." He grinned. "I just hope he sleeps on the way back too."

RUDD SCOWLED AT AVERY. "It's you again. How come you keep turning up like a bad penny?"

On any other day Avery would have reacted and bitten back, but he didn't have the energy to defend himself. He was tired, it was an effort to string one thought to another, so he said nothing.

Rudd suited up and pulled his latex gloves on before entering the building. Avery could hear him barking orders. Then: "I hope for your sake no one has destroyed vital evidence by climbing around here before we arrived. And where's that photographer? Why are we always waiting for him?"

Copeson pulled his mobile out and phoned Jono. "He'll be here in ten minutes," he reported. Rudd humphed.

THE ESR CAR pulled up and first out was Emma, the leggy blonde. Copeson glanced admiringly, trying not to be too obvious. One day he would muster the courage to ask her out. He gave her a casual wave, turning away pretending to do something important on the phone, while trying not to show the scarlet glow he could feel spreading to his ears. Gathering himself, he joined Rudd who was busy at work, which meant he had to concentrate and be quiet.

The ESR team was examining the area closely, logging anything that might be relevant in relation to the victim's body. When Jono arrived Rudd unleashed his wrath. "Good, you turned up then." His mood had not improved at all, especially since the temperature in the tin-roofed building was climbing and he was sweating profusely.

It was clearly Pick On Jono Day. Not that it did seem to faze him. "I could only drive so fast to get up here," he said calmly.

The funeral directors would arrive soon and the body had to be ready for transportation. They put bags over hands, feet and the head, keeping eventual trace elements contained. If they were lucky, they would find DNA in the form of hair, fibres or bodily fluids. One of the junior officers would then accompany the body to the mortuary at Auckland Hospital, ensuring that all was by the book.

Bill went over to Avery who was sitting on the bench. "You are free to go, but we'll want to speak to you again, you understand."

"Whatever I can do to help," Avery said.

Bill waved Isaac over. "I need you to come by the station."

"No problem. I can swing by before I head back to Auckland this afternoon." Isaac was eager to get back to Avery's and on his way home.

"Sounds good. See you both later." Bill hoped he had done the right thing.

Avery and Isaac walked back to the car, both relieved to leave. "I get that you need to go home," Avery said.

"I feel bad leaving in the middle of all this shit, but I think you and Lexi could do with some time on your own. The last few days have given me some clarity on what's important in life. I need to do all I can to save my marriage. Just look at James and Tina — they don't get a second chance."

33

There was nothing more they could do at the crime scene so with heavy hearts Bill and Niko drove into Warkworth. It was their duty to inform Tina, James's estranged wife of his tragic death. It was never easy to let people know that their loved one had been killed. For Bill, having had a family of his own it got worse as the years went by and he got older. Niko had made enquiries, and Tina was at work. Driving to the supermarket, they were both thinking about how such a tragedy would affect the small community. It was imperative to get hold of her promptly as terrible news like this had a tendency to spread like wildfire. Niko had spoken to Clive, the store manager, on the way. He was standing outside waiting for them, his black shirt and pants with a thin belt hugging him slightly, making his overhanging stomach more pronounced. His short grey hair and generous walrus moustache made him look every bit the granddad he was.

Clive took them straight into his small office. The cramped room barely had enough space for a small desk and two spindly kitchen chairs. He asked them to wait while he got Tina from the checkouts.

"Tina, I'm afraid we have some terrible news," Bill said.

"My god, what's happened? Are the boys all right?" she said, her face rapidly losing its colour.

"The boys are fine, but you'd better come and have a seat." She sat down on the empty chair, steeling herself for what was to come.

"I'm sorry to tell you, but James is dead," Bill said, weighing each word carefully.

Tina just stared at him with a blank expression. A moment later and as the realisation set in, she let out a gasp followed by loud sobbing, her body rocking back and forth.

"I know it's an enormous shock. We found him this morning at home," Bill continued.

From Tina's expression she seemed unable to comprehend what Bill was saying. Clive came in and put his arms around her, comforting her like a child, as she burrowed her face into his shoulder.

"I'll call St John," Niko said, helpless at the emotional breakdown of the woman in front of him, then left the room to organise the ambulance.

"How did it happen?" Tina said between sobs.

"It was not accidental," Bill said, careful to not give her any gruesome details. As the reality set in, Tina was hyperventilating, her body shutting down, spinning her into a deep void. She didn't take any notice when the ambulance officer walked in.

THE UNIFORMED WOMAN in her fifties spoke softly to her. "Let's get you looked after, my dear," she said, guiding Tina out to where a gurney was waiting. "I'll give you something that will make you feel more relaxed. How about that?"

Tina nodded weakly, her body tightly curled up and her hands clenched as she lay down on the hard stretcher, her entire existence ripped away like a rug under her feet. She had seen James just a few days ago; he had seemed happy and content. There would be no second chances.

They carried her through to the waiting ambulance. Her entire body protesting and shaking, she could no longer hold it together and let out a long wail. She thrashed about, kicked the wall and medical supplies went flying. Hands physically restraining her, holding her down. Cold liquid being injected into her body. Fuzzy edges, her body letting go, engulfing her in the deepening sinkhole of grief and regret.

34

Back at the station, Bill sank into his chair. It had been an intense start to the day; the adrenalin had flowed and exhaustion was creeping in.

He looked at the board with the assorted photos from this morning. "The priority is to get hold of Peter Evans in Martinborough. He might well be in danger."

"Perhaps the mobile number we had for him was out of date," Niko said. "I'll call Martinborough and get one of their cops to knock on his door."

"Great. In the meantime I'll take Lexi's Audi to the boys at the workshop. They might well have something that'll take the paint off the bonnet. Otherwise it's a complete repaint."

Niko dialled Martinborough. "Sergeant Lawson speaking," a cheerful voice sounded.

"Hi there. I'm Niko Sopoanga, calling from the Matakana police station. How are you?"

"We're all good down here. Did you say Matakana, as in the playground for the rich and famous Aucklanders?"

"Yes, that's the one. But it's not as glamorous as it sounds." Niko's voice dropped. "Especially not right now. We've had some trouble here, possibly linked to a man living in Martinborough. Peter Evans, at 23 Penfold Drive. Can't seem to get hold of him."

"I'm afraid you're a little too late," Lawson said. "We found him dead in his house on Tuesday."

Niko froze. "How did he die?" Bill was staring at him now.

"We found the body on the floor in the basement. He'd been stabbed multiple times, ultimately causing severe blood loss," Lawson replied. "Interestingly enough, his left hand was missing. Severed post-mortem."

"I think we've got your missing hand," Niko said. "When does the pathologist estimate the time of death?"

"Sometime between last Friday late afternoon and early Saturday morning."

"We found a male left hand on Sunday morning. It could well be a match, if you could send what you have, I'll make sure you get what we've found so far."

"Absolutely. Look forward to working with you. Let's keep in touch."

35

Isaac was just out of the shower and scrubbed clean, and in a rush to get home. He looked in a complete daze as he carried his bag to the car after the morning's horrors. Lexi and Avery walked with him in silence to the car.

"Thanks for having me," Isaac said.

"Sorry that you didn't have a very relaxing time, mate." Avery's attempt at a joke went flat.

"Don't worry. I loved seeing you guys but I've got some shit to sort. You never know when your number is up. I just hope they catch this maniac soon."

Lexi's stomach was churning. What if they were all in danger?

"Keep safe and take care of yourself mate," Isaac shook Avery's hand then gave Lexi a hug.

"Give Petra our love. I hope you two work things out," Lexi said. A pang of hurt was festering in her chest. She wished that Avery would have come to the same insight, but shook it off. There was no place for self-pity on a day like today. Poor Tina and the boys.

"Thanks guys, it means a lot." Dust whirled around the sleek sports car as Isaac drove down the driveway.

Avery's phone buzzed in his pocket.

"You can pick up Lexi's car this afternoon. The paint came off relatively easy," Bill said.

"Thanks very much," Avery said. "We appreciate it."

"No problem. See you around three thirty."

"That's brilliant news," Avery told Lexi. "The car will be ready for pickup soon, so you can take it to Orewa when you drop the children off."

"Come on, kids," Lexi called from the bottom of the stairs. "Let's get going."

Pushing and jostling, the kids piled down the stairs, an array of colourful sports bags piled at the bottom.

"You'll only be away a few days, you're not moving out of home," Avery said, trying not to laugh.

"It's all essentials apparently," Gabriel said, rolling his eyes. "I tried."

THE CAR WAS UNUSUALLY QUIET, not even a peep from the back seat. The emotional roller-coaster of the last few days had taken its toll.

"Mum and I will see Bill at the station. You guys get yourselves an ice cream from up the road. We won't be long," Avery said, grabbing Lexi's hand. "Everything will be okay, I promise," he said.

She was unsure if he meant what was happening around them or the state of their marriage. The nagging feeling was still there in the pit of her stomach. She hoped her gut was wrong.

They didn't talk as they passed the Four Square supermarket then crossed the road to the police station overgrown with bougainvillea blooms. Lexi found the combination of a sweet scent and sunshine strangely comforting. She had not been inside the Station for years, and this was her second visit in a matter of days.

A cheerful summer tune was playing on the radio as they went inside. Niko got up and greeted them with a smile. Bill was sitting down at the back. "It's been an upsetting day. How are you both holding up?" he asked.

"Still in shock. Can't believe that James is dead," Avery said.

Lexi looked pale and drawn, Bill thought. "Lexi, you're welcome to have a coffee in the lunchroom while you wait," he said, "or sit on the terrace in the sun if you like."

Avery sat down at the meeting table in the middle, his back to the front door, while Niko gathered his things.

Walking through to the kitchen Lexi looked to the right and saw a couple of large noticeboards in The Incident room to the side. A few graphic photos caught her off-guard and she hastily looked away. In the lunchroom she filled the jug, pressed the button and waited for it to boil. A mountain of used cups and plates cluttered the small sink and bench, you could tell there were two males working here. She found the last clean cup in the cupboard above the sink. The jug clicked off in a cloud of steam. A half-empty jar of freeze-dried coffee and some dodgy-looking tea bags sat on the bench. Deciding on the lesser of two evils she opened the coffee, took a whiff and tipped some into her cup. The fridge was in an equally interesting state and needed a good clean. The milk didn't smell too bad; she checked the expiration date before pouring it in.

Her eyes wandered around the room. A half-dead Ficus in an enormous pot needed some love and attention; dozens of industry magazines were piled on the lunch table and a mop and bucket alongside an ancient vacuum cleaner sat idle in the corner.

They weren't looking her way. Lexi didn't know what possessed her, going into the Incident Room. she knew she shouldn't be there, but curiosity overtook her. Some photos were from home. The warmth of the afternoon seemed to have disappeared and she shivered. She took in the photos from James's house, culminating with the violent images of his battered body. Nothing could have prepared her for the sight. The close up of his face beaten to a pulp and the vast amount of blood on the floor made her swing around and race back into the lunchroom. Hands shaking, she flung the bi-fold doors open to the patio and grabbed hold of the trellis fence, focusing on a compact bird house a few metres behind. She was relieved Tina wasn't the one that had found him like that.

The images replayed before her eyes. As Avery had said, it seemed the killer had wanted James to suffer. Would that be their fate as well ?

36

L exi took a deep breath to compose herself before rinsing her cup out and adding it to the pile in the sink. Avery was still talking to Bill. Niko was back at his desk on the phone.

Bill looked up from his notes. "We're just about done here."

"That's great. I bet the children are wondering what's taking so long." Lexi was eager to get going.

"There's just one more thing," Bill said. "I'm very sorry to have to tell you, they have found Peter Evans dead at his house in Martin-borough."

"What?" Avery stood up abruptly, the blood draining from his face. "Why the hell didn't you tell me as soon as we arrived?" he said, anger overtaking shock, his neck muscles and jaw tightening.

"I'm sorry, but I needed you to think without your head being clouded by more tragedy."

"What the fuck is going on? First James and now Peter." Avery shook his head.

"Actually, we think someone killed him on Friday or Saturday," Niko said. "His body is missing a left hand. Tests are being run as we speak to see if that's a match to the one under your house."

Avery's anger boiled over. "Of course it's his fucking hand! What are you going to do about it?"

"We are taking the threat to your family extremely seriously, but you need to calm down, Avery," Bill said. "Protection will be organised. Under no circumstances do we want you to stay there on your own."

Lexi was standing in the door way, her face was white. "I won't let anything happen to you or your family," he told her. "First things first. Did you say you were taking the kids down to your parents?"

"Yes, I'm driving them down straight after this," Lexi answered, still a bit dazed.

"Niko is organising some cops from Warkworth to come and stay with you two at the homestead as a precaution," Bill said.

Avery and Lexi nodded. The air had gone out of them both — they were merely bobbing along in the current. Lexi had never felt more vulnerable and lonely.

~

OUTSIDE THE STATION the afternoon sun had some heat in it and the pavement radiated it back like a heat gun blasting them from below. Avery headed down the road and Lexi had to sprint to catch up, grabbing his shoulder to get his attention. "Stop," she gasped.

"Why?" Avery said tersely.

"I know you're upset, but so am I. Can you just stop and take a moment? We have just had the second lot of tragic news today, Avery. The car and the children can wait for a few minutes."

They perched on the stone wall in the shade of an old oak tree. Avery put his arm around her shoulder and pulled her close. He wiped his eyes and sniffed, feeling self-conscious, a grown man getting emotional in public. It terrified him that he could be the next victim, not so much for his own sake but leaving his family all alone.

Seeing his sensitive side was rare, but it gave Lexi hope.

By the time she got down to the corner, the children were looking bored and overheated, sitting in the shade outside the Four

Square. "You took a long time. We've been waiting for ages," Evie said, exasperated and on her way to having a meltdown.

"Sorry, guys. It took longer than we thought. Dad's just picking up the car, then we'll be on our way to Orewa." There was no need for the children to know the whole story.

Evie and Samantha started bickering and Gabriel raised his voice telling them to cut it out. To Lexi's surprise they did, and she shot him a grateful look. He was growing up and it made her heart swell.

Avery pulled up beside them, the Audi looked brand-new after its cut and polish and was gleaming in the sun. "Are you sure you're up to driving the kids?" he asked.

"I'll be fine. I promise to take it easy."

"Give my love to your folks." Avery pulled her close and hugged her, his broad shoulders swallowing her up. "Everything will be fine," he said, kissing her gently. "I won't let anything happen to our family, I promise."

Lexi couldn't speak for the lump in her throat.

"Don't worry about dinner," Avery said. "I'll pop into the butchers down the road and pick up some steaks, I'll have dinner ready by the time you get home."

Avery followed the car as they drove away, hoping he could protect his family.

37

O *rewa*

THE TRIP to the Orewa Gardens Retirement Village took twenty-five minutes. Lexi was preoccupied with the images she had seen on the wall at the police station. What had triggered such a vicious murderous spree — and why?

The sub-tropical gardens were buzzing with activities. They didn't call it active retirement for nothing, she thought. On the nearby Pétanque court a competitive game was being played; next to it a group of residents were pottering around their allotments with laughter and chatter. Outside the café, others sat enjoying a late afternoon tea in the flower garden. Opposite, through large panoramic windows, she could see women in brightly coloured swim caps were enjoying their aqua aerobics to loud music.

"Look there's Grandma, she's in the pool," Sam said excitedly. Lexi phoned her Dad, who said he'd be right down and would meet them at the café.

"Grandad!" Evie shrieked, making several residents jump, and ran into his arms.

"Lovely to have you here," Bob said. "Hey kids, the exercise class in the pool is just about done. Do you want to jump in?" He didn't have to ask the girls twice, but Gabriel was playing it cool and walked casually behind his sisters.

"Come on, love," Bob said to Lexi, "let's sit down and have a cup of tea while the children are having fun." The feeling of calm and safety only a father can provide spread through her being. Bob came back with a tray of beautiful old china cups and saucers and a plate of freshly made blueberry muffins. The smell reminded her of her childhood.

Bob put his weathered hand on Lexi's arm. "Now, start from the beginning," he said. He listed intently without interruptions, his eyes betraying the sorrow and fear when she told him that James and Peter were dead. "I remember those lads well. They were decent blokes, not shy of a hard day's graft and helped with the harvest several times, if I rightly recall."

"Remember when Avery organised the pig on a spit one year?" Lexi said. "We'd set up that long table outside, the music on full volume and dancing into the small hours."

Bob smiled at the memory and offered her the butter and a knife. Lexi smothered a thick layer on the still warm muffin, realising she hadn't eaten since breakfast.

"Bill's organised police protection," she said. "We are grateful you and Mum can have the children for a few days. It makes me feel better to know that they are safe with you."

"They're welcome to stay as long as they want," Bob said. "Listen, I want you and Avery to be careful. Don't take any risks. Why don't you stay at your sister's beach house in Matheson Bay? It might be wise if no one knows your whereabouts. I have a spare set of keys. Let me give them to you before you go. I know she wouldn't mind."

"Thanks, Dad, that's a lovely thought, but you know how particular Avery is about his grapes. There's no way he would leave this close to the harvest."

"All right, but it doesn't mean I have to agree with it," Bob said, shaking his head. "Now, let's see your mother. Surely the Aquacise ladies must be out of the pool by now."

Elsy wore a bright pink fluffy bathrobe, flip-flops to match, and her beautifully manicured toenails were painted in the same shade.

"Hi Mum," Lexi said.

"How are you doing, sweetheart?".

"We're okay," Lexi said, but knew she didn't sound convincing. "Thanks for having the children stay. That's a huge load off our mind."

"We're glad to help, but I'd feel better if you could stay somewhere else for a few days until this terrible mess gets sorted out."

"I wish we could, but you know how stubborn Avery is. The harvest is days away and we really need to be at home."

"Just make sure you are careful."

Lexi could see the worry in her mother's eyes. She said goodbye to the children, who were having a ball in the pool, then Elsy and Bob walked her to the car.

"I nearly forgot," Bob said. "Let me run and get the keys to Clara and Brett's beach house."

While they waited for him to return, Elsy took Lexi's hand in hers. "Take Dad's advice and stay at the Bach."

"Thanks, Mum. I promise we'll be careful."

Bob came back with the key. "Call me any time and I'll come up straight away," he said and hugged her tight.

As Lexi drove away, she struggled to keep it together. Seeing how worried her parents were had been tough. Tears welled up in her eyes so much it was hard to see the road, so she pulled over at the next petrol station. The last few days of stress and built up anxiety had taken its toll. She filled up and went inside to pay, the cashier barely gave her red-rimmed eyes a glance but the short break worked wonders, and by the time she arrived home a plan had hatched in her head.

38

Bill was staring at the graphic photos of the murder victim from Martinborough. The investigation had been forwarded from Orewa, and he was pleased to be kept in the informed.

"Let's assume we connect the cases. According to the timeline the perpetrator was in Martinborough at the end of last week, possibly killed Peter Evans on the Friday or early Saturday. He or she must have then driven the seven hundred kilometres north." He looked at the map. "I'd say the drive would take eight or nine hours of steady driving if you did it all in one go."

"If he was killed on Friday," Niko said, "it would have been after the housekeeper had been there. According to the report, she left the house in the early afternoon. They always had lunch together on a Friday as Peter worked from home."

"This would mean the killer possibly drove through the night to get up here, depositing the hand late Saturday or early Sunday at the McCall homestead," Bill said, thinking out loud.

"Big gamble," Niko said, looking confused. "It's not like it was left it in plain sight."

"I think the perpetrator sabotaged the water pump, thus ensuring someone would go under the house and find the appendage," Bill said. "But that's just a theory. I could be wrong."

The shrill signal of the phone ringing shattered the peace. Niko ran for it.

"That was Orewa," he reported after ending the call. "They rate the threat level as low, but have dispatched a patrol for Isaac's house for the next day or so. Now we just have to wait for Warkworth. Hopefully they can spare some people to stay at the McCall's. If not I guess it's you and me."

"Let's focus on the two victims," Bill said. "Why so many stab wounds? And why mainly in the legs when he could have hit a major artery and made it quick?"

"It looks like the killer enjoyed inflicting excessive violence. When do you think they'll send the preliminary medical report through?"

"Your guess is as good as mine. Orewa will receive it, but they've agreed to keep us informed. Let's hope they do," Bill said. "Listen, I'm dashing home to get a change of clothes in case we have to stay the night at the McCall's. Why don't you do the same, then we'll meet back here."

BILL PULLED up at home less than three minutes later. Annika wasn't in the house, judging from where the loud music was coming from, but in the barn where her studio was. A playlist of eighties' songs he had grown familiar with over the years was blaring. Annika had her back to the door, was singing at the top of her voice and didn't notice him walking in until he shouted to get her attention. Her ponytail bobbed as she looked up beaming.

"Productive day by the looks of it," he said. The large canvas reminded him of a Jackson Pollock, but with thick smears of paint shaped into flowers on top, the 3D effect was astounding.

"Yes, it's been a brilliant day. I've got lots done." She pointed to three canvases in different stages of development.

"That's terrific, but I'd feel better if you'd lock the doors. You didn't even hear me coming in with the music blasting at that volume," Bill said. "They found James Smith dead this morning."

"Oh, that's just awful! Those poor wee boys," she said, covering her face with her hands. "How did he die?"

Bill filled her in on today's events from the crime scene to the hand belonging to a man killed in Martinborough.

"It all sounds too far-fetched to happen here in Matakana," she said.

"I'm here to pick up a clean shirt and some things," Bill said. "I might have to stay the night at Avery and Lexi's place. Are you picking the twins up from dance practice?"

Annika glanced at her watch. "I still have a couple of hours before I have to be there."

Bill grabbed some clean clothes and a toothbrush. Driving off, his mind wandered. Although many killings born of hatred had been committed by women, his gut told him they were dealing with a male.

The phone rang, diverted to his mobile from the station. "Matakana police station, Granger speaking," he said.

"Hello, it's Smith here from Warkworth. We have had a request from Orewa for protection at the McCall house. We've sent Trenton and Rose."

"That's great. Thanks for letting me know," Bill said. "I was thinking I'd have to go myself."

"How are things going?" Smith asked.

"You know what it's like. The Feds from Orewa have taken over. We are merely minions. I appreciate your help, though."

Bill thought of what James had hinted at yesterday and drove over to Matakana Valley Wines. Avery was in the office and jumped when Bill walked in. "Jeez, mate," he said, clutching his chest.

"Sorry, I didn't mean to startle you," Bill said apologetically.

"No worries, mate. I think we all just feel jumpy. I mean, you read about shit like this, but I never thought we'd be in the middle of it here in Matakana."

"You've tidied up, I see."

"Yeah, thought I'd better sort it out," Avery said. "What can I do for you?"

"Do you know if someone could have tampered with the water pump?"

"Now that you mention it, it kind of looked like someone had been having a go at it through the guard. There were scratches on the front," Avery said.

Bill pulled out his notebook. "James mentioned that there might have been an incident at the vineyard in Martinborough all those years ago. Can you shed some light on that?"

Avery leaned back in his chair, letting the words sink in. "It's such a long time ago," he said. "There were many issues. The labour laws weren't exactly in our favour. Being seasonal workers, they could do what they wanted. One thing sticks out, though, and to this day I still believe we did the right thing all those years ago."

Bill's ears pricked up. "Continue," he said.

"The winery had been doing well. They even had a successful export operation, sending wine all over Europe and to the USA, which was something unheard of back then. The so-called New World wines were only just emerging. From what I understood the winery extended themselves and their operation significantly, then the 1987 stock-market crash happened."

"Yes, I remember it well," Bill said.

"Maurice Stott, the owner of the vineyard supposedly had trouble with mortgage repayments and things were getting desperate. I only know this because Robert, the winemaker, got pissed with us one night and let a few remarks slip. Apparently the premium wine sold well overseas, but they were relying on the rest, the moderately priced wines, for their bread and butter. Anyway, the boys and I discovered that Maurice and Robert had resorted to bottling the cheaper wine and labelling it as the premier. The wine got shipped overseas, lessening the chance of discovery and getting caught."

Bill couldn't believe his ears. "How did you discover that?"

"We were having a few drinks one night and took a few bottles of wine as we usually did. Maurice knew and didn't seem to mind. We only ever drank the entry-level wines but on this occasion, as it was the end of the season, we grabbed a few of the export bottles. Isaac being the accountant had no idea, but Peter and I picked it up immediately. We even opened a few more, uncorked them and had a taste. They were all the same, cheap wine labelled as premium."

"Where was James?" Bill asked.

"Not sure. He might have gone back to Auckland to visit his parents that weekend. He wasn't there anyway, I'm sure of that. The next day, Peter and I approached Maurice, telling him there had been a terrible mistake made with the labelling. He didn't seem surprised at all. We accused him of being a bloody crook, threatened to go to the police. Maurice pleaded with us and asked us not to get the authorities involved, said he would put a stop to it immediately." Avery said.

"What happened?"

"I'm not entirely sure. It was the end of the season and we were finishing. Maurice gave us his word and a good reference and off we went."

"Do you know if they put an end to the scam?" Bill asked.

"I would imagine so. Maurice was a decent bloke, and it was a tough time for everyone in the industry." He leaned back in his swivel chair. "Funny, I haven't thought about this for years."

"What was the name of the vineyard?"

"Stott's Landing. It was one of the first vineyards in the area."

"You mentioned the winemaker. Have you had any contact with him over the years?" Bill asked.

"No. I heard he was working in Central Otago, but that's at least fifteen years ago."

The sound of tyres on the gravel and squeaky brakes in desperate need of lubrication alerted them to the new arrivals. Officers Gary Trenton and Laura Rose waved as they stepped out of the patrol car, Lexi was just behind them.

"We need to establish a few things before I go," Bill said. "Under no circumstances will either of you leave the property on your own. You will be in the company of an officer if you need to tend to something on the farm."

The look on Lexi's face said it all, armed police at their door — would this nightmare ever end?

39

There was no sign of Niko when Bill got back to the station. He wandered into the Incident Room and tried to read the reports Orewa had sent them, but had trouble concentrating. Lexi had looked so small and vulnerable, not like the capable woman that he knew.

He stared at the board. Who had an agenda to kill these men and why? If it was related to something that had happened when they were all together in Martinborough, why hadn't Isaac received the same threats? James wasn't even there when the wine scam was discovered, so did it relate to something else? He made a mental note to call Isaac, but first he would talk to Orewa about the burnt-out pump. Before he could dial the number, the phone rang.

"Matakana police station," he said.

"Hi, it's Archie from Martinborough," a cheery voice rang out.

"Hi Archie, I'm Bill Granger, the Sergeant here. You've been speaking to Niko. He's not here at the moment. Can I help in any way?"

"I have some information that might interest you," Archie said. "Not sure if you are aware, but we couldn't locate Peter Evans's mobile phone. Anyway the telco has just got back to us with the data, so we have a clear picture of where it's been."

"Yes?" Bill said impatiently.

"According to them, the mobile went from Martinborough late Friday evening, and was pinged by cell-phone towers travelling north via Taupo and Auckland. The last ping was on Sunday, but it's likely it's switched off now or the battery has run out. I'm not sure if it's still there but we can say with certainty that they located the mobile north-east of Matakana in the small settlement of Point Wells on Sunday night."

"Point Wells?" Bill scrambled for paper and a pen. "Did it give an exact location?"

"Yes. The last ping showed it to be at the corner of Dunbar and Kowhai Roads. The last known location was number thirteen or thereabouts."

~

BILL CALLED NIKO'S MOBILE. "Where are you?"

"At the gym. Thought I'd get a quick workout in case we need to pull an all-nighter with the McCall's."

"Be ready in two minutes. There has been a development. The last location Peter Evans's phone signal pinged was in Point Wells. I'll swing by and pick you up," Bill said.

His adrenalin was surging; could this be the place where the perpetrator was hiding?

Niko was already waiting outside the gym, buttoning his shirt and vest up, his wet hair slicked back. He threw the gym bag in the back and jumped in.

A gust of Lynx deodorant filled the car. "Think you've put enough deodorant on?" Bill said.

"Better than sweat." Niko grinned, holding on to the handle above his head. The dust flew as they took off, cutting through the carpark at RD6 and turning down Omaha Road towards Point Wells.

Bill knew the street well. It was down by the water on the landward side, not the expensive part. Slowing down to a crawl, turning left into Dunbar, he drove past the small cottage, parking further down the street. There was no obvious movement that they could see. Bill popped the boot and they got the Glocks out of the lockbox. The street was still, with only a slight rustling from the overhanging tree branches and the lazy hum of a generator. Bill felt trepidation as he always did when he held his gun.

The glossy grissellinia hedge gave them suitable cover. Still no movement.

The tiny house looked uninhabited; its sad exterior oozed gloom with the grey wooden boards in desperate need of a lick of paint. The net curtains had seen better days, making the insides dreary as they tried to look through. Bill signalled to Niko, and in a few swift steps they were both standing with their backs pressed against the wall of the house, a faint damp and mouldy smell seeping through the wood. The sparsely furnished living room reminded Bill of his grandparents' home. It was as if someone had walked out of the house fifty years ago and never come back.

Front and back doors were locked. Bill could see into the kitchen, the pantry door was slightly ajar, a couple of cans and a cereal box visible. Perhaps it was just used as a holiday home, he thought. It didn't look as though someone lived there full-time. The gravel driveway at the side of the house was scattered with weeds and in desperate need of spraying. At the end was a rickety old garage, the red paint long since faded by the harsh sun, exposing the wood grain.

He pulled the thick metal tab on one door of the garage. It creaked and protested as sunlight filled the cavernous space. A workbench took up the entire back wall, old hand-tools hanging neatly above. Up in the rafters were building materials and old bicycles in various states of repair. The garage at first glance seemed empty, but as Bill and Niko walked in and their eyes got used to the dim light, they could see neatly stacked boxes, a pile of suitcases, an old lawn mower and various other bits and pieces. A large drop-cloth covered something in the back. Niko lifted the corner. To his surprise, underneath was a modern all-terrain motorbike that clearly hadn't been there as long as the old junk.

Bill had just got his torch out when the door shut with an almighty thud. Suddenly everything went dark, and the latch lowered on the outside. Niko threw his 118-kilogram frame at the door, making it bulge under the impact.

"Fuck!" he yelled as the door bounced him back.

Bill was just as angry. They had played right into the hands of this person, who'd made them look like complete rookies.

There was only one small window, high above the workbench. Both Bill and Niko were too big to get through it. Niko felt around the door to find its weak point. When he put his shoulder into it, a slight crack appeared. Bill could see the wooden latch slid across. If only they could find something thin and strong to slide between the doors, they could lift it up. A rusty machete was hanging on a hook. Niko put all his weight onto the door while Bill slid the machete through the narrow opening. The angle was awkward and the catch was heavier than he expected. Swearing under his breath, his hands struggling to get a grip.

With one powerful movement upwards, the latch lifted. The door groaned as the warped piece of wood released its hold and swung open. They drew their weapons, but no one was there.

"Fuck, I'm glad the Feds didn't see us like this," Bill said. "We'd never live it down." Propping both doors up and removing the wooden crossbar, he went back into the garage. Something had caught his eye. A new-looking sports bag was sticking out from behind a pile of junk. Pulling a pair of gloves on, he put the bag on an upturned crate. "It's probably nothing, but it seems out of place," he said as he opened the zip. Someone had rolled up a paper-thin bundle. Carefully lifting it Bill could see it was disposable overalls with rusty-red stains on the sleeves.

"Bingo! If that's not blood splatter, I'll eat my hat," he said. Using a screwdriver from the bench, he pushed the garment aside and spotted a mobile phone and a toolbox at the bottom of the bag. He couldn't wait to get these items to the lab.

He called Brian Rudd. "Bill Granger from Matakana here. We'll need you to come up to a property in Point Wells and have a look. We've found a bloodstained disposable suit and other things of interest at the address where Peter Evans' phone signal was last picked up."

"I hope for your sake that you haven't touched it," Rudd barked.

Pompous little prick, Bill thought. Did Rudd really think that because they were from a small town that they wouldn't put gloves on when handling potential evidence? "It's all free of our DNA, ready for you to come and pick up and analyse," he said curtly.

THE FIRST CAR from Orewa pulled up. "The house appears uninhabited, but we have located a stash of things possibly connected to at least one murder. You two stay put until the SOCO's turn up, we can get on with some door-knocking," Bill said.

He and Niko each took a side of the road. As it was late afternoon the only people home were retirees or stay-at-home mums. The only person who was mildly helpful was Albin Andersson, a retired schoolteacher who lived directly opposite. He normally spent a lot of time in his study, which faced the street. "I have seen someone occasionally," he said with a distinctive accent.

"Are you Swedish, Mr Andersson?" Bill asked.

"That's a good guess. I was born in Sweden and met a wonderful English woman in my early twenties. We were part of the Ten Pound Poms who emigrated to New Zealand in the early Sixties. Both being teachers, we already had jobs to come to. Sadly, we had no children of our own," he said, his voice tinged with sorrow. "But we had the honour of teaching many children over the years, something we both treasured very much."

He coughed to clear his throat. "Anyway, back to the business across the road," he said nodding in that direction. "It was a few days ago now. I had received a package of rare stamps from a collector down country and was putting them into my album when I saw a person walk down the driveway. No one has lived in the house since Mrs Bell moved into care, about five or six years ago.

"Do you remember what the person looked like?"

"He had blue jeans and one of those oversized zip-through hooded jackets. I think it was dark grey with some white print on the back. He also had a sports bag thrown over his shoulder."

"Did he stay long?"

"No, he left after a few minutes, barely enough time to walk around the house."

"What about a vehicle? Did you see one parked nearby?"

"No, I'm afraid not. Sorry I can't be more helpful."

Niko hadn't come up with anything of interest as he had mainly talked to young mums, who were too tired or too preoccupied with toddlers hanging off their legs.

Rudd and Copeson pulled up shortly thereafter. "No dead body this time?" said Rudd.

"Thankfully not," Bill replied, having to clench his fist to not be rude. He didn't know why he let Rudd get to him.

"Show me where you found the bag," Rudd barked.

Niko stepped in while Copeson rigged the lighting. "You can leave, we're here now," he said dismissively and turned his back to them. "We are the ones doing the bloody work and this is the thanks we get," muttered Bill under his breath.

Copeson, sensing their ire, turned around and rolled his eyes as to apologise for his colleague.

As he and Bill got into the car to drive away Niko said, "Someone wants to torment not only the victims, but us. Why on earth lock us in the garage? He'd have been better off leaving us to have a quick look. We mightn't have even found the bag. I'm no psych, but at a guess I would think this person thinks they are far superior to other people, with a rather large dose of arrogance mixed in."

· · ·

"You can see it in the killings," Bill said. "Excessive violence, torture, wanting the victim to suffer."

Back at the station Bill finished up the paperwork from the day and Niko checked if anything had come from Orewa. "There's an email here from The Feds. Apparently the preliminary findings from the autopsy on Peter Evans should be out soon, but they found Heparin in his bloodstream."

"Isn't that a blood-thinning medication?"

"Correct. Apparently he had a huge dose in his system, which ensured he would have bled to death with so much as a paper-cut. A cruel form of torture, if you ask me."

"The ferocity of both attacks lend themselves to being inflicted by a man. This is about so much more than just taking someone's life," Bill said. "I'll go and ask Harry about the Heparin."

Harry the pharmacist had been there since Bill was a child and was now pushing seventy-five. His kind face creased into wrinkles as he smiled in greeting.

"Hey, Harry, Bill said." How difficult is it to obtain Heparin?"

"It's commonly used for stroke victims to prevent further clots forming, or to treat conditions such as deep-vein thrombosis and angina among other things," Harry said.

"Prescribed by a doctor, I presume."

"Absolutely. It's a restricted medication that needs careful monitoring. In fact, most pharmacies don't stock it. It's more an A&E drug, but since we are rural we carry a small supply here. Why do you ask?"

"Just something that came across my desk," Bill said and thanked him for his help.

When Bill walked through the door back at the station, Niko said, "Copeson just rang. They've finished at Point Wells and will come past here shortly on their way. Also, the preliminary autopsy report has come through. It's on the printer."

Bill was at his desk flicking through the report when Copeson and Rudd came through the door.

"I haven't been in here for years," Rudd said. "I see you've received the report. To save you reading it, Peter Evans was tortured, and it was his hand we found here in Matakana. His hand was nailed to the wall while he was still alive. Whoever did this broke his right arm in two places, injected him with blood-thinner, then stabbed him repeatedly."

Niko scratched his head. "But why?"

40

A *uckland*

ISAAC AND PETRA had enjoyed an early dinner at O'Connell Street Bistro, one of their favourite restaurants. After walking his wife to her car Isaac had a spring in his step as he continued down the street to stop by the office. They had sat in the corner, with no through traffic, and he had let her talk. For the first time in ages, he just listened. Petra really opened up to him, told him how she felt. He felt embarrassed that he'd lacked so much in empathy. She said she understood, didn't blame him, they each had their own demons to deal with. She had smiled at the end, so there was a glimmer of hope for them to rebuild their marriage. He invited her for dinner at home this weekend, and he would do the cooking. It wasn't his forte, but he would try.

Back at his desk, the office was empty and an enormous pile of paperwork had mounted up over the days that he had been away. Even that couldn't dampen his mood. It had been the strangest day, from the morning's horrific find of James's body to Petra calling him out of the blue wanting to talk.

The display on the phone lit up, not a number that he recognised. He picked up.

"Is this Isaac Miller?"

"Yes. Who is calling, please?" Isaac thought it the height of rudeness when people didn't introduce themselves first.

"This is Constable David Tuffey from the Auckland Central police station. A patrol car will be stationed outside your house this evening as a precaution after what happened in Matakana this morning."

"I don't think that's necessary," Isaac said.

"As I say, it's merely a precaution, nothing to worry about. We'll monitor the situation overnight. Constables Stephenson and Goode will make contact and introduce themselves."

All the happiness Isaac had felt a moment ago was suddenly replaced with despair and the beginnings of a headache pounded at his temples. He went to the coffee-vending machine a level down. He needed to think. What on earth was happening here? And how could it have anything to do with him?

When he got back to the twelfth floor, he called the McCall's. "Hi, Lexi. How are you guys doing?"

"It's weird, kind of surreal," she said. "We're getting police protection after what happened to Peter and James."

"I know how you feel. I just had a call from the cops. They are placing some plods outside my house tonight. I don't understand how this business has anything to do with either of us."

"The police seem to think it may stem from the summer the four of you worked together at Stott's Landing in Martinborough," Lexi said.

"That's preposterous," Isaac said, feeling the throbbing headache tightening across his forehead like a vice. "It was thirty years ago."

"I know it seems strange, but perhaps there's something in it. Avery mentioned there was some upset at the end of summer, that you guys caught the winemaker bottling their cheaper wine and labelling it as premium."

"Jeez, I had completely forgotten all about that. Old Maurice didn't bat an eyelid when we told him, he was in on it. But I'm fairly sure they discontinued it when we threatened to take it to the authorities."

"Do you think Maurice is out for revenge?"

"After all these years, I doubt it. Besides, we never called the police to report it. We should have, really, but we were young."

"Have you spoken to Petra yet?" Lexi asked changing the subject.

"I have. We had a meal out and haven't communicated like that for years. I let her talk and really tried to listen. I'm cooking dinner for her on Saturday night. Can't wait."

"Remember, it's not the food that matters, it's the effort you make," Lexi said.

Isaac decided the rest of the paperwork could wait until tomorrow when he was feeling better. He popped two headache tablets and drank the rest of his coffee, hoping that the combination would ease his discomfort.

41

The shrill ring of the office phone interrupted the concentration at the station.

"Hi, Niko," Annika said. "Can you send Bill home as soon as possible?" She said sounding close to tears. "Someone has killed three sheep in the front paddock."

"Shit. Are you all right?"

"I'm fine, but the other sheep are cowering in the corner. I was on my way out when I saw them lying down, which is strange at this time of the day. I stopped the car and got out to check on them. There was so much blood everywhere."

"Stay put," Niko said. "Get back in the car and lock the doors. We're on our way."

He stood up. "That was Annika. Someone has killed three of your sheep."

"What?" Bill said. He and Niko rushed to the ute, the engine protesting as they sped away.

Annika was sitting in her car, halfway up the driveway, only just visible over the dip from the main Leigh Road, pale and a little shaky. The negligible amount of mascara that she had put on this morning having run down her cheeks like a horror painting. Stepping out of the vehicle on unsteady legs, she wiped her eyes as best as she could. There was no hiding the fact that she had been crying. Niko climbed the timber fence and went over to the dead livestock. Three dead sheep, one severely butchered with sizeable chunks of meat gone. The smell of blood and lanolin hung in the air.

"They're still warm, Sarge," Niko said.

Bill bent down and put his hand on one of the dead ewes, its eyes still open. What a horror they'd had to endure, he thought.

"You think it was an order job, someone wanting something specific?" Niko said.

"Probably, but who knows? One thing is for certain, something has disturbed them. Why else leave the meat behind?"

Niko took some photos while Bill had a wander round. The ground was bone-dry and the little grass left was short. This time of the year they got supplementary feed.

"Hello, what's this?" Bill whistled and bent down to pick up a checked flannel rag. The unmistakable smell of sweet liquid triggered memories from his high-school chemistry class. "I'll be damned, it's chloroform."

"Well, that explains how they could kill three large sheep in the middle of the day with no one noticing," Niko said.

"As a controlled substance it would have to come from somewhere."

"Sure, but if I rightly remember, labs, dentistry clinics and veterinarians all use it. Tracing it might be like looking for a needle in a hay stack," Niko said. "But it wouldn't hurt to see if any has gone missing locally."

~

"WHO WOULD DO SUCH A THING?" Annika wiped her nose on the back of her hand. "It's just such a waste."

"What time does dance practice finish?" Bill asked, to get her to think of something else.

"It's done in about twenty minutes." She wiped her nose again.

"Let's sit here for a minute, then I'll get them," Bill said putting his arm around her protectively as they got back in the car.

"I know we're off the main road, but you'd still be visible. Why take the risk in daylight?" Bill said, his anger turning to sadness. Cattle rustling was big business, especially further up north. There had been a few cases around the district over the last six months, mainly on remote farms, with sizeable head counts taken away on transporters in the middle of the night. This was three sheep, in a small herd. It made little sense. This was the fourth instance of killed or mutilated stock in the area as far as he knew, but it had a different feel to it. It was a lot riskier than plain thefts. Unless it was a warning.

"What are we going to do with them?" Annika said. "They will spoil lying out in the open like this."

"I've already called Fred. He'll be right over and take them away."

"Please tell him we don't want the meat. I couldn't possibly," Annika said.

BILL ARRIVED at the school hall just before the session finished. The twins were loud and excited and chatted non-stop on the way home, which was a welcome relief. Pulling into the driveway at home, he let out a sigh as he looked out over the dry paddock. The eerie stillness sent a shiver down his spine. The dead sheep, just visible, looked as if they were resting. The ones remaining huddled in the far corner beneath an oak tree with a low-pitched chorus of bleating.

Once home, the girls ran off upstairs. Annika was sitting at the kitchen table, a million miles away. She jumped when he touched her elbow. "What happened today?" he asked.

She told him that she had spent the entire time in the studio, except for a quick break at lunch when she had come into the house to make a sandwich.

"You didn't hear anything?"

"No, nothing at all. Mind you I had the music turned up as I do when I'm working. The dogs heard nothing or they would have let me know." Maggie and Finn were snoozing in their baskets. They were brilliant guard dogs and would take any opportunity to bark at and challenge anyone who set foot on the property. "Here I am worrying about my sheep when James is dead. I don't know about you, but I've had enough for today."

42

Lexi was holding the phone in her hand contemplating as Avery came inside after his evening chores. Gary had trailed behind him on his own quad bike. Laura had stayed with Lexi in the house. It felt strange having someone following your every move.

"Isaac just rang. The police will be at his house tonight," she said.

"That's good. Did he seem okay?"

"He's fine. He was excited at having met up with Petra for dinner. Things seemed to have gone well. Let's go to Rusty's for dinner. I don't know about you, but I'm too tired to cook."

"What about the steaks I bought earlier?" Avery tried but with little enthusiasm. "I can throw them on the barbecue."

"They'll keep for another day. You'd better get changed into something tidier, though," Lexi said with a weak smile.

At the eatery Gary and Laura seated themselves at the back, having a view of the entrance, while Avery and Lexi chose a table for two by the window. "If it hadn't been for what's happened today and the fact that we have two armed police officers sitting there," Avery said, "this would have felt like a date night, and it's sure been a while since one of those."

Lexi nearly choked on the mineral water as she laughed at the ridiculousness of the situation. "I know what you mean," she said. Over the meal they chatted about this and that, but could always feel the eyes of Gary and Laura on them.

"Let's have coffee at home," Lexi said, keen to get going. "We can do some research on our own."

"Research about what?"

"Do we still have that box of old photos?"

"I think so. It's probably piled up in the attic with all the other boxes."

Lexi's eyes lit up. "Let's keep it on the down-low for now. We may not even find anything."

Avery glanced towards the back of the room. "Perhaps we shouldn't be digging about on our own and should let the cops handle things."

Lexi frowned. "Are you serious? We can't just be sitting around, waiting for the killer to come and pick us off, one by one."

"I suppose you're right," he said and looked at her admiringly.

BEAU WAS beside himself seeing them home again and wagged his tail. Lexi had made the guest beds, Gary and Laura would take the night shift in turns. Beau kept Laura company in the kitchen while the others went their separate ways to bed. Avery continued up to the attic.

Lexi sat in bed with her laptop in front of her, searching for anything she could think of in relation to Stott's Landing. There was nothing at all about any wine scandal but less than a year after the harvest Avery and his friends worked at, Maurice the owner had died. The vineyard had sold, but it seemed only a few years later it had closed down. Lexi wondered why his wife Jenny hadn't kept it going. Perhaps she hadn't been involved in the day-to-day running of the vineyard?

Lexi was busy making notes when Avery walked through the

door, balancing an armful of old photo albums. They spent the next hour going through the albums and notes. "These are from the vineyard when I used to come and visit you on the weekends," Lexi said, nudging Avery. "Look how young we were! Bad perms and massive shoulder pads were all the rage," she laughed.

The next few pages featured photos of the group scattered among the vineyard crew at various barbecues and get-togethers, busy harvesting, sampling the wine, but nothing stood out as unusual. The last photo in the album was a family shot of Maurice and Jenny, her arm around their son Benjamin — all smiling at the camera, seemingly without a care in the world, with no sign that Maurice would be dead within the year.

43

Bill picked up pizza for dinner. Annika didn't really have an appetite, but forced a few slices down. As quickly as they started dinner, it was over and the children had scattered. Bill and Annika cleared the plates and tidied up. "Fancy a glass of red?" she said. "It's still warm outside. We could sit on the veranda and glimpse the setting sun."

"Sounds nice," Bill said. "Just let me get out of this uniform and into something more comfortable."

Annika poured them a glass each and put a few crackers on a plate with some of Lexi's double-cream brie. She sat on one of the light-blue Adirondack chairs, a large grey sheepskin softening the hard back. The tight curl of the pelt reminded her of the poor slaughtered sheep. Bill came out looking more relaxed in shorts and a faded T-shirt. He reached across and held Annika's hand. There was no need for words.

BILL DIDN'T HEAR the phone ringing on the bedside table. Annika had to elbow him in the ribs which made him sit bolt upright, answering the phone with his heart in his throat. The call had been transferred from the station, and he rubbed sleep out of his eyes to wake up. The clock radio display showed it was eleven-thirty.

"Matakana police station," he said, willing his voice to sound more awake than he was.

"Hi, Bill. Sorry to be bothering you so late. It's Harry from the pharmacy in the village. There's been a burglary. The alarm went off fifteen minutes ago, and the security firm phoned me. I'm on my way down. Thought I'd better let you know first."

"I'm on my way," Bill said, feeling a bit more awake. "I don't suppose there's any sign of the perpetrator?"

"From what the security boys are saying, I'm afraid not."

"Okay, I'll see you there in a few minutes," Bill said, fumbling his way to the wardrobe for a clean shirt. "Someone's broken into the pharmacy," he said to Annika who was leaning on the pillows and wondering what was going on. "I shouldn't be too long."

In the village not a soul was around apart from the small gathering outside the pharmacy. The security guards had turned the alarm off and were standing to the side, completing paperwork. Niko, who was first on scene, had already been down to the station and got the basic kit and the camera and was photographing the mess in the shop. Harry had been told to keep out and was pacing on the pavement. After talking to Harry and the security, there really wasn't much for Bill to write in his notebook, neither of them had seen anyone leaving the shop. By the time the alarm had gone off and Niko got there, no one was there.

"Niko will finish soon," Bill told the security guards, "but in the meantime we need to find something to board up the shop. Or are you able to stay?" The two burly men looked like body-builders with gang connections, tattoos covering their bulging arms and up their necks.

The taller one said, "We're happy to stay here until the morning, when someone can come and repair the glass door."

"Thanks, that's great. Are you happy with that, Harry? I know you have a lot of medication in there." Even at this ungodly hour, the older man was immaculately turned out with a crisp blue-and-white checked shirt and high-waisted beige trousers with sharp creases at the front; his shoes were polished to perfection and shone in the light of the street lamp.

"Sure, I may keep the boys company. I sleep little nowadays anyway. I might go home and make a few sandwiches and a Thermos of strong coffee. It will make the time pass quicker." If he didn't trust the guards, he didn't let on.

"That's very kind," the shorter man — shaven head, hay-coloured beard — said. They were both well-spoken. Perhaps he shouldn't be so quick to judge a book by its cover, Bill thought. He slipped his business card into Harry's hand, with Niko's mobile number on it. "In case you need it," he said quietly.

"On the face of things, not much damage," Niko said as he came back outside. "The mess is in the back where the prescription medications are. Most of it's been ripped off the shelves."

"Just about done?" Bill asked.

"Just about, then I'll pack the equipment up."

"We might as well head home and try to get some sleep," Bill said. Niko was looking worse for wear and, he knew, it would take ages to get back to sleep.

44

After abandoning the pile of papers and photographs, Avery and Lexi called it a night. Avery had just settled in to bed when Beau started barking ferociously. "Who would this be at half-past midnight?" Lexi said.

Avery leapt out of bed, pulled on a pair of shorts and raced downstairs into the kitchen. Gary Trenton came running out of the spare room, weapon drawn. Laura Rose was already outside, her Glock glinting in the moonlight. Beau had followed Laura outside.

"Stay inside," Trenton shouted as Avery and Lexi appeared in the kitchen. A guttural howl echoed through the night followed by two loud shots. Then all was still. Ignoring Trenton's instructions, Avery grabbed the largest kitchen knife from the block and went outside. The moon highlighted the shape of someone on the ground, motionless.

"Call an ambulance! Laura's been stabbed!" Gary yelled, trying frantically to stem her blood loss.

Avery ran inside and shouted at Lexi to call for the ambulance then went back outside to see if he could help. Gary was administering pressure to the gaping wound on Laura's neck, the rhythmic spray of the major artery squirting warm blood between his fingers, soaking the T-shirt he had pulled off to plug the wound.

"Please, I need something else," Gary shouted. Avery ran inside and got hold of an armful of towels.

Gary rolled them up and wrapped them around Laura's neck, speaking softly to his partner, trying to reassure her but there was so much blood. The stab-proof vest had provided little protection, and an ominous red stain was soaking the top of it.

Sirens sounded in the distance, then the Warkworth police and first responders arrived just before the ambulance. The medics ran over followed by two police officers. Gary told them he had fired two shots and was sure one had hit the offender. They set off in the direction he pointed.

The ambulance officer said to Avery, "The rescue helicopter is on approach. We need to clear a landing area and get some lights rigged up."

"The safest spot to put the chopper down would be in front of the barn. And I've got some spotlights we can use," Avery said.

Gary nodded and reluctantly left Laura with the ambulance officers.

Avery got the lights and Gary had some powerful torches in the back of the patrol car. It took less than two minutes to set up the landing area. They could hear the rotor blades in the distance, but Laura was only just hanging on and, due to the massive blood loss, no longer conscious.

Lexi had covered her in warm blankets, but didn't know if Laura was still breathing. The medics kept working on her, administering fluids and pain relief. Lexi guessed that it was the pain medication that made her unresponsive, but knew in her heart that she was grasping at straws.

The officers from Warkworth searched the immediate area, but reported that the offender had vanished: "The dog unit is on their way. Hopefully they can get a scent and track the prick."

The engine noise of the rapidly approaching rescue helicopter filled the night air, its strong lights sweeping the valley as it prepared to land. Dropping straight down, the pilot set the BK117 twin-engine down in front of the winery, the draught of the rotors whipping up dirt and debris. Lexi covered her ears and closed her eyes until she heard a slight slowing of the blades and the declining whine of the jet engines. The crewman and the paramedic jumped out and took over from the ambulance personnel.

Lexi turned away and saw the unmistakable shape of Beau lying perfectly still a short distance away.

"Beau! What's wrong, boy?" she called. She went over and knelt next to him. His breathing was merely a rustle and a large wound on his stomach had parts of his intestines spilling out of his body. With every desperate breath his body shook as he struggled with the pain.

"No!" Lexi's scream was drowned out by the rotor blades as they loaded Laura into the helicopter. She raced over and grabbed a spare towel, wrapping Beau up tight around the middle, stopping the blood loss and comforting him. "Come on, boy, don't give up on me now." Beau calmly stared at her, his brown eyes trusting her. This would not be the end.

A large pool of blood had seeped out of his wound. She called out for Avery, who with one swift motion picked him up and carried him to the car as the helicopter lifted off, covering them in exhaust-laden rotor wash. Driving off, she realised they hadn't told Gary that they were going. That would have to wait. The priority was to get Beau looked after.

Lexi had the phone number for the veterinary clinic in her phone. As it was after hours, the call was diverted to the vet's home. Beau had his eyes closed and was barely breathing, lying on the back seat with his head in Lexi's lap. Avery sped through the traffic light at the Hill Street intersection and pulled up outside the clinic. Ronald and his wife were waiting for them outside. Beau made no sound as they put him on the stainless-steel operating table in the back room and sedated him . The door to the operating theatre was closed and all Lexi and Avery could do was wait.

The compact waiting room doubled as the reception area and shop. They sat down in the corner on padded seats surrounded by a variety of dog food and a myriad of toys and accessories; a small table offered some out-of-date magazines. In the background was the rhythmical sound of the ventilator controlling Beau's breathing. The smell of burning flesh was mixed with disinfectant.

Avery put his arm around Lexi. "He'll be all right."

45

When Bill got home, the house was quiet and he boiled the jug to make himself a cup of tea. Getting a head start on the paperwork, he sat down in the old chair in the lounge and put his feet up while he scribbled some notes. Maggie and Finn settled by his feet and were soon snoring away. Bill was wide awake. It would be hours until he could go back to bed and fall asleep, so he thought he might as well use the time productively.

The shrill ringtone from his mobile made him jump, making him knock the cup of tea over in his rush to answer before it woke the whole house up. "Bill, we have an officer down at Matakana Valley Wines," the duty officer at Warkworth station said. "Can you make your way? A car has already been dispatched along with ambulance and dog unit."

"I'm on my way," Bill responded. Adrenalin pumped through his body as he threw his vest on and got the two Glocks out of the lock-box, putting one in the holster and the other on the passenger seat. All his fatigue blown away, he rang Niko from the car. Not strictly by the book, but there was no way they would arrive and fumble around for their weapons like idiots. Niko met Bill at the roundabout, saving them time.

"Officer down at Matakana Valley Wines. No details as yet," Bill said, trying to control his breathing. "Odd, it can be months between armed responses. This is the fucking second one today."

"Just like South Auckland, mate," Niko said, slotting the weapon in his holster.

The rescue helicopter had already left as they pulled in.

Gary met them as they got out of the car. "The offender is still on the loose," he said. "We've searched the immediate area. He took off behind the barn and I assume through the paddock to the north-east. The dog unit should be here shortly." He paused to catch his breath. "Laura is critical. I'm not sure if she'll pull through. Her injuries are bad and she was unresponsive," he continued.

"All we can do is hope," Bill said.

Gary looked down at his bare chest and hands, stained with Laura's blood. Niko took him by the shoulder and sat him on a chair in the garden. Gary shook his head and stared aimlessly into the night.

"Where are Lexi and Avery?" Bill asked.

"Not sure. I told them to stay inside, but Avery came and assisted with Laura. There was so much blood. It was a deep wound." Gary shivered in the cool air. The temperature had dropped and shock was setting in. Niko went over to the medics who were packing up and got a blanket to put over Gary, whose teeth were now chattering. "I'm fine, really. It's Laura who needs the help, not me." Bill asked Niko to check in the house for Avery and Lexi, then asked Gary, "Are you sure it was a male offender?"

"Yes, absolutely it was a bloke. In all the commotion I didn't get a good look at his face, but he wore dark pants and a hoodie. Average height and athletic build, I'm guessing mid-thirties or around. I fired two shots. I'm sure one hit, at least grazed him." Gary paused. "Perhaps this wouldn't have happened if I'd taken the first shift, but Laura was stubborn and insisted she'd take it."

Bill patted him on the shoulder. "No one could have predicted what would happen."

Niko returned. "I've searched the entire house. There's no sign of either of them."

What if the attacker had taken them at knifepoint?

A phone rang. The sound came from Gary's back pocket. He snapped out of his trance and answered. "Thanks for letting me know," he said. "I'm glad you're safe. Keep us posted." He looked up at Bill and Niko. "That was Avery. They're in Warkworth at the vet's. Apparently the dog got cut badly trying to protect Laura and is being operated on now."

Bill knew how much Lexi loved that dog. "Thank Christ they're safe. Hopefully Beau will be okay too."

Niko returned with a cup of heavily sugared tea for Gary who was still very pale. "Drink up, it will make you feel better," he said.

Before long the dog unit turned up with three armed officers and Bismarck, a giant German Shepherd. "If the attacker's around, Bis will flush him out for sure," the lead handler said.

"I'm not sure we'll be that lucky," Gary said. "I don't think it was more than a flesh wound. He was still able to run."

"Do you know where you hit him?" Bill asked.

"I think his upper right arm."

"Okay, we'll alert local medical centres and Emergency Departments to look out for a gunshot wound."

Half an hour later there was a radio call from the dog unit. The scent Bismarck had picked up led to Sharp Road. The offender must have had a vehicle parked there as the trail then went cold.

46

The waiting room was dimly lit and quiet, just the odd clinking of stainless-steel instruments. Poor, fun-loving old Beau, Lexi thought. The gaping wound with the spilling guts, the rank offal odour, the faint whimpering as they lifted him into the car. She had been frantic; he had been the calm one. Avery had taken charge; it was all a blur how they had got to this point. The stress from the last few hours was manifesting itself in a nasty headache that had started at the base of her neck and gone up to squeeze her skull. Lexi massaged the back of her neck to loosen her muscles. "Thank God the children didn't get to see this," she said shakily.

Avery — rumpled, dark circles under his eyes — nodded. Lexi wished he would put his arms around her, the way he used to. She needed him and wanted everything to return to normal. The glimmer of care and tenderness, the togetherness they'd had when they scooped Beau up, was now gone, overtaken by exhaustion.

"I just hope Laura pulls through. She's still so young," Lexi said. Tears flowed down her cheeks. Avery inched closer and put his hand on hers. The slight gesture made her emotional floodgates open and she started sobbing loudly. Avery pulled her towards him and she leaned on his shoulder. Lexi took a deep breath, savouring the familiar scent. How she had missed their closeness.

She knew Avery was putting on a brave face, that he was worried too. Someone had come to their house intending to hurt them. The thought made her shudder.

"I'm sure Laura will pull through," Avery said, letting go of Lexi and running his hands down his legs nervously. In an instant the magic was gone.

A text message lit up her screen. It was from Bill:

Glad you and Avery are ok, sorry to hear my mate Beau got hurt. Hoping he makes a speedy recovery. I'll come past tomorrow.

Lexi quickly replied:

Thanks, he is still in surgery. See you tomorrow.

It was another hour before the vet came through the double doors. His scrubs were bloodstained and his grey hair was standing on end. Ronald wiped his brow. "It's fortunate that Beau is a healthy dog," he said. "He might not have survived the blood loss otherwise. The cut was deep, his stomach perforated and the blade severed his small intestine. Thankfully I was able to save most of it. He's got a drain in, and we'll monitor him for the next few days before you can bring him home again. Providing infection doesn't set in, he should make a full recovery. But he's not out of the woods yet. He is comfortable and we have him hooked up getting a blood transfusion at the moment, but the prognosis is good."

"We can't thank you enough," Lexi said.

"You are very welcome. It's rare that I get a call in the middle of the night, but I'm always happy to help," Ronald said. "He's still asleep, but you can see him. A pat and a few words whispered in his ear would do him good."

As Lexi walked through the operating theatre and into the back of the surgery the smell of disinfectant tickled her nose. Beau looked comfortable in a padded cage, IV fluids and a bag of blood slowly dripping into his veins, tucked up with a blanket mostly covering his bandaged stomach. "Hang in there, boy," she said. "You'll be home before you know it."

Avery put his hand on her shoulder, signalling it was time to go. They all needed rest, not least Ronald who was leaning on the door-frame, struggling to keep his eyes open.

Driving home in silence, neither of them had the energy to talk. As they pulled into their driveway, two uniformed officers greeted them. The older one introduced himself as Constable Dave Green, the other one as Constable Justin Biggs. Light was blazing across the lawn, crime-scene tape flapping against the tree trunks.

"Any word on Laura?" Avery asked.

"The last we heard, she was still in surgery," Biggs said.

As Lexi walked past the cordoned-off area, chills went down her back when she saw Gary's blood-soaked T-shirt crumpled where Laura had fallen.

47

The heavy door slammed behind him, the windows on either side vibrating, making the wooden frames creak and complain. He winced. The adrenalin had all but worn off and he was exhausted and furious with himself. The evening hadn't gone to plan. The top of his shirtsleeve was blood-soaked and he was in agony. That stupid cop had shot him!

He had felt the bullet go in. It wasn't at all what he had imagined it would feel like when a metal projectile was ripping through your flesh, just an initial burning sensation. The pain had come later. Not knowing how badly hurt he was, he had run for it, escaped through the vines and the paddock heading north. The backpack slammed against his body as he traversed the hilly landscape. The moon obscured behind thick clouds, his hands sweaty, he stumbled on the uneven ground, falling face-first, dropping his knife. It was impossible to find it in the dark.

He knew the cops would be on his trail soon, he had to keep going. He could feel the blood trickling down his arm and grimaced as he made his way up the steep incline to where he had parked the car.

As he pulled the blood-soaked sweatshirt over his head, the pain ripped through him, so intense and searing. He needed to stop the bleeding. Reaching into his backpack he grabbed a bandanna, flinching as he had to contort his injured right arm to hold onto one of the ends, tying it as best he could with his other hand, nearly passing out as pressure was applied. He then slipped a jacket on, covering the blood-stained sleeve of his t-shirt. He needed to get home.

He gripped the steering wheel tightly, taking a deep breath to compose himself, concentrated on his driving. No other traffic was on the road, which he was pleased about. Getting home was an effort. The cupboard door protested on its hinges as he reached in to grab the only clean glass on the shelf, a large opaque tumbler, its rim slightly chipped, not that he cared. He reached into the bottom cupboard, pushing the sparse selection of tinned goods and a bottle of tomato ketchup to the side, searching for the cheap blended whisky at the back. The woody aroma hit him in the face as he put his nose into the bottle, savouring it. Pouring it with a trembling hand, he took a large gulp. The burn down the throat and into the bottom of his stomach took his mind off the increasing level of pain. He knew it would not last long.

Swallowing another generous mouthful, he felt the warmth spreading through his insides. He knew what he had to do, he'd seen it on television. Reaching for a packet of cigarettes, he pulled one out, finding it awkward using his left hand to light it. Finally getting it lit, he took a long drag and blew the smoke out slowly. Feeling light-headed, he took a deep breath, then with one swift move he stuck the burning tip into the entry wound, cauterising the blood vessels.

The new pain was so intense that he could no longer hold the cigarette, and dropped it on the floor. The smell of burning flesh caused an automatic gag reflex. He ran to the sink and let it all out. He screamed and smashed his fist into the Formica bench, sending the glass up in the air. Before mustering the courage to repeat the whole procedure, he poured another whisky and downed it in one go, coughing and spluttering as his throat protested. Bending down, he picked up the still smouldering cigarette. A black burn had etched itself on the wooden floor board.

He closed his eyes as the red-hot cigarette once more connected to his exposed flesh. Every fibre in his body protested. Shaking wildly, he both dreaded and cherished the pain. Putting the bottle to his lips, he poured what he could down his throat. Losing consciousness was a welcome relief.

As the morning light came through the dirty net curtains, he woke up freezing, his body stiff from spending the night on the bare wooden floor. Shivering, he got himself to an upright position, holding on to the bench to steady himself. Dried chunks of vomit were left in the sink; flies buzzed around while the rancid smell wafted into his face. His stomach threatened to repeat the eruption.

He sat down and cast his mind back to yesterday. He had most likely killed that woman cop; she had got in the way. So had the damn dog. Why did she have to come out, her pistol drawn? New Zealand police didn't carry guns, he knew. She was the one that had surprised him. But she had got what she deserved. Served her right for sabotaging his plan. He hoped the bitch was dead.

48

The alarm woke Bill at six o'clock, exhausted and feeling as though he had only just gone to sleep. His fatigued body and mind refused to function. Turning over, he realised Annika's side was empty.

He rolled out of bed and his bare feet on the cool floorboards woke him up. He stumbled into the shower. The warm water on his tired body felt good.

Walking into the kitchen he stifled a yawn then he smelled freshly cooked bacon. He hadn't realised how hungry he was.

"Morning," Annika said. "Thought you could do with a decent breakfast this morning." She handed him a plate of poached eggs and bacon with baby spinach and sliced orange on the side. He knew better than to comment on the greens.

"What time did you get up this morning?" he asked while tucking into his breakfast.

"I had trouble sleeping and finally gave up at about five," she said with a weary smile. "The killing of the sheep... But on the upside I've done a heap of baking." She pointed to the production line of lunch boxes lined up on the bench. "You were late home."

Bill filled her in on the events at Matakana Valley Wines. Annika was shocked. "Oh my god, I hope that Laura is okay."

"So do I. The guy who did this is panicking and will make mistakes. It's just a matter of time until we catch him. I can feel it in my gut."

"I just hope when you and Niko come face to face with this lunatic you are prepared."

"We'll be fine," Bill said. "Don't you worry about that."

"Just promise you'll be careful," Annika said, planting a warm kiss on his lips.

The peace was shattered with shrieks from upstairs and noisy footsteps racing down the stairs. The twins piled through the door, quarrelling non-stop who had won the game they were playing. Getting their cereal and fruit for breakfast was deafening. Zac and Katie followed suit.

"Have a good day everyone," Bill said, hugging them on his way out. As he was putting his shoes on, the shrill ringtone of his phone rang out.

"Morning, Andrew Copeson here. We'll be on our way shortly to Matakana, just wanted to let you know. Terrible business what happened."

"Hi Andrew. Yes, you could say that again. Thanks for keeping us in the loop. Really appreciate it."

"No worries. Now we just have to make sure we get the bastard."

Bill was just about to leave when Annika handed him a basket of baking still warm from the oven. She had wrapped the knotted Gotland buns in a red-and-white checked cloth. "I thought you could take these over to Lexi and Avery's. I'm sure there will be a crowd of people there," she said.

The sweet yeasty smell took him back to his mother-in-law's house in Sweden. "Thanks, darling, I'm sure they'll appreciate it," Bill said as he rushed out the door.

Arriving sharply at seven, he parked outside the pharmacy. The security guys looked worse for wear in the unforgiving morning sun as they tucked into toasted sandwiches from the Rigawera Bakery next door. The melting cheese on the outside of the thick slices of bread made Bill's mouth salivate.

"How long have you been here?" he asked Niko as he climbed through the broken front door.

"A while. I had trouble sleeping and thought I could use the time to get started."

"Good work," Bill said and went back outside to the guards finishing their breakfast. "Anything of note happen overnight?"

"It's been dead as a doornail," the taller one said.

"What about Harry the pharmacist? Did he come back?"

"He returned with some coffee and sandwiches that were well received," the shorter one said.

"Did he stay long?"

"No, not really. He kept us company for a while, then went home just before I saw your colleague arrive back," the taller one said.

Bill went back into the shop where Niko was sorting through things.

"Something isn't adding up here," Niko said, surveying the damage. "As soon as the alarm sounded, I came downstairs from the flat to investigate and there was no sign of anyone here."

"Perhaps it was just kids."

"No, I think it's more than meets the eye initially. They would have had max thirty seconds after the glass broke. I was here straight away."

"Unless they'd got hold of the alarm code," Bill said thinking out loud, "but then why break the glass door? Why not just slip away into the night?"

"I guess we'll see what's missing when Harry does the stocktake this morning," Niko said.

"Morning, officers," Harry said from the footpath.

"Morning, Harry. How are you doing?" Bill said.

"Well, on reflection, I'm so pleased no one got hurt. You hear about aggravated robberies going wrong all the time. We can easily clean this up."

People never stop surprising you, Bill thought. Most of the time people looked at things with a glass half-empty attitude.

"Although it's a little peculiar," Harry said walking through. "They've torn down the prescription drugs off the shelves, but if drugs were what they were after, why leave things like Tramadol?"

"Yes, that's odd," Bill said.

"I'll get the girls to go through the stock to see what's missing as soon as they get in. We should know fairly quickly," Harry said.

Bill wrote down the details of who had what responsibility, which turned out to be shared between the two women who had worked there for years and whom Harry trusted.

"Do they lock up, and if so have the code for the alarm?" Bill asked.

"Well, of course," Harry said. "We change the alarm code every month."

BILL AND NIKO stopped at Ravish on the way to Matakana Valley Wines, picking up two flat whites. Back in the car, the phone rang.

"Matakana police station," Bill said, the phone on hands-free.

"This is Roger Willis from up on the ridge by Matakana Valley Wines."

Bill's ears pricked up. "Hello, Roger. What can we assist you with?"

"Well, after finishing the milking this morning, I found a big blood-stained Bowie knife in the paddock."

"What did you do with it?"

"I didn't touch it. Put a tin bucket on top of it so the cows wouldn't trample all over it."

"That's good. Any chance you could move the cattle to another paddock? We need to preserve as much of the surrounding area as possible."

Niko smiled. "Well, there you go. With any luck that might be the weapon used last night. Hopefully we're one step closer to catching this scumbag."

49

The morning sun streamed into the room, making the air hot and stuffy. Lexi's mind was foggy from last night. She wondered if it had all been a dream, until she saw the bloodstained T-shirt thrown in the corner, and she remembered. They had fallen into bed last night, the bottom of her tresses still matted with Beau's dried blood.

She rolled over and glanced at the time on her mobile; it was already after eight. She showered and put on a clean T-shirt and denim shorts. In the mirror she scrutinised the fine lines on her face and pulled the skin around her eyes. The stress and lack of sleep was showing. She sighed. She felt she had aged ten years in the last week.

As she walked down the stairs the aroma of freshly brewed coffee tickled her nose, making the kitchen feel homely, despite the five police officers sitting around the dining table.

Bill gestured to the basket of knotted Gotland buns. "Annika made these this morning." "That's so kind. I love them." Lexi cut a soft, pillowy bun in half and spread a generous layer of salted butter on top, finishing it with some of her own cheddar. It was the comfort food she needed.

A call came in from Orewa, with an update on Laura's condition.

She was still critical, and in an induced coma. The room's mood slightly improved with the news — she had survived the operation and the night.

~

"THE FEDS and the SOCO's should arrive shortly. I'm sure old Ruddy will bring his bright sunny disposition," Bill joked to Niko. It wasn't like him at all to talk badly of other people, but this guy really got under his skin.

The sound of tyres on gravel alerted him to Rudd pulling in, followed by Jono, the photographer.

Bill braced himself before going outside. Rudd got out and strutted in front of the car like a peacock. "I might have to take up residence here in Matakana with all the mileage we do backwards and forwards," he huffed. Well, let's get started. Which of you were here last night?" His grey eyes peered at them all.

"I was the first on the scene," Gary said.

Rudd pivoted on his heels. "Right, the rest of you remove your-selves from my crime scene."

Bill steeled himself and went over. "I had an interesting phone call earlier from a farmer whose land borders this property." He pointed up the gentle slope behind the winery buildings. "He found a knife in one of his paddocks this morning. The attacker might have dropped it as he fled. Niko and I will have a look. I'll let you know if we need you to come by."

Rudd grunted. "I hope you told the farmer not to touch anything."

"I did, not everyone's stupid," Bill snapped and walked away.

Copeson had already followed the blood trail behind the winery. "See you up the hill," he said.

50

To get to Roger Willis's farm, they had to head back towards Matakana, turn right by Ravish then carry on for half a kilometre along Sharp Road. Roger Willis was waiting for them on the wrap-around veranda reading the paper. He had a firm handshake and a fit frame for his age. His weathered face had a few visible skin cancers and white scars from the ones already removed.

"Thank you for coming by," Roger said, the laugh lines around his eyes creasing.

"No trouble at all. Where's this knife you found?"

Niko had brought the stepping plates from the car and was taking care where he placed them, approaching the bucket slowly. Once there, he carefully lifted it up. The knife lay flat on the ground, its black handle and long blade smeared with blood. He could just make out a smudge mark or two in the dried blood. He could only hope the prints would be viable.

Bill back-tracked along the metal path, carefully balancing on the plates, then turned to Roger, who was peering over the fence to see what was going on. "Mr Willis, I'd like to ask you some questions. To start with, before the helicopter landed did you hear anything unusual?" .

"No, I don't think so, although Kip was barking and carrying on just before we went to bed. He's getting a bit senile and we brought him inside."

"What time was this?"

"Not long after we heard the sirens," Roger said. "We didn't think much of Kip barking until this morning when I found the knife."

"Anything else you have noticed?" Niko asked.

"Not really. The only thing I can think of was the other day, we'd been out and when I went to check on the cows I saw bike tracks in the dirt across the paddock. Peculiar, as I don't ride these days. No one ever comes up this way through the paddocks."

Bill and Niko stood up to leave. "Here's my card, should you think of anything else," Bill said.

The sound of another vehicle pulling into the property caught his attention. Copeson and Rudd stepped out of the car. Bill walked over and gave them the lowdown on what they had found.

"Granger, I see that you used stepping plates," Rudd said. "Well done."

Bill nodded, not accustomed to praise. Perhaps it had been good that he'd bitten back at Rudd before.

"We are expecting the autopsy report on James Smith later today. I'll let you know as soon as we receive it."

"Thank you, that would be great," Bill said, still slightly wary.

"I spoke to the lab this morning," Rudd said matter-of-factly. "The blood on the overalls and gloves found in the sports bag in the garage in Point Wells matches Peter Evans. ESR also retrieved DNA from the inside of the gloves and the collar of the suit. We now have a comprehensive profile of the killer."

This was a breakthrough. "Any hits in the system?" Bill asked eagerly.

"Unfortunately not," Copeson said. "This person has no prior convictions, although the indications of the crime suggest that this might not be the first act of violence he has committed."

Bill's feeling of slight elation waned.

"Hopefully we can give you more information later today."

Bill could not believe his ears. Rudd was talking to him like a normal person without the tiresome sniping and excessive rudeness. It was as if the man had undergone a personality change.

51

A s the police car pulled in to Matakana Valley Wines, Trevor came roaring up their rear on his quad bike. Despite being in his mid-seventies he jumped off with the vigour of a forty-year-old and swaggered over to the officers. "I demand to know what's going on and why the police are still here," he said. "Are the rest of us in any danger?"

Lexi, who had been talking to Gary, turned towards her irate neighbour with some annoyance. Dealing with Trevor was the last thing she needed. Gary stepped forward and gently guided the old man back toward his four-wheeler, talking to him as they walked. Trevor got back on the bike and waved as he drove off.

"What did you say to old Trevor?" Lexi asked curiously.

"I just told him as he lives on top of the ridge, we appreciate his help, and if he would keep his eyes and ears open and report to Bill if he sees anything, the police would appreciate it."

Lexi laughed. "Well, as long as it works. He is such a bloody nosey bugger."

Before Gary could reply her phone rang. It was Annika. "What a terrible night you must have all had. Bill told me about the attack on Laura Rose and Beau."

"I can't believe what's happening."

"I'm not sure if I'm allowed to tell you, but apparently they received the autopsy report regarding Peter. It was his hand they found under your house," Annika said. "It seems he had Heparin in his system. You know, the blood thinner. It was injected to make him bleed out."

"It's so sick," Lexi said. "The police are doing their best, but I'm not sure if it's enough. I don't feel very safe here."

"I know, but you have to trust them," Annika said.

AFTER TIDYING up the breakfast dishes Lexi went upstairs to make the bed and sort out some washing, anything to distract herself. She saw the pile of notes and photos from last night. Then it had seemed like a blurry mess, but this morning she was looking at it with fresh eyes and from a different perspective. On the top was a faded photo of the owners of Stott's Landing, the husband, the wife and the adolescent son. She wondered whatever happened to the wife after Maurice's death.

Her mobile buzzed again. It was Ronald the vet. Beau was doing well, had even eaten something and been outside for a minor comfort stop. Lexi smiled, food had always motivated Beau. Ronald said if he kept recovering well and there was no infection, he would be home in a few days. A warm glow spread through her chest, her boy was on the mend. Hopefully Laura Rose would be as fortunate.

She sat down and thumbed through the notes, choosing to do some research instead. There was nothing else to do, the farm shop was closed and the cheese production was on hold indefinitely.

Based on what they knew, which wasn't much, she did a psychological assessment, digging deep into her nursing training. A phone call to an old colleague now working at a psychiatric clinic in Auckland confirmed that she was on the right track. She did a Google search and found out everything she could about the now-defunct vineyard. She even tracked down the winemaker who had worked for the family and was now in Central Otago. On a whim she dialled the listed mobile number. There was no answer but she left a message, hoping he would call back.

Using Google again she found the vineyards around Stott's Landing and made a few phone calls to see if anyone remembered the family. The first call turned up nothing — the people were new to the area. The second call was more helpful. The man remembered the family well. They had sold the vineyard, he said, not long after Maurice's tragic death.

"If you don't mind me asking, how did he die?" Lexi asked, her curiosity piqued.

"Old Maurice killed himself. The boy found him in the study. It was a terrible thing really."

"That's awful," Lexi said, her heart going out to the adolescent son.

"Jenny and Benjamin stayed on in the house, even though they sold the vineyard. Last I heard, might be a year or two ago, Jenny suffered some major health issues and moved to a care home."

"What about the son, Benjamin? What happened to him?"

"I'm not sure. I know he finished his schooling in the district, then moved to Australia, he might still be there."

Lexi thanked him, giving him her number should he think of anything else. When Avery came back inside, she relayed the information she had compiled.

"Outstanding work," he said. "I'm sure Bill will be happy to get some help with the investigation."

"I hope so. As soon as I have a few more things sorted out I'll pass it over to him," she said, feeling rather pleased with her effort.

Lexi's stomach growled. "How about we get some lunch and pick up some groceries in Matakana?"

"Sounds like an excellent idea," Avery said.

They took Lexi's car, Avery was driving. Biggs and Green followed behind in their own car. Lexi switched between radio stations until she found a song that she liked. The Pub was the obvious choice. Sitting down outside in the courtyard, the sun on their backs, she felt at ease. The air at home had seemed suffocating. The two cops sat a few tables over, which she was grateful for. It was tiring to be under constant observation like a goldfish in a bowl.

"What do you remember about the owners at Stott's landing?" Lexi asked, putting her fork down. Avery wiped his chin, the juices from his burger going everywhere. "They were a pleasant couple, hardworking folks. I felt the wife might have been the long-suffering woman. I don't think Maurice was that easy to live with. If she wasn't looking after the workers at the vineyard, she was out cleaning houses, from memory. I don't think he involved her in the vineyard's running, more the logistics of cooking and feeding workers and things. A full-time job in its own right, really. She always looked exhausted, poor woman."

"What about the son?"

"His name was Benjamin. He might have been about ten or eleven, I suppose. I remember thinking it was strange him spending every day of his summer holidays working in the vineyard, never having a friend around. He was a peculiar boy, introverted, almost morose."

They paid the bill and Lexi went into the Four Square supermarket to pick up a few groceries while Avery got takeaway coffees from Plume across the way. When they met back at the car, Lexi stopped dead in her tracks. There was a piece of paper tucked under the windscreen wiper like a parking ticket:

YOU THINK YOU ARE SAFE — I CAN STILL GET TO YOU

THEY DROPPED the note off at the police station and by the time they were home again, Lexi had regained some colour in her cheeks. "Why don't you have a rest?" Avery said. "Neither of us got much sleep last night."

"No, I'll be fine, thanks. I might have another look at those notes again, see if I can spot something new." She went upstairs to the bedroom, spreading the papers out in front of her. She decided to try phoning the winemaker again. Robert answered this time and was more than happy to help. Thinking on her feet, Lexi made up a story about writing an article on the founding wineries in Martinborough.

Robert didn't wait for her to ask, told her he'd been at Stott's Landing for nearly ten years. Maurice and Jenny were lovely and he got on well with them. Unfortunately, after Maurice died, Jenny didn't have the skills or the money to keep it going. Robert had stayed on as new owners took over, but it got quite run down and there wasn't much money about. He left, and the business folded shortly after. "It was a real shame. The land produced superb wine. It's what in the industry we call *terroir*, the perfect growing conditions."

"Where did the wife and son go?" Lexi asked.

"Benjamin went to high school in town and as far as I know Jenny continued to work as a cleaner until she fell ill with a severe stroke two years ago."

"What about Benjamin now?"

"He went to Australia as soon as he was old enough, but as far as I'm aware is back in Auckland since a couple of years," Robert said. He didn't have an address, but suggested she'd try the care home where his mother was living. What a lovely man, Lexi thought, as she hung up after having asked a few more questions about the neighbouring vineyards to not arouse suspicions.

If the son was living in Auckland, that was an excellent start. She called Bill to tell him what she had found out. "Not sure if it's of any use to you, but the son of Maurice Stott apparently lives in Auckland."

"That's interesting." Bill sounded intrigued and impressed. "How did you find that out?"

"Oh, I just did some googling and thought I'd pass it on to you." She wasn't sure he believed her story, but he promised he'd look into it. She looked at the Stott family photo again and pondered their fates.

52

Annika had some errands to run in the village and went past the police station. Bill was busy reading the autopsy report on James Smith. Annika went in to the lunchroom and glanced at the wall in the Incident Room on the way. She listened to Bill and Niko discussing the report, comparing it to the previous one. "Had they injected him with the same drug as Peter Evans?"

Bill didn't flinch. He was used to discussing cases with Annika. She was a great sounding board and more often than not came with up with brilliant solutions, making him see things from a fresh angle. She would have made an excellent investigator.

"Yes, they did," he said.

"Most killings are crimes of passion, violent and swift," Niko put in. "This feels different. The killer is cold and calculated, and wants his victims to suffer. It doesn't fit the normal profile. It's like the killer has a different genetic makeup. No remorse, seemingly."

"Any DNA found at the crime scenes?" she asked. "Or perhaps any viable prints?"

Bill thought for a moment, then decided it wouldn't hurt if she knew more. "Orewa might pull some prints off the knife we found on the neighbouring property. They may compare with the ones found on the overalls in the sports bag."

"I think it's the same killer," Niko said. Bill nodded in agreement. "Good to see you boys. I'm heading over to Lexi's," she said.

Her mind was working overtime. What did all this mean? She stopped at Ravish on the way and picked up some raspberry and white chocolate muffins. As she pulled into Matakana Valley Wines she missed Beau's friendly welcome. An officer greeted her on the path.

"Hi, I'm Annika Granger. I'm here to see Lexi," she said.

A smile replaced his suspicious look as he realised she was Bill's wife, one of their own.

Annika called out to Lexi who came downstairs, her pale face and loosely tied-up hair a far cry from her usual tidy self. "I'm so glad you're here," she said and threw her arms around Annika.

Annika held up a brown paper bag. "I brought afternoon tea."

"You are the best," Lexi said. They sat down at the kitchen table and Lexi recounted what she had dug up.

"Have you googled the son, Benjamin, yet?" Annika asked.

"No, I haven't had a chance. Let's have a look now." Lexi went upstairs to get her laptop. Annika cleared the table and made room for the notes that Lexi brought with her.

"Wow, you have been busy," Annika laughed. Lexi typed the name Benjamin Stott in, but there weren't many hits.

"Has he been living under a rock?" she said. "It's virtually impossible to live without a digital footprint being created."

"Let's try Facebook. Everyone's there," Annika said. There were two hits on that name, one in Europe and one in Auckland. It was a public account so Lexi clicked on it. Minimal information, nothing current; the last post was three years ago.

"Shame there's no photo of the guy," Annika said.

Lexi closed the lid to the laptop and sighed. "This is impossible. There must be another way. Let me call Zac. He's a whizz on social media. Perhaps he'll have some ideas," Annika said, pushing speed dial on her phone.

"It's worth a try, I guess," Lexi said but didn't sound convinced. Perhaps they could help Bill.

Lexi could hear some of the conversation, but was eager to get the entire story when Annika had finished. "What did he say?" Lexi said. Annika smiled. "Facial recognition."

"What, like in the spy movies?" Annika nodded. "Precisely." She searched the App Store on her phone for the software Zac had suggested. "Oh, come on. Why is the Internet so damn slow when you want something?" she said impatiently obvious. Going through the steps was fairly easy, you had to scan an existing photo, input it, and the program would do the rest, searching the Internet for a match.

"Look at you, Mrs Technology," Lexi said. She scanned the photo from the vineyard they had, editing out the people they didn't need, just leaving Benjamin Stott, loaded it and pressed Enter. The nervous tension buzzing in the room.

Then just as Avery walked in with the officers the program dinged — it had found a match. Annika quickly closed the lid of the laptop while Lexi collected up the pieces of paper spread across the table. Annika wasn't ready to admit they had been doing some investigating.

"Annika bought some delicious muffins," Lexi announced to deflect the slightly uncomfortable situation in the room.

"Thank you," Avery said and turned to Annika. "I could get used to all this lovely baking turning up at our house."

Lexi and Annika looked at each other and burst into giggles like naughty schoolgirls. "I feel sneaky digging around like this, but we're only trying to help, really," Annika sighed. "I'm not sure that Bill would appreciate us sticking our noses in."

Lexi opened the laptop and gasped. It was eerily like him. It wasn't a great photo, perhaps a few years old. He had longer hair and a slightly fuller face, but the piercing eyes were the same. *It can't be.* Fear spread through her body.

Annika stared at the screen, her eyes wide. She had to call Bill.

53

He had lain low all day. There had only been two calls from numbers he didn't know and he let them go to voicemail. He was in no mood to talk to anyone. His arm was swollen and aching and definitely infected. He couldn't go to the medical centre; they would ask too many questions. He had to be strong and push through, even though his plan had gone awry.

Walking to the bench he held his arm for support, as at every step a sharp pain radiated up through his shoulder. He found some antiseptic under the sink and rolled the sleeve of his T-shirt up as far as he could. At least the bullet had gone clean through his triceps and not hit the bone. The seeping through the dirty bandage had stuck to the burns and he had to yank it off, causing unbearable pain in the process. He cleaned up as best he could, but the astringent antiseptic smell made him queasy. Being right-handed didn't help the situation either. Clearing up the mess on the bench, he knocked one of the ceramic cups which shattered all over the floor.

"Fuck!" he shouted and kicked the cupboard door in frustration, his heel sending waves of pain through his battered body. Holding on to the bench, he forced himself to calm down and splashed cold water on his face. He paced across the floor. He needed to think. Get his head out of the fog that had taken a firm hold of him like a cold, wet winter's day. He had to get away from the cottage. It was just a matter of time before they put two and two together and came looking for him. He knew just where to go.

54

Bill looked weary. "Any security footage at all?" he asked.

"I spoke to Bob from the Business Association," Niko said. He looked remarkably fresh, having youth on his side. "Unfortunately the block of shops in and around the pharmacy doesn't have cameras up. It's been on the agenda for years but nothing has happened. But he did say that the pub is the only place with cameras that are working."

"Hopefully Matt from the pub has got something we can use." Bill stifled a yawn. His eyes were heavy and full of grit. "I'll walk down to see how Harry is getting on.

The builder had repaired the door frame and the glazier and his assistant were changing the broken glass pane. Harry and the two female staff were inside trying to get on with business as usual. The glazier looked annoyed when Bill squeezed through the half-open door.

"Hi, Bill," Harry said. "Trying to get everything back to normal." He looked exhausted. The women were a little younger than Harry, perhaps in their early sixties. Pamela wore mint-green slacks with a crisp crease and a green-and-white short-sleeve jumper, showing she still had a nice figure. A single string of pearls hung around her neck. She would have been a beauty in her youth, Bill thought, and still was. Lindsay was more like a little grey mouse. Her blonde hair was cut short, a practical style flattering her face. She wore a simple summer frock with a short sleeved cardigan to match.

"Have you got an idea of what they took?" Bill asked.

"Yes. It's rather curious. It seems that all they have taken is one drug, Heparin," Harry said.

Bill's ears pricked up. "You'd think if someone took the risk of breaking in, they'd grab handfuls of different prescription medication."

Harry nodded.

"Heparin, that's the blood thinner isn't it?"

Harry nodded again.

"How much did they take?"

"We only had four vials, all on pre-order for a customer."

It was late afternoon when Bill walked back to the station. He was hoping something would show on the security tapes and was feeling better for the walk. It had got his brain into gear and he could think again.

Niko put the phone down as he came through the door. "That was Rudd. Even though we don't have a DNA match yet, looking at the stab wounds, calculating the angle and force, it's likely its the same killer."

"The question is, when is the killer going to strike next?" Bill sank into his chair, groaning as it dug into his back. Before he could fill Niko in on the conversation at the pharmacy, Matt the publican walked through the door. He was a tall man in his late forties with broad shoulders and sandy hair.

"Bob said you were looking for footage from last night," he said, putting an iPad on Bill's desk.

"That's right. Please tell me the cameras are in working order and you have something recorded." Bill was always exasperated with businesses that put dummy cameras up as a deterrent.

"We have got the footage all right," Matt said. "I've had a look at the recording, and something's strange about it."

"What do you mean?" Bill asked, gesturing for him to take a seat.

"Well, you look at this sequence and see what you think." Matt pressed Play. A grainy image showed a person walking towards the pharmacy on the opposite side of the street. He — assuming it was a he, Bill thought — wore a hoodie which disguised his face, and a long overcoat, far too warm for this time of the year. Work boots with heavy socks on a pair of stocky legs showed. It was difficult to distinguish any other details as the camera was a good thirty or forty metres away across the road. The person looked around before tapping in the security code and opening the door, quickly closing it behind him.

"What! That means he knew the code," Niko said.

"Just watch on," Matt said. Less than two minutes passed with minimal movement in the dark pharmacy before the person came out, closed the door and keyed in the code again to reset the alarm. Suddenly, from under the large coat he pulled out a hammer and smashed the glass and lock in the door frame, which would have activated the alarm and strobe light. As quickly as the person appeared, he sprinted down the road towards the wharf. The tape kept running another thirty seconds before Niko burst out on the pavement in shorts and T-shirt.

"Strange to first use the code to get in, then lock the door and smash it when he could have just left," Bill said.

"Could it be an inside job, someone connected to an employee?" Niko said.

"Yes, it might be worth investigating who might have access to the keys and entry code, other than the employees."

"I'd better get back to work," Matt said. "We have a function on tonight, and tons to do. Hope this was helpful."

"Can you email me this?" Bill asked.

"Sure thing."

As Matt was walking towards the door Niko said, "The question remains, if the offender already had the code, why go to the effort of smashing the front of the shop. Seems unnecessary."

Matt poked his head back through the door. "I forgot to say, we are all creatures of habit and do the same things every time."

"What do you mean?" Bill said.

"I can't be sure, but Harry isn't taking much precaution any more. I've seen him coming and going to the shop, punching in the code in plain view for anyone to see. I meant to tell him the other day when I saw it again, but got side-tracked and forgot."

"Thanks, Matt, you've been a great help. We'll talk to Harry," Bill said deep in thought.

"PERHAPS THE OFFENDER didn't think Harry would keep a good stock-take system and just wanted it to look like an ordinary robbery," Niko said as they were alone again.

"Or it was purely diversion." Bill's mobile buzzed. It was Annika who was speaking so fast that he couldn't understand a word she was saying. "Slow down, darling. Take a deep breath and repeat what you just said."

Annika started from the beginning. Bill listened intently, looking more and more perplexed as the conversation continued. "Send me the information through, please," he said, and hung up.

"Annika and Lexi have done a bit of amateur sleuthing and have come up with the possibility that Benjamin Stott, the son of the vineyard owner in Martinborough, might be the same person as Ben Wilson," Bill said.

"The electrician?" Niko said. "You're kidding, right?"

"It might be a long shot," Bill said. "Or is it?"

The email pinged.

The two photos were hardly telling. One was from thirty years ago and the other was more recent.

"It could be half the male population," Niko said. "Besides, it's not illegal to change your name."

"They put it through some facial recognition software and it came up as a likely match," Bill said. "Perhaps we should have a chat to Ben and see what he says. There might be a perfectly logical explanation."

Niko looked up the address in Point Wells and they got in the car. Ben Wilson had been an exemplary member of the community in the brief time that he'd lived there and had got involved in local projects, donating his time and expertise for free. They parked the car on the kerb by his driveway, the scorching sun blazing in contrast with the eerie quiet. There was no one around.

Ben's work van was parked in the driveway of the small white cottage. The heavily laden apple and pear trees surrounding the house made it look homely.

Niko knocked on the front door but there was no movement inside. While Bill stood at the front, Niko walked around the back. He pressed the door handle down. It was unlocked and the door creaked and gave way, opening inward. Niko peeked in and called out. Making a split-second decision he stepped through the door and inside. Not strictly legal, but as Ben's van was parked out the front, for all they knew he could be hurt inside. It was a flimsy excuse, but the opportunity was too good to pass up. "Ben, are you here," Niko shouted, but got no answer.

The compact kitchen had the original pale-pink Formica bench tops and plywood cupboards; no modernising since the 1960's. Looking through the rubbish bin was always the first thing Niko did while doing a search, no one ever expected you to look there. He slipped on a pair of gloves and lifted it out from under the sink. Bloodied gauze strips thrown on top of takeaway containers and a handful of soft-drink cans. Leaving the bin on the floor, he walked through the two sparsely furnished bedrooms and lounge. Ben was nowhere to be seen.

He unlocked the front door. "Sarge, I found something that might be of interest."

Looking at the bin Bill said, "There might be a perfectly plausible explanation." Continuing through the house they found nothing of significance, and hardly any personal items. There wasn't much in the kitchen cupboards either, just some tinned goods, placed in alphabetical order. The small and dimly lit bathroom was squeezed in between the two bedrooms, most of which was taken up by an apricot toilet suite comprising a large bath with a shower above it and a toilet with a fluffy seat cover on top. There was a soiled mustard yellow carpet covering the floor.

"Who would carpet a bathroom?" Niko said, shaking his head. He opened the mirrored bathroom cabinet above the pastel sink. There wasn't much in it apart from a container of prescription medication made out to B. Wilson from a pharmacy in Warkworth. "Zypine" it said with bold letters. He wondered what it was for. The absence of a toothbrush and other toiletries struck him as odd. It looked as though the occupant had just up and left.

BILL GOOGLED THE MEDICATION. "It's an anti-psychotic drug." He rummaged through the cupboard under the basin and found a box of three month's supply of the medication. All dispensed just over four months ago and unopened. The first bottle was more than half-full which didn't bode well, he thought.

If Ben was off his meds, that put an even more serious spin on the situation. It was dispensed by a pharmacy in Warkworth. He dialled the number on the packaging, the pharmacist mentioned patient confidentiality but could clearly hear the urgency in Bill's voice.

"Let me check in the computer," she said, putting him on hold. After a minute she came back. "That bottle was the last he collected. We've been trying to get hold of him. His repeat is sitting here."

"How serious is this for the patient?" Bill asked.

"Abruptly discontinuing medication like this can lead to a range of adverse effects such as paranoia, confusion and aggressiveness. I don't recommend going cold turkey."

"We need to locate Ben Wilson," Niko said.

Bill nodded and looked at the pill bottle again. The prescribing doctor was psychiatrist Dr Stan Webber.

NIKO WENT through to the larger of the two bedrooms, the one that looked lived in. An old rag rug covered most of the wooden floor. The double bed, pushed up to the back wall, had a ghastly animal print duvet cover that looked mismatched with the rest of the old-fashioned furniture. On the bedside table was an ornate lamp with a pink frilly lampshade and a pile of books on Sleep and Mindfulness, and a blue notebook with a pen on top.

The drawer protested when Niko opened it to reveal a bottle of Sleep Drops, magnesium tablets and a sleep mask. Niko struggled to picture Ben wearing a sleep mask to bed — he was such a surfer type. Closing the drawer, he flicked through the notebook. It was a sleep diary, dating back to last year. According to this Ben was a chronic insomniac and slept only a few hours a night if that.

He opened the built-in wardrobe. There was an old wetsuit hanging up and a smell of dust and stale clothes. And —

"Hey, Sarge, look what I found on the shelf in the wardrobe, covered by old blankets." He held up a dark-stained wooden box. It was the same size as a shoe box; its carved lid and two hinges looked handmade. The ornate sides were delicate and intricate, less chunky than the lid. It had a tiny vintage padlock on the front.

"It looks like it has been special to someone," Bill said.

Niko pulled a Leatherman multi-tool from his pocket and picked the lock. "Child's play," he said triumphantly as he opened the lid.

"Put it down on the table," Bill said, his curiosity rising. Inside was an assortment of faded photos, old school reports, birthday cards and a stack of red leather-bound notebooks.

Niko opened the first one. It was a journal with a dedicated page for each day, cursive writing flowing on each page. He turned to the front. "Hey, it's got a name on it," he said. "Maurice Stott." Bill stared at him as the penny dropped.

55

A nnika wasn't sure that Bill was thrilled to hear that they had been doing their own research.

"I'm sure he'll get over it," Lexi said, hands on hips. "We're only trying to help."

Annika wasn't so sure, but this case had her intrigued. In high school she had seriously considered a career in the police, but after speaking to the guidance councillor and her parents at length, she had gone into teaching. A decision that she didn't regret for a moment, although it would have been more exciting doing policing. Then again, she thought, she might not have met Bill.

"Come on, Lexi, you spent some time with the Stott family. What were they like?" she asked.

"It's such a long time ago. Besides, I only visited on the weekends." Lexi walked over to the enormous window. She stretched her arms up above her head and did a slight back bend, taking a deep breath in, the bones of her spine readjusting with slight cracks. She exhaled slowly and sat down again.

"I suppose they were like any other family, working hard at their business," she said. "What life experience did I have anyway? I was young, still a university student." She massaged her tight neck muscles. "Although I remember Maurice. He seemed to have demons — huge highs and deep lows. He could be very buoyant, then at other times glum, barely able to make eye contact or even talk."

"I suppose Jenny, the wife, and the adolescent son can't have had it easy either, especially after Maurice's death," Annika said.

They let their minds wander until Annika looked at the time and realised she had to get home and organise dinner.

As she drove away, she wondered what was Ben's part in all this. Or was it just a coincidence? She didn't really know him, the few times that she'd had dealings with him he'd seemed like a lovely guy, and half the women in the village swooned over his rugged good looks.

She turned left at the roundabout and called in at the police station. Bill and Niko had papers spread all over the two lunch tables, in some order by the looks of the different piles.

"I see you've been busy," she said with a smile.

Bill raised an eyebrow. "So, it seems, have you. We have confirmed that Ben Wilson is the same person as Benjamin Stott, and have put an alert out. He changed his name by deed poll a couple of years ago"

It surprised Annika that her hunch had been right, and she was pleased that she'd been able to help.

"Who would have thought?" Bill said, still grappling with the discovery. "Niko has checked with New Zealand Transport and the toll road cameras, and received confirmation that his van headed south last Thursday morning. We're trying to place him in Martinborough at the time of Peter Evans' death sometime on Friday afternoon or evening."

Niko looked up. "Footage has already been requested from the petrol stations along State Highway One."

Bill filled Annika in on the find at Ben's cottage, the old journals and how they'd have to sit down and read at least the last few years before Maurice's death.

"I could help," she said, thinking back to the essays and assessments she had marked in her career as a teacher. "I'm good at deciphering handwriting and should get through the text quickly."

She sensed Bill wasn't sure — it wasn't police procedure to let civilians look at the gathered material, but then again what could it hurt? They could trust her, and could do with an extra pair of hands and eyes. Orewa hadn't put priority on the diaries, deeming them sentimental and not important to the current case, so they were still in Matakana.

"Let me just get the twins from after school care. Zac and Samantha will be home soon. They can sort out an easy dinner," Annika said, already heading out the door.

BILL WASN'T sure he'd done the right thing in agreeing that Annika could help. He could almost hear his superior in Orewa giving him a bollocking, but it might be worth the pain and wrath if they got the case solved and saved lives. Anyway, it was too late now. She was very determined, very stubborn, and there was no way she would change her mind now.

56

The exhaustion and pain was at the limit of what he could cope with. As he rested and tried to slow his breathing down, he leaned against a gnarly old Ponga. Closing his eyelids for a moment to get rid of the flickering lights dancing in front of his eyes, he was on the verge of collapse. It would be dark soon and he had to concentrate and gather all his strength to carry on. His arm was aching and waves of nausea rolled over him like the wild breakers in the secluded bays below. He was still too far away to see them, but he could sense the familiar taste of salt in the air.

Having laid low all day, he had parked his Mazda RX-8 at the back of one of the many empty holiday homes on the main road. He tipped up his near-empty water bottle and drank with urgency. Trekking on the edge of farmland initially, then having to go through almost impenetrable dense bush on the sloping hills of the Tāwharanui Peninsula, he had definitely underestimated the terrain. As if the steep incline wasn't bad enough, the warmth of the sun didn't penetrate the vast canopies sheltering the damp ground. He was unsure if it was the slight fever he was running or the air temperature that made him shiver. The smell of wet leaves underfoot, ginger and Ponga trees was comforting. When he inhaled it he felt as if he was back in his childhood's Martin-borough.

Feeling the damp coming up his legs he stepped on the soft ground of earthy fungus, which made him slip and struggle through the thick undergrowth. It was getting more challenging the further he ventured, so he was glad he had brought a compass to ensure he was walking in the right direction. A flashback to a camping trip in the Australian rainforest brought memories of spiders and the occasional snake he had encountered. He was thankful that he was back in New Zealand rather than in the critter infested Australia, where he had spent a good part of his adult life. A brief memory of his beloved Clementine flashed through his mind before his backpack slipped off his good shoulder. This made him lose his balance and he fell face-first, the pack landing on top of the injured arm he was trying to protect. Catching his breath, he attempted to stand up, falling again, rolling headfirst into a patch of thorny bushes down a gully. "Fuck!" His body was on fire. He eventually got up into a sitting position, his breathing laboured, beads of sweat running into his eyes.

He brushed himself off and checked his bearings, relieved that the compass was still on the string around his neck. As he walked on, the bush began slowly clearing and he could feel the surrounding air changing and taste the sea salt in his mouth; he knew he was getting closer.

Arriving on the edge of the bush behind a row of eight or nine houses, he surveyed the small, gated bay. There was no one in sight, but he stuck close to the tree line just in case. He had done a job there not so long ago and had a place in mind. Most properties came with a hefty price tag and were owned by retired folk. The house at the far end had weatherboards and was in Cape Cod style, with a wrap-around veranda. He remembered the alarm code and knew where the spare key was.

He lifted the planter by the front door and picked the key up. He looked out over the pebbled beach, soaking up the calm. The mirror-flat water looked inviting, not that he would take the chance. A rowboat and some kayaks lay deserted on the grass verge. The salt-tinged breeze was pleasant; he could relax a little. Leaving the pack, he unlocked the front door.

The alarm panel was on the left, he remembered. Pressing in the code he held his breath as he hit Enter, what if it was the wrong sequence? Silence. He breathed a sigh of relief, closing the door and dumping the backpack. He made his way down the hall past the lounge and into the kitchen. It had all the essential appliances befitting an upmarket beach house. There was even a plumbed-in Italian coffee machine on the granite bench. You'd need a pilot's licence to operate it, he thought. He opened the double pantry door, looking for some plain tea bags instead.

Mug of tea in hand, he walked through the house. It was getting dark so he left the blinds at the front closed. No need to advertise his presence should someone be around. He would have to rely on his torch. The pantry was well stocked with non-perishable food left behind from the summer. There were even some bottles of wine and a box of chocolates on the top shelf. He reached for a packet of chocolate-chip biscuits and dunked two in his tea, not something his Victorian grandmother would have condoned. Smiling, he remembered visiting his grandparents who had lived close, his mother not minding if he dunked his biscuits or not. She had been the sunshine in his life, as opposed to his father and his controlling grandparents. Maurice had been a dutiful father, just weighted down by all the financial worries, and very absent during his formative years, the time when he needed his Dad. His mother had always been there and interested in school and other aspects of his life. The grandparents died well before he became a teenager, and his Dad not long after. That completely broke his mother.

A stab of guilt came over him as he remembered going to Australia as soon as he finished school. She had been so happy he was learning a trade and making a life for himself. He had lived the dream, meeting a terrific girl and having a great job. His mother stayed on in the house after they sold the vineyard. He visited every year; she was always so proud of him. Then it all crumbled and he fell into a gigantic hole. His heart squeezed with the weight of the memories flooding back. Suddenly it was difficult to breathe.

He made his way to the back door and sat on the wooden step in the pitch-black night. The silent grief bubbled to the surface and an overwhelming desperation sneaked up on him. He couldn't remember when he last cried. Probably when Clementine died. By the time he calmed down he was trembling with cold and despair. The lemony scent of the Ponga fronds hung in the air, the blackness of the night bringing an assortment of creepy-crawlies from the surrounding bush. There was a rustling at the edge of the garden, snuffling coming closer. He pointed the torch and a reflection of eyes from a stunned possum stared back. He shivered. His dirty clothes were getting damp from the night air. It was time to go inside.

Cold to the bone, he stripped off and jumped into the double walk-in shower next to the master bedroom upstairs. The hot water soothed his battered body. Dirt and blood trailed off him, pooling on the white porcelain tiles. A pile of large soft towels sat neatly folded on the freestanding unit in the bathroom. He wrapped himself in one and put another on the floor to mop up the excess water. He looked in the mirror. Apart from his infected and angry-looking arm, he had scratches on his face and neck. A large cut on his forehead gaped ominously. In the bathroom cabinet he found a first-aid box and taped up the cut on his head as best as he could, pulling the two edges together. The pain was unbearable as he applied antiseptic on to the swollen bullet wound, wrapping it up tight again.

His stomach growled, he needed to eat something. He opened the heavy oak floor-to-ceiling wardrobe. Colour-coded, folded neat piles of shirts appeared. They were not really his style but they were warm and dry. Once dressed, he looked through the deep freeze and found some ready meals and put one in the microwave. He took a bottle of wine and sat down at the oak dining table. He poured a generous amount of wine and swallowed a couple of paracetamol tablets. The microwave dinged and he pulled out a steamy dish of roast chicken, potatoes and gravy. The delicious smell made him forget that it came out of a store bought packet. He washed each mouthful down with more wine before rinsing his plate and sticking it in the oversized European dishwasher. Finishing the last mouthful of wine he walked into the lounge and pulled the curtains open.

The moon reflected on the calm water in front of the house. He spotted a decanter of whisky on the sideboard. Finding a crystal tumbler and pouring a good slug he sank into the plush sofa. The smell of whisky took him back to his childhood and his father's den where he used to have his drink every night while writing his journal entries. Many years later when his mother had suffered her stroke, he had returned to his childhood home to stay for a few days, and had found his father's notebooks. He knocked the whisky back, his knuckles whitening around the glass.

57

Annika arrived back in Matakana after organising the children at home. She was buzzing with energy and looking forward to getting stuck in and being able to help. Bill and Niko seemed pleased to see her, although she sensed some regret and apprehension on Bill's part, and could understand why. That she had brought in some leftover lasagne pulled out of the freezer seemed to seal the deal, she was now one of the team. "You can come and help any time if you bring in home-cooked food like this," Niko said.

While they were eating, Annika got started with the diaries. The well-thumbed notebooks felt precious and conjured up memories of her own diary writing when she was an adolescent. It felt intrusive opening them up to read something so private as Maurice Stott's inner thoughts. She put her feelings aside and started reading. The cursive handwriting was beautiful, a joy to read. It didn't take long until she came to the summer of 1987.

Each day there was an entry where he described the weather and the work they had done, as well interesting anecdotes. She soon discovered a common thread running through the entries, the constant conflicts and disagreements with Robert the winemaker. He came across as arrogant, unlike Maurice himself who seemed meek and mild-mannered. Maurice described his wife and son in loving terms, expressing how pleased he was the son was taking an interest in the business. He had been a kind man, she thought. She wondered what could have pushed him over the brink. What could have been so bad that he took his own life, leaving his adolescent son and wife behind?

To digest what she had read so far, she walked around the room. It felt good to move after sitting hunched over the diaries for the last hour or two. There was still a lot to get through and it would be a long night, she thought.

Delving further in, she could sense Maurice's mood change. The sentences were now short and urgent and his language more blunt. Nothing personal and no interesting anecdotes, he was like a deflated balloon, the joy gone and the undertones of despair and gloom shone through.

"MATAKANA POLICE STATION. GRANGER SPEAKING," Bill said as the phone rang.

"This is Dr Stan Webber. I've been at a conference all day. My secretary gave me your message to call back regarding one of my patients."

"We have grave concerns of the mental state of Benjamin Stott, or Ben Wilson as he calls himself now."

"I don't know what kind of operation you run, but I'm not in the habit of breaching my patient-doctor confidentiality," Webber huffed. "There are proper channels to go through for this."

Bill was in no mood to be lectured. "We believe that the suspect has killed two people already and slashed the throat of a police officer," he snapped. "At this stage we are unsure if she will survive. We can get a court order in the morning and you will still have to give us the information we need." Bill was getting louder and more animated. "He has a hit list of at least two more victims lined up. You tell me if that warrants me asking some bloody questions!"

There was silence on the line. "All right, you win," Dr Webber said. "Benjamin is my patient. He trusts me, so I would like to oversee the matter and be involved in his subsequent care."

"I see no problem with that. The station is in the main street of the village. You can't miss it."

"Thank you, Granger, I will be there first thing in the morning."

Niko stifled a laugh. "Did I hear that he is coming up to our humble station?"

"He'll be here in the morning." Bill looked around the small office. "I just hope he won't get in the way."

The phone rang again. It was the petrol station on Tongariro Street in Taupo. After going through their footage from the forecourt they had found a clip of the vehicle of interest. No close-up, unfortunately, just a grainy wide-angle of a person making the transaction at the pump. Within minutes they'd emailed the images through to Niko who printed some still frames, clear enough to confirm the vehicle registration of Ben's work van and that the person more than likely was him.

Bill drummed his fingers on the table. "Well, this places him in Taupo on his way home on Saturday afternoon, then going through the toll cameras at Puhoi in the evening the same day, which makes it possible for him to have placed the hand under the house at Matakana Valley Wines in the early hours of Sunday morning. Plus, he would have had the knowledge to sabotage the water pump."

ANNIKA HAD READ through most of the diary notes for the summer of 1987. She stood up, stretched and wandered out on the deck at the back. The cool evening breeze was refreshing but made her shiver. It was a clear night and the stars shone brightly, competing with the light of the full moon. She could hear Bill's voice in her head; "Full moon means all the loonies are out in force." She did some yoga stretches to get the blood flowing in her tight back and neck, then pulled her mobile out of her pocket and dialled Lexi.

"Hi, is everything all right?" Lexi said, sounding concerned.

"Yes, we're all fine. I'm at the station helping Bill. They found Maurice Stott's diaries today. I'm reading through the summer of eighty-seven, looking into why Ben might be aggrieved."

"He was so young. I can't say I remember any specifics about him," Lexi said. "He was an awkward child and kept to himself. He seemed to struggle to relate to other people," .

"There are lots of entries about the winemaker, Robert. It seems all was not good there, quite a lot of difference of opinion," Annika said. "You spoke to him earlier today. What was he like?"

"I thought he was very nice. He answered my questions as best he could, genuinely wanting to help. I got the impression he was fond of the family, had even visited Jenny in the care home several times after she had the stroke. I guess, on reflection, he was a bit gushy and I do know he was in on the the wine scam?"

"What wine scam?"

"Oh, just something Avery mentioned in passing earlier," Lexi said. "Apparently the guys had discovered how the winery was scamming their export wines by selling their lesser-quality wines at the premium price."

"You're kidding me!" Annika said. This put a spin on things.

"Avery and the guys thought there had been some mistake and went to tell Maurice, who didn't deny the fact, and was in fact well aware of the goings-on. Maurice must have seen sense and put a stop to the operation when they threatened to go to the authorities. Avery assumed he had made good on his word. Maurice seemed like a respectful guy, realising the error of judgement made. There was never anything in the media. Everyone thought it had ended."

ENGROSSED in the information that Dr Webber had sent through, Bill couldn't help feeling sorry for the man. It was young Ben who had discovered his father's body. According to the notes they ruled it suicide; Maurice had shot himself in his study. That alone was enough to screw someone up for the rest of their life, Bill thought. After finishing school, Ben had moved to Australia where he completed an electrical apprenticeship. He got married and lived a normal life until his young wife died from meningitis. Ben's world fell apart, he lost his job and went off the grid in the Outback, until he was found wandering a dirt road to nowhere, malnourished and incoherent. He was hospitalised, then committed to a mental-health facility, where he recovered sufficiently to travel back to New Zealand. Settling in Auckland, he got back into the trade, and part of his ongoing recovery was to meet with Dr Webber regularly. Bill glanced at the date in the margin, Ben had been going to therapy for nearly three years on and off.

Annika came back inside and sat down at the table, relaying the details that Lexi had just told her about Robert the winemaker.

"Avery told us about the wine scam when we spoke earlier, but well done on tracking down the winemaker," Bill said. "We ought to speak to him next. This might well be our elusive motive."

The shrill signal of the office phone cut through the air. Bill reached for the receiver. "Matakana station, Granger here."

"Hi, Bill. I'm afraid I have some terrible news. I'm very sorry to have to tell you Constable Laura Rose passed away earlier this evening. She never regained consciousness."

The words hit Bill straight in the guts. "She was an outstanding police officer and will be greatly missed," Bill managed to get out. He turned to the others. "She didn't make it," he whispered.

"I'll make you a cup of tea to take to bed. You just head on up," Bill said. Annika did not protest and went upstairs. When Bill carried the tray of tea upstairs, Annika was already sound asleep. He was wired and wide awake, thoughts swirling around his head, tormenting him. From experience he knew it would take a while to wind down. He went back downstairs, taking care to avoid the creakiest step and went into the pantry, taking the half-full whisky bottle from the top shelf. He poured himself a generous slug, more than he usually had, but he felt it was warranted tonight. He sat down in the La-Z-Boy, and swirled the whisky.

He sighed and took his first sip, enjoying the pleasant warm feeling in his throat as it went down. Picking up the remote he turned the television on, channel surfing until he came across an old black-and-white Western. Maggie and Finn were happily snoozing by his feet. He reached for a refill and felt calm settle over him.

58

He parked the Toyota HiAce on the overgrown grass verge close to the entrance to Matakana Valley Wines. The tinted windows wouldn't raise an eyebrow — he looked like any tourist travelling around the countryside. Even though it was late in the season, there were still plenty of backpackers and seasonal workers around. Reaching into the backseat he pulled one of the thick-cut sandwiches out of the small chilly bin. The evening air was cooling off and a swarm of mosquitoes, keen for a warm body to land on, buzzed around trying to get in. Pulling the window up, he swatted a couple that had already got in. He reached for the Thermos on the floor and poured coffee into one of the hard plastic mugs that he had brought along. The coffee was disappointingly tepid as it had sat in the flask for a while. The plastic tinge from the mug didn't help. Still, it was better than nothing.

As the darkness set in, he took his Bushnell Equinox Z2 night-vision scope out. There was no movement inside that he could see. He was happy with its range of more than a hundred metres. He rummaged in his bag and found the Nighthawk camouflage stick, winding the three colours by a slight twist at the bottom. Applying the soft cream paint onto his face, neck and hands, making sure he would remain unseen, he pulled up his hoodie, then did a last-minute check of his gear bag. It was amazing what you could buy without any questions on the Internet.

He made his way parallel with the tree-lined driveway. The moonlit landscape was eerily quiet, apart from a chorus of crickets that got noisier the closer to the homestead he drew. Standing in the shelter of an old eucalyptus tree he could look straight into the lounge at the back of the house, twenty metres away. The light from the television flickered on their faces.

With his bag firmly strapped to his back he climbed up the tree to a vantage point a few metres above the ground. The minty scent was calming as he settled under the vast canopy. His scope was Army-issue. Switching off the night-vision mode, he could easily make out the smallest detail in the room. The two police officers looked relaxed; Avery had a deep frown. Climbing back down he took out a packet of nicotine gum, chewing vigorously as he settled in for the long night ahead.

59

Bill woke early, his head heavy from a night sleeping in the chair and fuzzy from too much whisky. His neck was stiff and his mouth as dry as the Sahara. He checked his watch, it was 6.15. His back ached from being at an odd angle all night. He shivered as he put his bare feet on the cold timber floor. The damp morning air was unforgiving, seeping into every inch of his crumpled uniform. He couldn't believe that he'd fallen asleep in his chair.

His oldest daughter galloped down the stairs. Bill groaned quietly while attempting to get up. He didn't want Katie to see him like this. He kicked the empty bottle under the couch and he poked his head in the kitchen and said good morning. Katie was cooking pancakes from the batter she had made last night. "I've woken up the twins. They're getting dressed. I'll make their lunches and get them sorted out." She smiled. "I thought I'd give you guys a break this morning."

"Thank you, darling."

"Dad, can you please wake up Zac? I daren't go in there. I'm afraid of the health hazards in his pit." Bill walked upstairs, every step reverberating pain through his dehydrated brain. He opened Zac's door, calling his name, getting only a grunt for an answer. It looked as though he had pulled a late one, just like his father, but without the alcohol. The stale air mixed with sweat and old socks hit Bill in the face. Shutting the door quickly and opening the nearest window, he pushed the pot plant aside on the wide ledge, the cool and slightly dewy morning air helping to settle his queasiness. *Teenage boys*, he thought. Desperate to get out of his grimy clothes, he walked into the master bedroom where Annika was still sound asleep. He wished he had made it to bed last night as he quietly tiptoed into the ensuite. He found a strip of paracetamol and popped two tablets then tossed his crumpled uniform in the laundry hamper.

He got into the shower, where the hot water slowly brought him out of the fog. Feeling slightly better, he got out and wrapped a towel around his waist and looked for a clean pair of uniform trousers and shirt before dressing and going downstairs. The kids were all having breakfast and it was unusually quiet, something he was grateful for this morning.

～

ANNIKA WAS EXCITED GOING to work with Bill. When they arrived at the station, Niko was already busy at work. "We've heard from the petrol station in Martinborough. There is footage of the van registered to Ben Wilson stopping and the driver entering the shop. It's grainy but he looks to be buying a bottle of water and a pie."

"That's him for sure," Bill said.

"The time on the film is one thirty-eight in the afternoon on Thursday, which corresponds to him coming from up north and through the toll cameras in the morning the same day."

Bill looked at the timeline. "We still need to establish what his movements were when he was down country."

"I'll call the care home where Ben's mother is living," Niko said. "They might have a log of visitors, or may remember if he came by."

"Annika," Bill called out, "if you wouldn't mind going through the diaries again, let me know what stands out."

"Sure," she said. She was enjoying doing the research. It felt good to engage her brain. On the odd occasion she missed her teaching career, the people contact, the students and the challenge and joy it brought. Not that she regretted giving it up — she was happy to focus on her painting and loved the freedom that she had — but sometimes she felt isolated. She picked up the diary and quickly immersed herself, reading through to the harvest time.

Maurice's entries and handwriting showed an urgency that hadn't been there previously, the script was getting more hurried and the entries even shorter. It was clear that he was struggling, the staccato sentences reflecting his state of mind. At the end of the harvest, some men had come to him, questioning him about his honesty and integrity. He didn't name them, but Annika knew who they were. Maurice expressed his embarrassment and anger into his journal, how he felt manipulated by someone.

The next entry was longer and he promised himself that he'd put an end to this practice, berating himself how he could have let it happen. For the few months following, the entries were more short scribbles, barely legible, the black mood increasing.

60

D r Stan Webber's beige trousers were a little too high in the waist, which made the pleats coming off the waist band pull across the top in the most unflattering way. Still, the razor-sharp creases would have impressed even the strictest drill sergeant. The light-blue polo shirt was a shade too tight and clung to his bulbous shape, perspiration already spreading under his armpits. He dabbed his ruddy face with an old-fashioned handkerchief and flattened his already slicked back hair with his hand. He looked ready to go on safari, Bill thought. All that was missing was a round pith helmet.

"Hello, I'm Dr Webber, we spoke last night." His handshake was firm.

"Welcome," Bill said and introduced Niko and Annika.

"Can't believe how quick it was to get up here," Webber said. "The toll road and tunnel have made a huge difference. It's only just over an hour from home now. That's incredible."

Bill gestured for Webber to take a seat and he perched his generous frame in the chair opposite Annika. Bill gave him a quick overview of events since Sunday. Webber leaned back in his chair, his arms resting on his generous stomach, his fingertips pushed together, nodding as he took it all in. It was obvious he was used to listening.

ANNIKA CONTINUED READING the journal until the last entry at the end of October. As far as she knew, Maurice was found dead much later, at the beginning of the following year. Her train of thought was disrupted as Webber came over. "Would you mind if I had a look at those journals?" he asked, looking over his reading glasses perched halfway down his nose.

"Not at all." Annika passed the last journal to him. "As you can see, I've put Post-It notes by the entries I thought might be of interest, but add your own notes."

Webber smiled and sat down again, absorbed in the task at hand. Bill and Niko were going over the latest material and Annika felt surplus to requirements. "I'll get some decent coffee," she said. "The Black Dog should be open by now."

"We have coffee here," Bill said with a grin.

"I'm not sure I would call that coffee," she laughed. Webber didn't even look up.

She enjoyed the walk in the fresh air. It was going to be a scorching day and the humidity was already hanging like a damp curtain in the air. Yesterday had been intense and she had slept like a log, yet she felt exhilarated, keen to understand what was going on. Dr Webber was more likeable in person than over the phone, reminding her of an absentminded professor. She had no idea what coffee he drank but got him a flat white, sugar on the side, just in case.

The mature trees lining the quiet street shaded the footpath as she walked back. It was strange, she thought, that amid such tranquillity evil lurked around the corner. It might be all right for hardened police officers to look at these horrendous notes and photos, but she was a civilian and a mother who cried at watching the news. She lingered on the porch for a moment, breathing in deeply to still her mind, willing the feeling of calm to stay with her before she walked through the door.

Over coffee Webber explained that Maurice Stott likely had a classic case of bipolar disorder. "Or, as it's also called, manic-depression. It brings immense highs and moments of elation and also immense lows, with almost non-existent communication. That's what Ben has. Often it's not just hereditary but also set off by a stressful event in the individual's life. The ongoing financial problems, the threat of exposure of the wine fraud, perhaps even being manipulated or blackmailed, wouldn't have helped."

"Perhaps we should call the care home where his wife Jenny lives," Bill said. "They might have some information that we'd find helpful."

"That's why I'm here," Webber said. "To help."

61

Waikauri Bay

FRANS MULLER, awoke early as always, sat on his front step looking out over Waikauri Bay, enjoying the first cup of coffee of the day. The gannets were feeding just off the beach, diving like projectiles, their long black-tipped wings tucked in, hitting the water's surface at speed. The fresh morning air made him shiver and he was glad he wore a woollen jumper his wife Dot made for him before she passed away three years ago. He could still feel her presence when he wore it, and it warmed his heart. Frans missed her terribly. She had been his high-school sweetheart and the love of his life. Not that he was alone. He had his two sons and their families, a handful of boisterous but delightful grandchildren, and his mates from the Blokes' Shed at Waitakere Gardens, the retirement village he lived at in Henderson. Dot had loved spending time here at the beach, and he had fond memories of carefree summer holidays here when the children were young. Now the grandchildren were doing the same, which pleased him immensely.

Frans had come up a few days ago to clean and close up the cottage for the season. Theirs was one of the older ones, not as large as next door with the sweeping veranda and all the mod cons, but he didn't mind. Looking across at the Watsons', he noticed that the curtains were open in the enormous bay window facing the beach. He could have sworn they had been closed yesterday. Strange, there was no car parked in front, and even if they had come and gone, he would have heard it as he was a light sleeper.

He walked over, stepped up onto the veranda and peeked into the living room. There was an empty whisky bottle on the coffee table. He could see the shape of a person sleeping on the couch, the bare feet sticking out from under an old blanket. Unsure what to do next, he made his way down the deck as quietly as he could, but nudged a small pot perched on the edge, tipping it down the steps. It broke into pieces at the bottom. Frans went across the grass back to his place as quickly as he could. Reaching his small deck he turned and looked back at Watsons' house, a familiar pain spreading across his chest. Looking back at him through the window was a man looking worse for wear. When their eyes met the man pulled back from the window. Frans hurried inside, slammed the door shut and locked it, barely able to breathe with the pressure across his chest. He rummaged in the small bag of medication that he carried containing blood pressure and angina tablets. He placed the nitro-glycerine tablet under his tongue and waited for the medication to take effect and slow his heart rhythm down. Then he dialled the police, all while expecting whoever he had seen to come stomping over and bang on his door.

62

The old man from next door who had peered through the window would certainly call the police. He had to get going. He swore as he threw a few things in his backpack, annoyed with himself for not pulling the curtains last night. Such a rookie mistake. He had planned to stay a few days to rest and figure out what the next step was.

He made his way through the bush, branches bashing him in the face as he hurried as fast as his battered body allowed. His shoulder was hurting a lot; the wound needed a proper clean and antibiotics, but he couldn't just turn up at the nearest medical centre and ask for help. Every step he took on the uneven ground shot hot pokers of pain through his upper body. If he could only get his car, but that was a couple of hours' walk at least. By now the local cops would have turned up at Waikauri Bay. He wiped sweat off his forehead. If they brought in the dog unit, he'd be screwed. If he could get hold of another car, he might be all right. So instead of walking up the valley he veered right. The terrain wasn't too steep, making it easier to get through. The trees thinned out and he spotted a small house through the clearing. Children's clothes were hanging on the washing line, a good sign. Strewn toys were on the lawn, a large sandpit next to the outdoor furniture under the shade of an old oak tree. On the table covered with an old fashioned table cloth were four place settings, a pitcher of red cordial, a plunger of coffee and a small milk jug set up. The large mug had Vote Labour on it. Out of view behind a tree he watched a couple of pre-school children tumble out of the back door, followed by their young mother, fresh faced and barefoot. One of the children spotted him. He waved.

The child waved back. "Come and have morning tea with us. We're having a tea party," she said. The three girls, in varying ages but all miniatures of their mother, looked at him curiously. The mother stopped in her tracks. By the time she had called out for the children to come back inside, the oldest girl had taken him by the hand and led him to the table. The mother set the tray of muffins and cookies on the table and snatched her girls into her arms to protect them.

"It's all right," he said, aware that he must look a mess. "I won't cause any trouble. I'm kind of in a hurry and just need to borrow your Mummy's car for a bit." He smiled at the girl who had held his hand. "You'll get it back, I promise." He crossed his heart.

The girl looked up towards her mother's worried face. "That's okay, isn't it, Mummy? You always say we should help those in need." She turned back to him. "Are you hungry?"

"I am a bit, you know."

"He could have something to eat first, then I could get the car keys from the hook in the cupboard. You will bring it back to us, won't you."

"I pinkie promise," he said.

"Well, that's all right then," she laughed.

Her mother nodded, frozen in fear. He understood her only concern was keeping her girls safe. She'd probably seen the news, that the police were looking for a killer. Her hand shook as she poured him a cup of coffee and nodded toward the milk jug.

"Thank you very much," he said.

"Mum always makes us use hand sanitiser before we eat anything. Here you go," the middle child said and put a small bottle of clear gel in his dirty hand. The tenderness and innocence of this small child touched him. If Clementine had still been alive they might have had their own family by now.

"Okay, we'd better do what Mum says," he said.

The oldest girl had fetched the car keys and handed them to him. "You shouldn't put them on the table. It's terrible bad luck, Mum says," she said. He nodded and put them in his pocket. He ate a couple of muffins quickly, all while the oldest girl told him all about how she was about to turn five soon. The mother looked on nervously, picking at a piece of muffin, not putting anything in her mouth.

"Have you got a mobile phone?" he asked, making her jump.

"We don't have a landline, so Mum carries it with her all the time," the middle girl said.

"Yes," the mother said, pulling it out of the back pocket of her shorts, knowing it was best to hand it over.

"You'll get it back," he said as gently as he could. "I'll leave it in the car when I finish with it."

As he stood up to leave, the oldest girl said she wanted to show him where the car was parked.

"Thank you so much for your kindness and your hospitality, but you stay here with your Mum. Is the car parked in the driveway at the front?"

The girl nodded. He walked across the lawn and turned around to wave. The girl waved back, her mother pulling her close.

63

M atakana

NIKO PUT THE PHONE DOWN. "There's a suspected burglary in Waikauri Bay. The offender is still in the house. A neighbour just phoned it in, describing the intruder as a male in his thirties to forties, he couldn't be sure. The male person had scraggly blond hair. It could well be Ben Wilson. We'd better take a look. The old man who phoned it in sounded rattled."

Bill drove while Niko put a call through to Orewa of a sighting of the suspect and the location. They dispatched the dog unit. Bill was concentrating on the narrow, winding, unsealed road as they drove towards Tāwharanui Peninsula. Around yet another blind corner an enormous rubbish truck appeared, making Bill stand on the brakes to avoid a head-on collision. The police car slid on the loose metal ending up sideways after the heavy braking.

The truck driver's eyes opened wide as they came to a standstill face to face. Bill waved apologetically and threw the ute in reverse, his heart thumping as he drove around the truck, this time a little further to the left, hugging the side of the narrow road. Niko didn't say a word.

By the time they arrived at the small gated community of Waikauri Bay they had both put it to the back of their minds. From here it was game on. Frans Muller had given them the gate code. The key pad was awkwardly positioned down the grass verge and Niko had to jump out to punch in the code. He swore under his breath, every second counted.

"I bet they run the this place with military precision," Niko said, looking at the luxury holiday homes on the right side of the driveway. To the left was a strip of grass, then the pebbly beach. Bill nodded. They rarely got callouts to places like this. Frans was standing on his front step waving to them. He was looking spritely, and in his late seventies. His grey hair was neatly parted on the side and his weathered face had visible sun damage, a lifetime spent in the harsh sun, Niko suspected.

"He was in there," Frans said, pointing next door. Bill asked the old man to step inside while they went over to have a look. Frans did as he was told and trudged the few steps and shut the door and went over to the window to watch.

Niko got the guns out of the lockbox and handed Bill his weapon. Bill motioned for him to move around the front while he took the back. There was no movement in the house. Niko wondered what awaited them.

64

Lexi was woken by the scurrying under the eaves outside the window. It was the second or third brood of young for the pair of swallows this season. She walked into the bathroom, running her fingers through her hair, avoiding looking in the mirror. She knew the dark circles were getting larger. She splashed some water on her face and got dressed before tying her hair into a ponytail and going downstairs.

Her mug was already on the bench with an Earl Grey tea bag in it, ready for the boiling water. A large plate of toast with all the condiments sat on the table amongst cereal boxes.

"I have a bit of work to do in the winery this morning," Avery said.

Green finished his cereal and reached for some toast. "Hope you don't mind if I take this with me," he said, buttering the toast and smearing peanut butter liberally.

"No problems at all." Lexi watched through the kitchen window as the two men walked into the winery. Cradling her cup, she took her first sip of tea. She longed to have this all put behind them. All she wanted was for everything to return to normal. Reaching for some ham, she knocked the side plate with her toast off the table.

"Damn it!" she yelled as frustration spilled over. Biggs bent down to pick up the bread off the floor and got her another plate, putting his hand on her shoulder. "Come on, why don't you have a seat on the couch. I'll bring your toast," he said, taking her into the lounge. The room was bathed in morning sun and the old couch looked inviting.

Lexi put her head down for a second and closed her eyes. When Biggs walked in again a few minutes later with the tea and toast, she was sleeping soundly.

BIGGS WALKED BACK into the kitchen and looked through the window. He was sure the door to the winery had been left open; now it was closed. He sent a quick message. *Everything ok?*

No reply. An uneasy feeling spread through his stomach. Something wasn't right. He slipped on his vest, grabbed his Glock and secured it to his belt. The pepper-spray canister was hooked on. It was just after seven-thirty in the morning, probably nothing, but he had to check. As a precaution he locked the front door behind him and pocketed the key. A gecko sunbathing on the wooden steps darted away as he came closer.

It was quiet, the dew glistening on both sides of the path. The only noise came from the crime scene tape, flapping ominously in the breeze. The gravel crunched under his sturdy shoes, as he walked across the yard. He opened the door slowly, still nothing. The light was on, but he couldn't see anyone. Stepping inside he peered down the corridor and slowly made his way inside, footsteps muffled on the concrete floor. He checked the rooms on each side. No sign of anyone. His heartbeat quickened. Entering the main area, his eyes were drawn to something a few metres in. Moving closer he realised it was a splattering of blood. There was another blood stain in the back of the room and a smear leading from it, like a drag mark. Inching closer, he unholstered his gun and moved forward.

A sudden movement from the side caught his eye, but there was no time. In slow motion his brain registered a cricket bat coming towards him. The last thing he felt before he blacked out was a crack to the side of the head and fear.

AVERY WAS SITTING UP, his head resting on his chest, when he opened his eyes. The room was fuzzy at the edges and he wondered what had happened. Why was he on the floor in the bottling room? His hands were tied behind his back. He shivered. The coldness from the concrete floor was seeping up his spine, and the back of his head hurt. The last he remembered was Green following behind into his office to turn the lights and computer on. Avery checked some email. After a few minutes he found it strange that Green had not come through and called out for him, with no response. He traced his steps back in to the winery, the hairs on the back of his neck standing up, senses heightened. He saw Green lying on the floor. Thoughts of CPR and calling the ambulance went through his head. The man must have had a heart attack and fallen — there was blood all around the back of his head. He was still breathing, which was a good sign. Avery stuck his hand in his back pocket for his phone to call for help, when a hard blow hit and everything went black.

Green was lying on his side a few metres away, unconscious in the corner, his arms now tied behind his back. Avery tried to make sense out of what was happening but his head hurt and focus was impossible. He had no idea how long he had been knocked out. His tongue was sore and swelling. He must have bitten it as he fell. He broke into a cold sweat, thoughts of Lexi whirling around his head, the fear paralysing him. Then he heard footsteps in the corridor and the door opened.

Light flooded in and a stocky man in a black T-shirt and camouflage pants entered, dragging Biggs by the feet. The downed officer was like a rag doll, his head hitting the corner of the door with a sickening thud on the way in. The man rolled Biggs over and bound his hands and feet the same way he had the other two. Avery's eyes were drawn to the heavy army-issue boots. Then looking up he saw ice-cold eyes staring back at him. The man looked as if he had come straight out of a US Special Forces movie; square jaw, steely gaze, cropped spiky hair and face paint.

The acrid smell of stress hung in the air. Green groaned as he began coming to. The man in fatigues walked over to Avery and stood there for a while watching him, then took a phone out of his pocket. Avery recognised the silly cover with Woody from *Toy Story* that the kids had given him as a joke for his birthday last year.

The man bent down and put the phone in front of Avery's face, letting the facial recognition unlock the screen. Once in, he scrolled for a minute before typing a message and pressing Send.

"Where's Lexi?" Avery said, his heart in his throat. "You fucking better not have hurt her."

"Don't you worry about her. She's fine for the time being. That's if you do what I say."

Anger boiled up. Avery tried desperately to get his hands untied but the tight knots wouldn't budge. *Where is Lexi?*

"We're going for a drive," the man said, his voice hard. He pulled a rag out of a plastic zip-lock bag, the sweet smell putting Avery into a restless void.

HE TOOK the long way around the orchard and crept by the dense oleander hedge to avoid detection. At the top of the stairs he pulled out the key he had taken from Biggs's pocket. There was no sign of the wife, but he knew not to underestimate a clever woman. He pulled the door handle gently, but as suspected it was locked. Inserting the key he opened the door as quietly as he could. The hinges were old but well-oiled. He was glad the dog wasn't around either. He couldn't understand people with pets. Animals were only there for work or as a source of food. A floorboard creaked as he slowly moved into the hall.

Lexi was still asleep on the couch as he crept up on her. The feeling of someone being in the room — a mother's intuition? — woke her. She sat bolt upright, eyes wide open.

He threw her down on the couch, pressing his weight onto her chest and putting the cold wet rag over her mouth and nose. Lexi clawed at him and took a chunk of skin off his bare arm before falling into a deep sleep a few seconds later.

He bound her the way he had the others, carried her over his shoulder and into the winery, then stalked down the driveway to collect the van.

The tarpaulin on the floor was new. He had made sure the ends went up the sides of the interior, so there would be no trace materials left behind. Leaving the two unconscious officers, he carried Avery and Lexi to the van, flung them in the back and slammed the door shut.

65

A *uckland*

Isaac had planned a lazy day off to prepare for dinner with Petra tomorrow. He had slept well and was in a buoyant mood, especially after receiving a text message from Avery.

Hi mate, we're going fishing. If you fancy coming along. Pop up to Leigh where we'll launch around midday. Let me know if you can make it.

An address in Hill Street followed. He thought, why not? It would be fun to go for a few hours' fishing with Avery. He'd be back in Auckland later tonight.

After reading through the recipe, he decided he was completely sorted and on track.

Sounds good, I'm on my way now, he replied.

Even though he had police stationed outside his house, surely they couldn't stop him going for a drive? He picked up the keys to the Aston Martin. It was only a weekend car, but what the heck, he thought. He changed into an old T-shirt and shorts, throwing a long-sleeved shirt in the bag along with a hat, sunblock and a change of clothes. He'd prepared a story to spin to the officer stationed outside, but needn't have bothered as the officer was snoozing away in the sunshine. Before leaving the city he stopped at a deli and picked up some filled rolls as he knew Avery would forget. It was just after nine when he was back on the road, revving up the Aston across the harbour bridge, the Bang & Olufsen music system belting out the Eagles, Isaac singing along at the top of his voice. He pushed the speedo a little. It felt good to stretch the beast's legs.

Another twenty-five minutes and he passed through Warkworth. Peak times the queues were a mile long, but not today. Driving through the Matakana valley was like being in the south of Europe, he thought. He slowed down as he came into the village, and thought of Petra. She had sounded like she was looking forward to dinner. Perhaps this was the beginning of something good for them.

Passing through the village and onto Leigh Road, it was back to open-road speed and he put his foot down. Coming into the charming small settlement he flicked up the GPS to locate the address Avery had sent him. Slowing down, he turned right on Cumberland Street by the dairy, then a left into Hill Street, looking for the last house on the right, a red-brick 1960s house. Apart from the van backed up to the garage, the place looked quiet. The letterbox was on a slight lean, the purple agapanthus was waist-high in the flowerbeds and the lawn needed mowing. Perhaps it was someone's holiday home, he thought.

Isaac got his gear from the boot and walked up the uneven path, its large cracks covered with weeds. When he knocked on the frosted-glass door, it was flung open and a giant of a man in fatigues greeted him like a long-lost friend. "Hi! So nice you could come up at such brief notice."

Isaac didn't know what to think. Had they met before? The man seemed familiar, but he couldn't place him.

"Come through. We're just about ready to get going," the man said. Stepping into the lounge Isaac could see into the kitchen and the corridor leading to the bedrooms. The smell of mildew hit his nostrils. The house didn't look very lived in. The hairs on his neck stood up and a feeling of unease came upon him. Before he could process the situation he was pushed head-first into the door frame and was out cold. The last thought that went through his head was, *Where is Avery?*

WHEN HE CAME TO, Isaac felt the barrel of a gun at the base of his neck. "Get on your feet," the man said, his friendly demeanour now replaced with hostility. Isaac struggled to gain his balance and tried to turn around but got side-swiped with a fist to his temple which broke the skin above his left eyebrow. He saw stars as he tumbled across the coffee table, landing hard on his side. He instinctively rolled up, protecting himself, and looked up at the figure standing over him.

"Stand up," the man growled, and kicked him in the ribs. Isaac groaned, coiling up in pain. "I said, on your feet, pretty boy," the man said, with a slight accent. He knew it was British, it seemed familiar. He had heard this man speak before, but where? With an effort Isaac got up on his knees, pain radiating through his sternum and ribs, he was sure a couple of them were broken. He stood up as quickly as he could, the last thing he wanted was another kick with those boots. A hard shove on his back pushed him through the house and outside, then in to the garage. All the windows were blocked out with thick black plastic. His eyes struggled to adjust to the dark for a minute. Having lingered in the doorway for a few seconds too long he received another push, making him fall face-first on the cement floor. The pain that followed was almost too much to bear. Shallow breaths were all he could muster between the waves of pain that kept rolling in. Relief flooded over him when the man left the garage, slammed the door shut and locked it. After a few minutes Isaac pushed himself into a kneeling position and his eyes fell on a crumpled heap of a person by the far wall. Half-expecting the body to be cold, he reached his hand out to touch the person's back, relieved to feel warmth and rhythmic slow breathing. He hobbled around the body and saw Avery's face.

"Avery," he said, but got no response. He slapped him a couple of times on the cheek to rouse him.

As Avery stirred, the back door swung open and the man in black was back. "Not as badly hurt as you pretended, eh?" He laughed. "We can fix that." The next minutes were a blur of kicks and punches. Isaac accepted his fate. He just wanted to disappear into the black abyss of pain.

66

W*aikauri Bay*

THE INTRUDER WAS WELL and truly gone. There were signs of someone having stayed in the house — no damage, just food and alcohol consumed. In the bathroom bin they found bandages and bloody gauze pads, just like at Ben Wilson's house. He couldn't have got far away since they got the call.

As they waited for the dog unit to arrive, Bill and Niko were having coffee and sausage rolls on the small deck in front of Frans Muller's house. He'd taken them out of the freezer as soon as he'd made the call, then baked them in the oven. "I'm on my own, you know. I've had to learn to find my way around the kitchen since my dear wife passed away," he said.

Bill reached for another sausage roll. "You said you came up a few days ago and have seen no one since you arrived."

"That's correct. I came up to tidy up for the season. No one really uses the cottage over the winter months, and I don't want to get vermin coming in. It's been a treat. I love the late summer days, and it's so peaceful here at this time of the year. If it hadn't been for the open curtain this morning next door, I would have been none the wiser."

Niko held up a photograph of a clean-shaven Ben. "Is this the man you saw?"

"It could have been, you know," Frans said. "Well, I hope you catch this fellow, at least I'll have one hell of a story for Happy Hour tonight," Frans said smiling.

It pleased Bill that they were on the right track. When the dog unit arrived, he gave them a brief rundown of the morning's events and the dogs were keen to get to work after picking up Ben's scent in the house, taking off through the bush with the officers in hot pursuit.

"Thanks for assisting us," Bill said, shaking Frans's hand. "It might be best if you get going home, as this man is still at large." Frans nodded.

When the dog unit returned the sergeant in charge reported that they had tracked the suspect to a nearby house. The woman there told them the suspect had "borrowed" her car and mobile phone. The oldest child seemed concerned the man had a sore arm, as he had been holding it. "I've radioed in the registration and the phone details. I expect they will nab him soon."

Niko and Bill jumped into the car and drove back to Matakana. The phone rang, it was a sergeant from Orewa station. "Someone spotted the Commodore station wagon driving towards Snells Beach. Warkworth will head towards Snells. You lot approach from the Matakana side. See if we can close the loop on this scumbag."

67

M *atakana*

DRIVING AWAY FROM THE HOUSE, he knew it was only a matter of time before he had to ditch the car and phone. He might have an hour, and he needed to find some medical help to keep him in some shape to continue running. He had a place in mind, not very far away. The old man had been an ambulance medic before he retired. He had been there two weeks ago, changed out a hot-water cylinder, and seen photos of him in his uniform. The old man had been more than happy to talk about his lengthy career in the service.

The house was on Sharp Road on the way to Snells Beach, but to get there he had to drive through Matakana. There was no option, he had to take his chances. There was a sun hat on the passenger seat and an enormous pair of Jackie O sunglasses in the centre console which he put on. He made it to Sharp Road without a hitch and into the old farmhouse of Barry Islington, pulling up alongside a beaten-up green Toyota. It would make an excellent switch. Out of the car, every step sent shock waves through his body. Barry had seen the car and opened the front door.

"Hi, Barry," he said, supporting his arm as he walked over. "I was wondering if you could help me out, like I helped you."

Barry stood on the steps, his leathery skin and white hair a stark contrast to his bright eyes. He might be in his late seventies, but he was a stickler for eating well, doing his morning exercise and hardly touching a drop of alcohol. "Well, let's have a look at you. Come in," he said. "What have you done to yourself?"

Once inside, he pulled his shirt over his head, wincing in pain as he lifted his injured arm. Barry couldn't hide his surprise when he saw the gunshot wound. "Right, let me get the first-aid box from the cupboard and we'll see what we can do."

He could hear the old man's shuffling feet as he went into the hall and rummaged in a cupboard for what he needed. He knew that Barry wasn't stupid — he would help him, then call the police as soon as he left.

"Well, there isn't much more than cleaning it that I can do." Barry leaned closer to get a better look. "You really need to go to a hospital to get it properly dressed and get some antibiotics. It's already infected." He went over to feel the outside of the electric jug, the water still warm from this morning's cup of tea. He reached under the kitchen sink for the bottle of disinfectant, poured a capful in a stainless steel bowl and added the tepid water.

"This is as sterile as you can get it at home," he said, washing his hands thoroughly and pulling on a pair of latex gloves.

"I'm grateful if you just do the best you can for now. I appreciate your help," he said, bracing for the pain than would follow. By the time Barry had flushed the wound and disinfected it, sweat was running down his face and he was close to fainting.

"Are you sure I can't drive you to the doctor? You need proper wound management and decent pain relief," Barry said. "If the infection spreads you will be in terrible trouble."

He looked up at the old man, realising how much he missed not having a father around. "I'm already in trouble," he said.

Barry nodded and put his weathered hand on his other shoulder. "I'm sure whatever you have done, it can be sorted out."

He shook his head. "I'm afraid it's gone too far." He stood up to go.

"Take care of yourself," Barry said and gave him a strip of pills. "These are the strongest painkillers I have, not that they will help much, I'm afraid."

"Thank you for your help," he said, opening the front door and grabbing the keys to the Toyota from the hook on the wall. Barry said nothing.

The bright sunlight blinded him for a second, and he thought he saw movement out of the corner of his eye. Then everything happening at once, armed police shouting at him to get down. Hands forcefully pushing him down, he dropped the car keys on the step. All the air went out of his body. He had known they would eventually catch up with him, but he hadn't expected it so soon.

68

Bill took charge and Ben did not resist when they put him in the back of the police car. The ride back to the station was a blur. They sat him down at the table in the meeting room. A steaming mug of instant black coffee and a slightly sweaty-looking ham and cheese sandwich wrapped in clingfilm were put in front of him. Staring straight ahead, he had no energy to pick either of them up. The room was closing in on him. It was nothing like in the movies where there was a small table and a couple of chairs and a two-way mirror covering the wall. This was like any office, but with no windows. He wasn't sure if he was dreaming or if it was real. The sound of the photo copier humming along with the muffled buzzing of the computer in the corner was almost hypnotic, but it magnified the shuffling of paper in front of him tenfold, hurting his ears.

"Have a sip of the coffee," Bill said.

"Have you got some water?" he said, desperate for saliva to return to his dry mouth.

"Sure," Bill said and gestured to Niko.

He was filled with a mix of fear of what was yet to come and relief that it had all ended. He was tired and just wanted to curl up and go to sleep. When Niko came back with a glass of water he drank it all in one go. Feeling better, he straightened his back. A week ago he was just plain Ben Wilson, the local electrician. Now they were referring to him as Benjamin Stott. It felt strange —that was a name and a life that he had left behind.

"We have someone who would like to see you," Bill said as he went to get Dr Webber in the room. Ben was surprised to see him there.

"Hello, Ben. How are you doing?" Webber said warmly.

"I'm not feeling that great, actually" he replied.

"I'm here to help you with anything that I can. You are safe here."

BILL PRESSED Record and asked him to start from the beginning.

He started by admitting that he had wanted to confront Avery about the role he played in his father's demise. That summer's day as a young boy he had overheard Avery's accusations of wine fraud. With a child's naivety, he had taken his father's side.

He flatly denied any involvement with any break-in or having anything to do with the murders of Peter Evans or James Smith, but showed some remorse for the accidental attack on the female police officer and for stabbing the dog, pleading self-defence in both cases.

Bill didn't know what to believe. There were so many loose ends.

"I didn't mean to do those things. I just wanted to talk to Avery that night. I didn't mean for anyone to get hurt," Ben repeated, tears were running down his cheeks.

"We have you on videotape going to Martinborough. Why did you kill Peter Evans?" Niko asked.

The repeat accusation made Ben shut down again. His distress was obvious, so Bill gestured for Niko to back off.

"I know nothing about that. I was only visiting my mother," Ben said, his voice barely audible. "He just turned up on my doorstep one day. I had to let him in."

Bill looked enquiringly at Webber, who signalled to let Ben continue without interruption.

"He wanted me to kill them all, but I couldn't," Ben said.

"Who wanted you to kill everyone?" Webber asked gently, but there was no response.

Webber pushed the sandwich closer. "Have a bite. I bet you're hungry." Ben picked it up but unwrapping the clingfilm proved difficult. Webber could see his frustration and leant forward, peeling the plastic wrapping off for him.

Webber tried to get him to open up, but nothing worked. There was no way of getting through to the broken man sitting in front of him, his sandwich untouched.

Webber had already recommended swift transport to a secure mental-health facility for immediate medical care and a full investigation. They would not get any further today, he knew; Ben had completely shut down.

Bill beckoned Webber outside. "What do you make of that?"

"I think he is slipping into one of his depressive episodes. In the lead-up to that can be symptoms of delusions, believing that something has happened that's not real, even though the person can see, hear, touch or smell what's happening. Psychosis usually accompanies episodes of extreme mania in these sufferers."

"Do you think we should look for someone else? He seems pretty certain there is another person involved."

"I couldn't tell you for sure, but I think Ben has gone through an intense period of mania, manifesting itself in blaming someone else for the horrific crimes that he has committed."

When they returned to the room, Ben was sitting on the floor, slowly rocking back and forth. No matter what they tried they couldn't get through, it was all over. Webber escorted him to the waiting car, Ben only just able to walk. The officer seated in the back with him had to lean across to fasten his seatbelt as there was no comprehension or emotion.

69

Annika was desperate for some air; it had been most unpleasant to see the man they had apprehended crumble in front of her eyes. She had sat quietly in the background in the office, privy to the entire thing, pretending to be busy at the computer. Now her hip flexors were as tight as knotted ropes and she desperately needed to move. As they put Ben in the car, she walked down to pick up a coffee from the bakery. While it was being made she popped across the road to the Four Square supermarket for more Post-It notes — she had used up the meagre supply at the station.

"Any idea where Avery and Lexi are?" a voice from behind said. It was Trevor, Lexi's nosy neighbour. Annika sighed.

"I've been trying to get hold of them." His eyes peered like a mongoose hunting its prey. "I have more of their mail. There must be a new postal clerk, someone who is both incompetent and blind and can't tell the difference between numbers," he huffed.

"I'm happy to give it to her," Annika said.

"Good. Just let me get it from the car." Annika followed him outside. The thick envelope had Avery's name written in bold block letters, urgency shining through its strokes. It was heavy — a thick catalogue of some sort, Annika guessed. Tucking the parcel under her arm she walked back for her coffee, wondering where on earth Avery and Lexi could be.

Back at the station, she dialled Lexi's number but there was no answer. Next she tried Avery's mobile, which went to voicemail. It worried her a bit, but she was sure there would be a simple explanation. She tidied up the notes, the suspect was in custody and things would soon return to normal. She just couldn't shake the feeling of something not being entirely the way it ought to be.

"I've tried to get hold of Lexi and Avery, but there's no reply," she told Bill, her worry obvious.

"I'm sure they're fine," Bill said to calm her. "The case is closed. We got the bastard."

"I still have this sinking feeling in my gut." .

"All right, I'll phone Warkworth station. They have regular contact with their guys." Annika had been around him and policing for a long time and her instincts were often right.

As Bill spoke to Warkworth, his face drained of colour. "We're on our way," he said and put the receiver down with a bang. "Warkworth haven't heard from them at the agreed time and can't get through. They've dispatched a car to investigate. Come on, Niko." Bill grabbed his vest from the hook by the filing cabinet and threw it on, zipping up the front.

"I'm sure it will all be fine," he said, his voice not entirely convincing. Annika knew her husband well. He was worried.

70

Speeding down Matakana Valley Road, lights and sirens blaring, Bill and Niko were glad the weekend traffic hadn't begun yet. Dust flew as they pulled up to the house. Parking in front of the winery building, they could see Avery's ute and Lexi's Q7 parked next to the marked police car. Even though the sun was beaming, the place was eerie and deathly quiet.

Niko shivered. "Sarge, this doesn't feel right."

"I know what you mean," Bill said. "Let's have a look at the house." Spreading out, they moved warily towards the homestead and inched their way up the wooden steps at the side. Niko tried the door; it was unlocked. After securing the bottom floor, they went up the stairs, bracing themselves, half-expecting to encounter something they did not want to see. Bill wiped clammy hands against his trousers, fearing the worst. But there was no sign of anyone; everything was tidy and in order, just like the floor below. He had a second look in the lounge — something was tugging at his mind. Tucked under the edge of the couch, just visible, was a white rag. He bent down to have a look and immediately recognised the sweet tell-tale smell.

"Niko, in here, can you bag up this chloroform-soaked rag," he said as Niko came in.

"Fuck, this ain't good," Niko said.

The patrol car from Warkworth pulled up. "Sorry we're late," a young constable said. "A boat came off its trailer and blocked the road."

"The house is empty, however there are signs that a struggle took place," Bill said.

"Chloroform," Niko said, holding up the evidence bag.

"We'll search the winery and adjacent buildings," Bill said, assuming command, already on his way down the steps. The officers nodded and followed behind Niko's broad shoulders. Bill indicated that he'd seen blood stains, signing to the others to be alert.

Further in, the air was stuffy and oppressive. Bill wiped his forehead and signalled to the men that he would enter the bottling room at the end of the corridor. Niko flung the door open and Bill followed closely behind, covered by the Warkworth officers. The darkness was dense until their eyes slowly adjusted. Grunts and movements in the far corner alerted them to two shapes lying facing the wall. Niko found the light switch and flicked it on, flooding the room in light to reveal Green and Biggs, bound and gagged. Niko bent down, quickly cutting the ropes and removing the tape over their mouths.

Apart from the knocks on the head and a few cuts and bruises, they reported, they were both okay.

"Did you see the perpetrator?" Bill asked impatiently.

"I didn't get a look at his face," Biggs said. "He knocked me out from behind and dragged me in here."

"One thing I noticed was his heavy footwear. They sounded like army boots," Green said. "He wore camouflage pants, like some Rambo character. I glimpsed him as he was bundling Avery out of here. He just flung him over his shoulder. He must be bloody strong to lift a grown man like that."

71

M artinborough

PAT WALKED into the local police station with the sizeable manuscript neatly tucked into her patchwork tote bag. Having left an unimpressed McTavish at home, she was on her own. She didn't know if they allowed pets in the police station and she would never leave him in a parked car. Today was a scorcher and who knew what dodgy low-lives were passing by. It would be her worst nightmare, losing her trusty companion.

She had to use both hands to pull the heavy glass door open, feeling that familiar shooting pain of broken glass up her wrists. The entrance was cramped, a sparsely stocked brochure rack on one side and an enormous umbrella stand on the other. A faint smell of fresh paint tickled her nose, making her sneeze. She had always been sensitive to certain smells. There were a few people in the reception room; two elderly men, a mum with a pushchair and a pre-school girl with long braids reading a picture book, a middle-aged woman with a sullen teenager, continuously picking at his acne-covered forehead, and the two people ahead of her in the queue. She had to wait for a few minutes while a mild-mannered man in his late sixties reported his bicycle stolen, filling in the correct forms. Next was a demanding middle-aged woman filing a complaint about damage to her letter-box. Someone had put fireworks in it and it had exploded, leaving most of the burnt remnants in the paddock across the road. She tapped her long manicured fingernails impatiently on the wooden counter as her details were entered in the system.

Pat felt sorry for the young woman at reception. She was barely out of her teens, but exhibited the patience of a saint. When it was Pat's turn, she walked up, every step of her sensible court shoes audible on the hard floor and leant against the reception counter. The name-tag said Maya. "Hello, my name is Pat Taylor," Pat said quietly. "I'm sorry if I'm wasting your time." The receptionist smiled patiently. "I have received something in the mail that might interest you regarding one of your cases."

Maya nodded, thinking if she had a dollar for every time someone said that, she'd be rich.

Pat leant forward, her voice hushed. "This is what arrived in the post. It's a manuscript." She hoisted the cloth bag up on the counter. "I haven't read it all, but it has to do with something that happened at Stott's Landing, one of the local vineyards. Long before your time, dear."

Maya opened the fabric bag gently to reveal a thick wad of manuscript pages. "What case would this have to do with?"

Pat leant closer. "The murder of Peter Evans. I was the one that found him, poor soul," she whispered.

Maya rocked back. The brutal attack had left the local community reeling.

"Mrs Taylor—"

"Don't be silly, just call me Pat."

"Very well, Pat. If you wouldn't mind taking a seat, I'll get someone to talk to you." She put the "Back in five minutes" sign on the counter.

72

M atakana

BILL HAD PHONED, letting Annika know there was no sign of Lexi or Avery. She was out of her mind with worry. Someone had taken them against their wills, but who? The prime suspect was in custody. A dull ache was spreading across her forehead and around to the back of her head, making her wince as she rubbed the base of her neck, trying to loosen the muscle. She rummaged in her handbag for two paracetamol, reached for the dregs of coffee left in her takeaway cup and swallowed. She grimaced. It was stone cold and unpleasant, but she would be no use to anyone if she didn't get rid of the headache. She went outside for some fresh air, trying to stretch her neck and relieve the pressure in her shoulders. Grabbing a glass of water on her way back inside, she went back to her table and started going through all the material again. What had they missed?

Dr Webber walked through the door. He had taken himself to the Matakana Market Kitchen for a celebratory late lunch before heading home. Having spent the day in Matakana, he told her he really liked the atmosphere, not to mention the proximity to Auckland, an easy drive up for weekends and holidays. A few of his colleagues had holiday homes around the coast. Perhaps he ought to consider buying a piece of this slice of paradise himself, he continued. On a whim, he said he'd popped into a real-estate office, picking up some information on current listings. He was close to retirement and could see himself spending time here. Stepping back into the station to say goodbye, the mood had changed. He sat down and let Annika fill him in on what was happening.

Bill sprinted up the steps and into the station, Niko not far behind. "Martinborough station just called. A manuscript exposing the wine scam was sent to Peter Evan's housekeeper as security before he was killed," Bill said, catching his breath. "She had opened it and had a look through before handing it over to the police. Interesting reading, apparently. They're going through it now."

Annika stared at the A4 envelope on her desk, flipping it over so she could see the sender's details. It was from Peter Evans. "Avery also received a copy." She held it up. "Trevor, their neighbour, handed me this just before. He'd received it in error and held on to it for a few days."

"Christ," Bill said. He took the envelope and tore it open. The manuscript inside was titled *The Great New Zealand Wine Scam*.

They divided the manuscript into four piles and each took one. As deep concentration set in, the only sound was the turning of pages, everyone focusing on what they were reading. Annika's headache had abated a little, but was still there in the background.

Niko's email pinged. "This just came through from the boys down the line," he said. On his screen was a driver's licence photo, with the name Robert Gibb.

Annika did a double take. "I've seen this man in Matakana. I remember thinking he looked in great shape for his age."

"Where was this?" Bill asked.

"He came into the movie theatre when I was setting up the other day. Then I think I saw him again yesterday. I'd stopped at the café on

Sharp Rd on my way to Lexi's. He was having a coffee and something to eat. I remember thinking he looked a bit out of place with the rest of us jandal-wearing locals. Immaculately ironed slacks, military vibe almost, polo shirt buttoned up, bulging muscles."

"God knows how long he's been up here," Bill said. He dialled Martinborough and scribbled on his pad throughout the brief conversation. "A vehicle registered to Robert Gibb was driven through the tunnel northbound, fitting the timeline. Niko, you check the motels around the area."

"I'll call Annie at Book a Bach. It's worth a try," Annika said.

"That's a brilliant idea," Bill said.

Annika picked up the phone and explained her unusual errand. She had known Annie since the twins were young — they had been in the same coffee group in the village.

"Oh I see," Annie said, cautiously. It wasn't every day the police asked questions, and really the client details were confidential, but since it was a matter of urgency she made a judgement call and agreed. "What was the name again?"

"Robert Gibb, but it's possible he used a different name to book the accommodation."

"I don't think so. We require a copy of a valid drivers' licence or a passport." Annika could hear the clack of Annie's keyboard. "Here he is," she said matter-of-factly. Annika couldn't believe her luck. "He's rented a beachfront property in Omaha. Booked and paid for until next week." She gave Annika the address.

"Thank you so much. I really appreciate it," Annika said, and hung up. "Jackpot!" she announced to the room. "He has a rented property in Omaha, the posh end."

"I'll call Orewa," Niko said. "We need the Armed Offenders Squad up here."

73

The helicopter landed on the meticulously manicured grass in the north end of Omaha, a few streets over from the target property. The AOS officers' black ballistic-grade vests and helmets were on and they carried an array of pistols and Bushmaster rifles. The smallest member of the team, but one of the toughest, was a woman with a distinguished career. She led the way holding a sniper rifle. No one spoke, as they'd had their briefing in the air.

The assembly point was set up on the street before the dwelling they were going to. Warkworth had dispatched two cars. The sun beat down from a clear blue sky and Niko could feel the sweat running down the middle of his back. Wearing the stab-proof vest was like being shrink-wrapped. The street was quiet; it was as if the beach settlement held its breath for the onslaught of happy weekenders turning up in droves after work on a Friday. Most of the holiday homes were larger than any city house, he thought. The gentle onshore breeze made the long grasses and native flax sway backwards and forwards like nosy bystanders gawking so as not to miss what was going on. The sandy beach was empty apart from a gaggle of large black-backed gulls, each leaving a trail of tiny footprints while searching for crustaceans or any other offering from the sea. Gannets circled the shallow waters, waiting for the right moment then dive-bombing into the unsuspecting shoals of fish. The houses nearby were mostly unoccupied, no doubt. Come this evening or tomorrow morning the place would be full of movement and noise, lawn-mowers and laughter in the air, children running around outside and adults congregating around barbecues.

THE NAVY VEST squeezed tight around Bill's middle. It didn't help that he'd put on a few kilos over the summer. Too many pies and deli sandwiches had taken their toll. He was paying for it now; the sweat-soaked uniform shirt rubbing against his skin, the seams under his arms chafing.

The Alpha team were in position; the Bravo team and the rest of the officers were awaiting further instructions. The radio crackled and gave the go-ahead.

Bill heard the crash of the door being smashed open and instructions shouted as the team entered the property. A minute later, the "clear" signal came from the radio and the sound of heavy boots on dry ground followed. The entrance was wide and majestic with polished concrete floors that seemed to go on forever. The vast open-plan kitchen and lounge was anchored by an impressive twelve-seater table and flanked by two separate seating areas with plush modern chairs and exotic rugs. Large abstract canvases covered the walls. Each to their own, Bill thought, as he walked through the ground floor. Four good-sized bedrooms, two on either side of the long hallway, all immaculate in presentation with just the right throws and cushions casually draped across beds and chairs. Upstairs, half the floor space was taken up by the master suite with an enormous gas fireplace, a movie room with seating for twelve, and two double bedrooms each with an ensuite. Who lived like this? It was like something out of a glossy magazine. The office next to the master bedroom was equipped with a sophisticated monitoring system with live footage from cameras angled in every room showed on a large screen. The place was like a fortress.

Bill spotted a briefcase by the desk and pulled a pair of latex gloves out of his pocket. The case was unlocked and had an assortment of surveillance photos, a laptop and a pile of paperwork. Before he could look through it properly he heard Niko's booming voice from downstairs, "Sarge, I'm in the garage. Come and have a look at this."

The double garage had a serious-looking home gym in the far corner. In the opposite corner some wooden framing had been put up, covered with thick plastic sheets. A couple of large plastic bins were set up in the middle. Protective clothing and a respirator were placed neatly on a table. Beside it was a chemical container. It was lye. This whole set-up was an acid bath for body disposal.

"What the hell?" Bill said.

Large plastic sheets covered the back wall by the internal stairs. Niko lifted a corner, peeked underneath and took a step back. The thick Styrofoam had been spray painted black, and a series of photographs pinned, not unlike what they had on the wall of the police station. "Sarge, come and have a look at this, will you," he gasped, staggered by what he was looking at.

"Fucking hell!" Bill uttered, gobsmacked. The photos pinned to the wall were not crime-scene photos in the normal sense. They were more candid snap and souvenirs, printed on normal paper and blown up to A4 size. "What a sick bastard." He struggled for words, not believing what he was seeing, "I'll call Rudd. They have to get the SOCO team up here, and fast. And we need to locate Robert Gibb." He was used to looking at crime scene shots, but the fact that these were trophies made him queasy. He pulled another sheet off the wall, a complete timeline revealing all the victims. There were pages of notes attached with pins. One photo showed the men in their youth, suntanned and invincible, having their entire lives ahead of them. It was exactly like the one missing from Avery's office.

74

nnika's phone buzzed. "Hi Annika, it's Annie again. Just thought you might want to know the person who rented the house in Omaha also rented a house in Leigh. The second booking is under the same name, but I guess I was only looking for the one rental and missed it."

"That seems kind of strange, don't you think? Why rent two properties?" Annika said, trying to make sense of the situation. She got the address and thanked her friend. Perhaps she could look herself. She knew she ought to wait for Bill and Niko to get back, Leigh wasn't far away, just five minutes by car. She dialled Bill's phone number, which went straight to voicemail. She left a brief message and said she'd wait for them there. It annoyed her slightly that she hadn't got hold of Bill. She tried once more but hung up when it went to voicemail again. It was probably nothing anyway, perhaps a booking made in error. Why on earth would a person book two houses for the same period?

She headed out towards Leigh and parked a short walk from the house. In front of the garage on the cracked concrete driveway was a large van with tinted windows, making it impossible to look in. In stark contrast was a low-slung silver sports car.

She hesitated for a moment and thought surely it wouldn't hurt to get a little closer, just to have a look. She crossed the road, taking cover by the bushy hedge of the neighbouring property. Getting down on all fours, she crawled the five or six metres from the hedge through the grass, pressing her back against the wall, the cool bricks calming her already rapid breath. Standing up, she peered through the venetian blinds into what appeared to be a small bedroom. The room was sparsely furnished, just a bed with a nightstand and a lonely chair in the corner. She couldn't see anyone in there and hunched down again, moving past to the next window. It was identical, but had no blind which meant she could see straight in. There was a person lying on a bare mattress. Annika gasped. She recognised the dark wavy hair — it was Lexi, hands tied behind her back. Perspiration was spreading under Annika's arms, soaking her thin top. Patting her back pocket, she fumbled to get her phone, but it wasn't there. Cursing under her breath, she realised she must have left it in the car. The sensible thing would be to run back to the car and phone for help, but she couldn't just leave Lexi there. She knew she should wait for Bill and Niko, but if there was a way in, perhaps she could get Lexi out.

She tapped gently on the window. A face drained of colour turned towards the noise. Annika signalled that she would look for a way in. Pushing herself up against the bricks, she looked cautiously around the corner to the glass door a few metres away. Saying a silent prayer she stepped up onto the deck and pulled the ranch slider open.

She braced herself for a squeak but the door opened effortlessly and she was inside the lounge. Holding her breath, half expecting someone to storm into the room, she waited a few seconds but no one came. The room was like a time warp. The Seventies turquoise synthetic lounge suite and veneer coffee table were like a look-back to her childhood. Underfoot the golden paisley carpet muffled her steps as she walked into the hall. Glimpsing the compact kitchen — its freestanding Shacklock stove, Formica benchtops and orange cupboard doors another journey back in time — she crept in and found a serrated bread knife. Her heart was in her throat as she navigated her way to the back bedroom.

She quickly removed the gag and Lexi eagerly sucked deep breaths in.

"Are you hurt?" Annika asked.

Lexi shook her head. "I think he drugged us," she croaked. "I can't really remember how I got here. There are just fragments of moments. I'm feeling a bit beaten up."

"Let's get you out of here. Lie still and I'll cut these ties off," Annika said as she pulled the knife between Lexi's wrists, the blunt knife eventually cutting through. Still in a daze, Lexi moved her arms to get the blood flowing. "Come on, we have to hurry," Annika said as she grabbed Lexi's hand, pulling her along. "Everything will be fine. We'll walk out of here the same way I came in, through the lounge and out the back."

Lexi walked on unsteady feet, holding on to Annika's arm. The sliding door wouldn't budge. Annika tugged at it with all her might. Holding on to Lexi with one hand, she tried the lock again, but nothing worked. Her hand was sweaty and slid over the handle.

"And what do you think you're doing?" a gruff voice sounded from behind them. Annika desperately pulled at the door. "There is no point," the man said coldly.

Looking down, Annika could see a steel rod along the length of the runners in the door frame. No amount of pulling would ever open it. Turning around slowly, mindful of not losing hold of Lexi, she recognised the solid man standing there. Lexi whimpered as he moved closer.

Annika lunged for him, but he overpowered her feeble attempt to strike him with the bread knife, knocking it from her hands before slamming her viciously into Lexi. He smirked as he made them hold their arms out in front, putting long cable ties around their wrists, tugging the strips tighter and tighter, their cries of pain seemingly adding to his enjoyment.

Avery was hanging upside down. His head felt about to explode as gravity carried every drop of blood towards the dirty garage floor, a few inches from his nose. Despite this, the smell of rat urine and mould was penetrating his every fibre. How on earth had he ended up here?

He drifted in and out of consciousness. The strain on his ankles from his body weight was enormous and he had lost all feeling in his feet. A slow trickle of blood from the cut on his neck ran across his face. Thoughts of Lexi and the kids popped into his head. He had not imagined his life ending like this.

Isaac was no longer moving. An initial attempt to contort his body to reach the ropes tied around his ankles had taken its toll. His wound seemed larger and the moving about had only increased the blood flow judging by the large puddle beneath his head.

Hanging from the rafters, the two men lost consciousness, awaiting their fate. Flies buzzed, feasting on the thick sticky blood pooling beneath, slowly trickling, draining the life out of them.

T he man pushed Annika and Lexi through the back garden and into the garage, the stench of blood and sweat overwhelming them as the door opened and he shoved them inside. Lexi hit her head and crumpled in a heap on the floor, but Annika remained on her feet as the door slammed behind them. As her eyes got used to the semi-darkness, she saw Avery and Isaac hanging suspended by their feet. Adrenalin surging, she rushed over to search for any signs the men were still alive.

Avery was breathing, albeit shallowly. Isaac was worse, his breath barely audible. Her shoes stuck to the floor, and realising she was standing in partially coagulated blood, Annika's stomach heaved. It was up to her now.

The cold emotionless eyes of the attacker haunted her as she frantically searched for a solution. She must hurry to cut them down, but first she needed to get the cable ties off her own wrists. Bill had showed Zac how to break free from these hand restraints after watching a hostage movie. Theoretically, she had to lift her arms above her head and push down. She gave it her best shot, but nothing budged and the plastic just cut deeper into her wrists. Then she remembered that the lock needed to be in the centre. She took the long ends in her teeth and dragged them across. Lifting her arms, she flexed her elbows, pushed down and the ties snapped. The small victory gave her courage to carry on. Her hands fumbled across the workbench on the far wall, dust and rat droppings and God knows what under her fingertips, looking for something sharp.

Avery groaned. She knew she had to hurry. Moving on to the shelves she found a rusty old saw. It would have to do. There was a stepladder in the corner. She positioned it between the two suspended bodies, hoping she was not too late. She took hold of Avery's legs for stability and pulled him tight against her body while frantically moving the decrepit saw back and forth on the thick rope. Because of the rust and missing teeth the saw kept snagging. Sweat ran down her back and her arm and back muscles were screaming from the effort.

Finally the rope gave way and Avery dropped on the floor like a sack of potatoes. The impact roused him out of his dazed state. Annika quickly moved on to Isaac. Her hands were clammy and the saw slipped out of her grip, crashing onto the floor with a bang. Annika froze. What if he'd heard them? She quickly picked it up, climbed the ladder and started cutting with more ferocity than before. The rope snapped and released Isaac.

Avery tied a rag around Isaac's neck to stem the blood loss and pulled him into an upright position with his back against the wall. Standing on wobbly legs he checked on Lexi, who was conscious but still dazed, when they heard footsteps.

The door was flung open. "I had a funny feeling something was going on out here," the man said. Avery stumbled forward to protect his wife, who screamed as the man struck him across the face. "As for you bitches, perhaps I should have strung you up as well."

77

Bill's uniform shirt was stuck to his upper body. Undoing his vest was a great relief. He sighed as the gentle sea breeze cooled him down.

The house was now overrun by Rudd and his team of SOCO's bagging the evidence. It was disappointing they'd not apprehended the suspect, but on the upside they had found the disturbing set-up in the garage . One thing was for sure, they were dealing with a psycho.

"Let's stop by the Superette around the corner and pick up something to drink. I'm parched," he said to Niko. They pulled up beside the small shop and Niko went inside for two bottles of water. Bill got his phone out to check for any missed calls or messages - there were several from Annika, and Bill's face paled as he listened to them, realising the danger she might be in. Honking the horn to get Niko's attention, Bill reversed out turning the car around.

"There is a second address in Leigh booked by the same Robert Gibb. Annika is there now," he spluttered. His mind racing as he sped towards the small settlement. He couldn't bear it if anything happened to her. Then anger overtook the fear. What the fuck was she doing there? He was acutely aware of the risks, but was she?

"I'll request backup from Warkworth and Orewa," Niko said, his voice steady as he called it in.

"Annika will be okay. She's a smart woman."

Bill nodded, concentrating hard on keeping the car on the road as they raced ahead, running a range of nightmare scenarios in his head. Niko gripped the handle above his head, his body thrown in all directions as Bill sped around the many bends on the road, racing through Whangateau, completely disregarding the fifty kilometre speed limit, blasting through, sirens on full. As the road straightened out and they came into Leigh, he switched the sirens off, keeping the lights flashing. Flying over the hill on the last straight with Little Barrier Island before them, then turned off the main road to the address Annika had given him.

Parking further down the street, Bill could see Annika's car on the road. His gut told him that all was not well. What if she was lying somewhere hurt — or worse?

They immediately recognised the Aston Martin as Isaacs, and Niko ran the registration of the van parked in the driveway on his phone. The van belonged to Robert Gibb.

The little colour in Bill's face drained away. "We're going in. I'm not leaving Annika with this fucking psychopath," he said. Just then a loud bang echoed across the street.

"Fucking hell, that was a gunshot." Bill grabbed his Glock and sprinted across the road. "We are going in, cover me," Bill said running along the dense hedge. He motioned for Niko to follow behind as he pressed himself up against the corner of the house. He could see no movement from inside. Staying low, they approached the front door in a few long leaps, grabbing the handle, pushing it down gently. The door sighed, the rubber seal at the base dragging on the floor as he opened it. The wooden floorboards in the entry creaked ominously. His shoulder brushed the wall, knocking a framed print off its hook, but he caught it before it hit the ground. They quickly moved from room to room before making their way out the back. Bill motioned for Niko to be quiet. They could hear loud voices coming from the adjacent garage.

78

"You are all responsible, the fucking lot of you," the man said.

Avery was confused. What was he talking about?

"If it wasn't for your meddling, it would have been a successful operation and made a shit-load of money. Your mate Peter was dead-set on digging up the past and writing an exposé about the wine we exported. He wouldn't give in. He deserved all that he got, the little chicken shit."

There was something vaguely familiar about this mountain of muscle, Avery thought. But where had he seen him before? And what wine export was he talking about?

"Besides, I dealt with it the first time. Maurice was about to crack, and I made sure it looked like he killed himself, the old arsehole. It was a pity his boy had to find him I suppose, but such is life."

The penny dropped. Avery knew where he'd recognised him from. Robert the winemaker at Stott's Landing had aged well; the muscle-bound man standing in front of them looked very different from all those years ago. He remembered the flabby young man with long hair, full beard and moustache, not at all like this man who was in astounding shape for being in his late fifties. "You look a shitload different today, Robert," he said.

"Took you long enough to figure out. I've been around for the last couple of weeks, watching you muppets, but you didn't have a clue."

"Why are you doing this? We've had nothing to do with Stott's Landing since we left all those years ago," Avery said, desperate to buy some time.

"It's all too late now. When your mate asked around, writing his exposé, I had to intervene."

Avery's blood froze. "Did you kill Peter and James?"

"They left me no choice. The idiot would publish it for the entire world to see. I wanted to make you squirm. That's why I placed his hand under your house. And now it's your turn to pay for sticking your noses into what didn't concern you." He pulled a gun out. "Sadly for you, the women are collateral damage. A shame really, such pretty things. I always enjoyed Lexi's visits back in the day," he smirked. "You two, Avery and Isaac, you started this and now I finally get to end it."

"We have notified the police," Annika said as forcefully as she could.

Robert grinned. "Don't worry, sweetheart. By the time they arrive here, it will be well and truly over."

"But what about Ben, Maurice's son?" Annika asked, realising that Avery was trying to inch his way closer to the implements leaning against the wall. "Was he in on it as well?" she continued, desperate to keep him talking and taking his attention off Avery.

"That idiot couldn't organise a piss up in a brewery. He's as weak as his father was."

Avery mustered his remaining strength, seized a shovel and took a swing. The rusty metal glanced off the back of Robert's shoulder. His gun discharged upwards, the bullet going straight through a canoe in the rafters above their heads. The ringing in their ears amplified tenfold in the small garage as fibreglass and dust rained down on them.

Robert shook his head. "That was incredibly stupid," he said, and cold as ice fired a shot into Avery's abdomen. Lexi and Annika screamed as he turned to Isaac, squeezing off another shot.

Lexi attempted to get over to Avery before Robert coldly took aim at her. "Don't fucking move. They both deserved it," he said calmly. "Besides, as I said, you two are just collateral damage."

79

Bill and Niko had made their way around to the garage when two more shots were fired in rapid succession. "Stay with me. I'm going in" Bill said, pulling the handle and slipping inside. Niko was right behind.

About to squeeze the trigger, Robert didn't see the movement from behind.

"Police, drop the fucking gun," Bill yelled. He could see Avery bleeding on the floor and Isaac slumped in the corner, blood oozing from a head wound. Avery looked to be alive, just. Isaac on the other hand was still. Annika and Lexi were cowering, but seemingly unharmed.

"I said drop the gun," Bill roared.

"Fuck off man, I'm finishing this," Robert hissed. He turned toward Lexi, raising his gun. Both Bill and Niko discharged their weapons.

Robert was thrown on to his back from the six rounds slamming into his body. Niko sprang forward and kicked the gun away from his hand. As Bill held his aim, Robert's eyes widened fighting against the certainty of death. A rasping rattle could be heard as his airway filled with blood and he gasped for a breath. In one final cough, Robert drowned in a mouthful of mucus and foaming red bubbles. "Now it's fucking finished," Bill whispered.

Bill checked on Avery, who was conscious but weak. His shirt was bloodied and there was a bullet hole in his right side just under his ribcage. Blood dribbled from the corner of his mouth so there was clearly internal bleeding. Putting pressure on the wound, Lexi joined him, her wrists still tied.

"Here, keep putting the pressure on," Bill said. "Let me cut these off." He could see how distraught she was, shaking like leaf, just keeping it together.

Annika was looking after Isaac, stemming the blood flow by tying her scarf around his head. The bullet seemed to have only grazed his left side, the ear being the major casualty.

"The air ambulance and first responders are on their way," Niko shouted.

The fire chief and another experienced medic arrived within minutes. Bill ushered Lexi outside to let the medics get on with tending to the injured men. Applying pressure on the wound and bandaging Avery, they administered IV fluids. "He needs an urgent blood transfusion. Please can you check on the ETA of the helicopter," the fire chief yelled.

Bill got through to dispatch as the back-up from Warkworth and the ambulance arrived. Annika joined Lexi outside, both shivering despite the warm sun while Avery was being prepared for transportation to the landing site by Leigh school.

"I want to go with him," Lexi pleaded with Bill.

He put his arm around her. "I'm sure that'll be fine. Come on. They're loading him up now." He hoped for Lexi's and the kids' sake that Avery would make it.

The ambulance made a quick turn-around to come back for Isaac, who after the IV fluids was awake and looking a little better. Unable to stand and with his head bandaged up, he was taken by road to Auckland.

Finally Bill could check on Annika, who was shaken, with minor cuts and abrasions but otherwise unharmed. He wrapped her in his arms, grateful that she was still alive. "How about I take you home? I think we've had enough drama for one day."

"Let's get out of here," Annika said.

"Granger," Rudd called out as the Orewa team pulled up. "Well done on containing the situation. I expect a full report by the end of the day."

"It might have to wait until tomorrow, I have to take care of my family. It's been quite a day," Bill said, opening the car door for Annika.

"All right," Rudd said. "Just get it done at the earliest, will you."

Bill got into the driver's seat as police from Orewa began securing the scene. He reached across and squeezed Annika's hand.

"It's been a hell of a week," she said slowly.

"You can say that again," he said.

EPILOGUE

M *atakana*

FIVE WEEKS later

NOT EVEN THE sideways rain could dampen Lexi's mood this evening. She took a breath, determined not to cry. Beau was pressed snugly against her leg, and hadn't left her side since he'd come home. The hardship they had experienced a little over a month ago was still raw. If it hadn't been for her parents, Elsy and Bob, she wasn't sure she would have coped at all. There certainly wouldn't have been a harvest.

Lexi stood in the doorway welcoming everyone out of the miserable weather, her slim silhouette a testament to the stress she'd endured. Tonight was about friendship and celebration, about coming together as a community after so much loss.

Words could not express how thankful she was for all the help she'd got after the kidnapping and brutal shooting of her husband. She had been completely lost, barely able to manage.

Music and laughter echoed inside the large concrete space of the winery, which was filling up with life. Crisp white cloths covered the food-laden tables. This was how she wanted things to be, joyous and happy.

Bob came past and squeezed her arm, checking that she was alright. She nodded, her heart swelling at how thankful she was for her parents having been there for her.

Bob had managed the harvest, the picking of the grapes, and organised the community and rallied willing workers. The fruits of their labour were now fermenting in the large vats along the back wall. Elsy had looked after the family and was now walking around making sure that everyone's glass was topped up. Bill was leaning against one of the old wine barrels chatting to Niko, who had driven up from Auckland after work.

"If you would all take a seat before the food goes cold," Lexi said and turned the volume of the music down a little.

Isaac took Petra's hand and pulled her close, twirling her around making her laugh in the process, the joy in their eyes visible to all.

Bill walked over to Avery, who had been watching their friends rallying around, and pushed his wheelchair closer to the table.

"I'd like to walk from here," Avery said. Bill lent his arm for stability and guided him to take a few careful steps to the seat at the head of the table.

"Thanks, mate," Avery said, his face as thin as the rest of his ravaged body. He was just out of hospital, still recovering from the gunshot wound to his stomach that had nicked his liver and pierced his intestines. He had been on a liquid diet until now.

"Friends and neighbours," Lexi said holding on to the back of the chair, pausing to compose herself. "Without you we would have been in a much different place now. From the bottom of my heart I want to thank each and every one of you who have helped us through this ordeal. To Mum and Dad — you have been amazing, helping us to get back on our feet. And to Annika, Bill and Niko —if it weren't for you we wouldn't be standing here today."

She looked at Avery. "And lastly, to absent friends."

**The story continues with *Rings On Water* -
Books #2 of *The Matakana Series*.**

AUTHOR'S NOTE

The Matakana area is located seventy kilometres north of New Zealand's largest city, Auckland. This picturesque region is famous for its many vineyards, artisan food and crafts as well as the superb weekend Farmers Market.

The crime thriller lurking inside me, has always sought the perfect setting. The inspiration for The Matakana Series burst into being over the last few years. Since the children were small, we have escaped to our own slice of paradise in beautiful Matheson Bay.

The area has it all; the local people, a rich amalgam of artisans, entrepreneurs, wine makers, creatives and proud hardworking folk with magical community spirit. An integral character of the book is the stunning scenery, breathtaking coastline and proximity to New Zealand's largest city. These elements combine to deliver an environment rich in motive, opportunity and the means to trigger a series of gripping crime novels. A great majority of the book have been written from our Bach in Matheson Bay, itself a treasure of local history.

REVIEWS

Dear Reader,

Thank you for reading *Blood On Vines,* the first in *The Matakana Series*.

If you enjoyed the story, please post a brief review or rating of *Blood On Vines* on your favourite digital platform. This in turn spreads the word and is incredibly helpful to an author.

Thank you,

Madeleine Eskedahl xxx

ACKNOWLEDGMENTS

Writing this book has been an interesting and sometimes challenging ride, and I have loved the journey.

My sincere thanks to the following :

My first readers, from the first draft to the last one, encouraging me to keep going, Adrian, Holly and Olivia you are amazing. Thank you for believing in me and the story, your love and support has been invaluable. Girls, I couldn't have done it without you being my technical support. From the bottom of my heart I love you all.

Robyn Stephen, thank you for your support and enthusiasm and for cheering me on. Your assistance, and keen eyes reading over the text, making sure everything is correct, has been invaluable. Any errors you find would be because I tinkered with the manuscript after she signed it off.

My fabulous critique partners Andrene Low and Kirsten McKenzie, thank you for being there for me, guiding me along, passing on your knowledge and making me a better writer. Your kindness and support means a lot, especially as I was going through many firsts.

My editor Stephen Stratford, your advice and guidance has been invaluable, and for wrangling the manuscript into the best it could be, I'm truly grateful.

Bede Haughey, thank you for showing me around the station and letting me ask loads of questions. Any errors you may find in here have nothing to do with his advice, rather my interpretation and creative freedom to fit the story.

Bev Robitai, proof reader extraordinaire, you are a huge supporter of New Zealand writers and I thank you for superb services and advice, I really appreciate it.

Jeroen ten Berge, thank you for designing the cover of the book. Your creativity and talent has no limits.

Lastly The Three Musketeers, Harry, Archie and Jemma for being outstanding co-workers and sleeping under my desk.

BOOK CLUB QUESTIONS

1. What was your favourite part of *Blood On Vines*?
2. What was your least favourite?
3. Did you race to the end, or was it more of a slow burn?
4. Which scene stuck with you the most?
5. Did you reread any passages? If so, which ones?
6. Would you want to read another book by **Madeleine Eskedahl**?
7. Did reading the book impact your mood? If yes, how so?
8. What surprised you most about *Blood On Vines*?
9. How does the book's title work in relation to the book's contents? If you could give the book a new title, what would it be?
10. Do you think you'll remember *Blood On Vines* in a few months or years?
11. Are there lingering questions from the book you're still thinking about?
12. If you could ask **Madeleine** anything, what would it be?

ABOUT THE AUTHOR

Madeleine Eskedahl was born and raised in Sweden on the beautiful island of Gotland in the Baltic Sea. Living a carefree childhood filled with adventures and surrounded by Viking remnants, her creativity was actively encouraged by her family.

Madeleine was a voracious reader from an early age, with a fondness for mystery, convinced she'd become a Private Detective or a Spy when she grew up.

Madeleine moved to New Zealand in the early nineties. Now married with two daughters, her family also consists of a trio of West Highland White Terriers — Harry, Archie and Jemma.

Apart from being a bookworm and a polyglot, she loves walking on the beach, her beloved Westies, yoga, painting, patchwork and spending time with family and friends.

Blood On Vines is the first instalment in the Matakana Series. The second book in the series, *Rings On Water* is underway.

To keep up to date with new releases and other information, please sign up to her newsletter at www.madeleineeskedahlauthor.com.

Printed in Great Britain
by Amazon